Sister of Sorrows

HENRY BALL

Sister of Sorrows

LOST IN THE WILDS OF SOUTHERN LOUISIANA

Sister of Sorrows
A Tumultuous and Remarkable Journey Through Life,
Love, and Lost in the Wilds of Southern Louisiana

For information about this title or to order other books
and/or electronic media, contact the publisher:

Storied Press, LLC
www.sisterofsorrows.com

ISBNs:
978-1-7357480-2-3 (hardcover)
978-1-7357480-0-9 (softcover)
978-1-7357480-1-6 (eBook)

Printed in the United States of America

Cover and Interior design: 1106 Design

Distributed by Civin Media Relations

This book is dedicated to April, my patient and loving wife. To Lori, Deborah, and Terri, my three favorite sisters, and to the memory of my dear mother, Dolores, may she rest in peace; I love you all.

Dolores Ellen Boone November 1, 1940—March 7, 2020

Special thanks to 1106 Design, Stuart Horwitz, Todd Civin, Jonathan Ellis, and Elsie Olesen for helping me to bring Sister of Sorrows to life.

Prelude: *You Have a Sister*
(Book One)

Part I: *Sister of Sorrows*
(Book One—Chapters 1–30)

Part II: *What the Monster Left Behind*
(Book One—Chapters 31–47)

Epilogue I: *Hold Please*
(Book One)

Contents

Part II What the Monster Left Behind

Prelude

"*You have a sister.*"

I was forty-three years old when mother unloaded that little nugget on me. I had been in a business meeting closing a large construction deal. She had tried calling twice so I was worried that something might be wrong. By the time I got her on the phone she was walking in to visit a sick friend at the hospital, and in a somber tone, she said that she had something she needed to tell me. It felt like she was going to inform me that she had a terminal illness or that something was wrong with one of my siblings. I braced for the worst.

I have to admit I wasn't expecting the kind of news she would deliver, rather nonchalantly, so when she unloaded a secret she had been keeping for almost five decades, that we had another sibling, a sister, whom she had placed for adoption, I was rather taken aback.

Though our call was brief, and I was left to wonder if mom was slipping into dementia, or if one of my (previously known) siblings had put her up to punk'n me, the obvious question that began to nag— other than why it took dear old Mom eighteen years after Elizabeth found us to let the rest of us in on the secret—was why did she give her up in the first place?

As the youngest son of a six-pack I had always known life in a big family. Four rough-n-tumble, take-on-the-world (and each other) boys and two slightly dramatic, if not defiant, giddy girls. We were all born within a thirteen-year period and there was a time, and some of my best—and worst—childhood memories, that we all endured beneath one roof.

And though the parade of homes got progressively smaller and more in disrepair as my father descended into alcoholism, abusiveness, and repeated business failure, one would think another mouth to feed or pillow to fluff would have hardly made much difference at all.

In fact, I did not have a room of my own until reform school, good old LTI (Louisiana Training Institute). Twenty-five years had passed since that chapter in my life by the time that I learned about Elizabeth, and I could have never guessed that a long-forgotten memory during that dark time would soon shed light on deeply buried family secrets. What I did know was that I felt the need to contact my new sister.

Mom couldn't or wouldn't tell me more than her adopted name, that she was a speech pathologist who worked with special-needs, mainly autistic, children, and that she lived somewhere in Oregon. Being somewhat resourceful, or more accurately, knowing how to find the Google search bar on my laptop, I began searching for Elizabeth Anne Boudreaux. I would locate my sister by her married name, Elizabeth Boudreaux-Aaron.

"Is Elizabeth Aaron home?"

Prelude

"She's not," the gentleman on the other end explained, "can I take a message?"

"Well, my name is Frank Hayden, I'm not sure if she'll . . ." I was trying to explain the purpose of my call.

"Are you Dolores's son Frank?" He questioned as if he knew exactly who I was.

"Yes, I am. Mom just told me about Elizabeth a couple of days ago, I hope it's okay for me to call?"

"Of course, she'll be so happy to hear from you. It'll make her day for sure!"

Elizabeth Anne 'Lizzy' Boudreaux, Dolores Crockett's fourth born, was conceived in the midsixties as the result of an ill-advised affair and would be the second child Dolores carried out of wedlock. She had been placed with an adoptive family, the Boudreaux of Gonzales, Louisiana, three weeks after her birth in 1966. As a curious and resourceful teenager, she would search for and learn her birth mother's identity but would not decide to make contact until 1996 at the age of 29.

She had wanted to know her birth family, especially her siblings. Dolores was not comfortable with revealing her long-held secrets, including the identity of Lizzy's father; so Lizzy promised to be patient and wait until Dolores was ready to make the revelation(s) to her children on her own time.

For the next sixteen years the two would correspond via cards and letters and Lizzy would learn all she could about her six biological siblings from afar. She wanted to know us, she wanted desperately for Dolores to open her secret diaries so she could forge relationships that she had been denied her entire life. After more than a decade and a half she had all but given up hope and since she'd promised Dolores that she wouldn't be the one to tell the six of us, she had resigned herself to the thought that she might never meet us.

Then, seemingly from out of the clear blue sky, Mother decided to spill the beans, to open those diaries and share her long-kept secrets, at least some of them.

It's not every day that you learn you have a forty-seven-year-old sibling, though this wasn't exactly uncharted waters for me. I received a phone call one day, ironically around the same time that Lizzy contacted Mother the first time, from a half-sister that had been fathered by dear old Dad, Beckett T. Hayden, prior to his relationship with my mother. Between the previously unknown half-sister, two actually, and at minimum a half-dozen step-brothers and sisters via multiple marriages, remarriages, and may-or-may-not-have-been-marriages before and after my mother, I could have my own reality show called *Twenty (or so) Siblings and Counting*.

This was different though; a lot of things did not make sense to me. My mother, despite many faults, which would have to include incredibly poor judgment in men, was *all* about her children. She worked, with little to no help, like a rented mule, to raise her brood. She sacrificed everything and anything she had and taught us that we had to look out for each other. Now well into her seventies, she still cannot say "no" to one of my sisters that desperately needs to hear the word "no." She loves her children like nothing else and for her to allow another family to love, protect, raise, and be responsible for one of her own, there had to be a story worth knowing.

To understand that story, the story I would tell my new found sister, I have to take you all the way back to 1957, 13 years before my own existence to a time before the free love and peace movements of the late 1960s, to a time when today's more tolerant and accepting views weren't all the rage in the Crockett family's little sliver of Louisiana, Livingston Parish. It all starts with my mother Dolores Crockett's first child, "illegitimate" as some called her—my wonderful

Prelude

eldest sister Anna Rae—the scandal from which my mother would virtually never recover.

Some of the names and events have been changed in order to protect the innocent, and maybe some were guilty, too, but this is that story as well as I know it, the one I told my long-lost sister and I thought maybe you, too, would enjoy getting to know from whence we came.

PART I

Sister of Sorrows

One

"The Devil's own daughter is in our sanctuary," screeched the bun-haired, sour-faced Sister Grantham when Dolores finally made it back to the Walker Church of Christ, the little evangelical congregation stewarded by the Right Reverend William 'Bible Bill' Grantham, during her pregnancy with Anna Rae.

Dolores's mother, the strictly faithful and ever judgmental Widow Kelli-Kay Crockett, had convinced her only daughter to come home to the Lord, to get right with God, and to bare her "sins" at the altar. She was going to bring a bastard child into the world and to the particular brand of fire-and-brimstone Christianity practiced by Brother Grantham's flock that was just short of personally driving the nails through the outstretched hands of the Christ.

When Dolores and the Widow Crockett made their way through the little portico that marked the entrance to the almost entirely wooden church—accented by the eight thin, tall, gothic-looking stained glass windows depicting, among other things, a stricken whore touching Jesus's garment to receive healing and the crucifixion of the Christ—the southern Louisiana evening sky was alive with electricity, thunderous rumblings, and the smell of an approaching megastorm.

The 1957 homecoming queen and would-be valedictorian of Walker High School had already been shamed into dropping out of her senior year and had by now thoroughly convinced herself that she would never fulfill her dream to be the first college-educated woman in her family and a successful businesswoman.

The boy, Jimmy-Jack Dempsey—homecoming king and stud shortstop for the Walker Wildcats—had promised that they would be together forever. Despite both their families' near violent protests, the two continued dating. They went to school holding each other's hand tight with their heads held high, even after their dirty little secret got out.

But now, Jack—as Dolores called him—was nowhere to be found. Rumor had it he had been shipped off to a boarding school in New Orleans to finish high school away from the scorn and scandal he and "that trashy little girl" had brought on his family's good name.

When Walker's principal, Martha Atmore, made the daily announcements over the school's brand new loudspeaker, she read from a previously unknown school policy regarding teen pregnancy that called it an abomination from hell and dictated that any student found to engage in such scurrilous and loose moral conduct must be banned from participation in any extracurricular activities and such a person would also not be eligible for honors bestowed by the school.

To make sure that every student, teacher, and staff member was perfectly clear as to just who might have been engaged in such activity, Principal Atmore announced that her daughter, Peggy Sue Atmore, who had been the runner-up in the homecoming court would now be recognized as queen in the school's yearbook due

One

to the unfortunate disqualification of one Miss Dee Crockett, as Dolores was known at school.

Dee had been one of four possible candidates for valedictorian, the only female, named just after the senior class began its final semester. More recently, Principal Atmore announced that Dee was recognized by the student council for her academic achievements and proudly read her scholarship letter as a way to celebrate that she would likely be the first female valedictorian for Walker High School. That message broadcast over the same loudspeaker system that she was now using to bellow the hateful condemnation of all things Dee Crockett.

Dee collected her books and walked quietly out of her homeroom class in tears. A straight A student just five weeks away from graduating top in her class with a promising academic future, she would never set foot on Walker High School property again.

Dee had never felt so humiliated. Just a few weeks ago, she was boss, she was the dolly on campus. After she aced her college entry exams, and with her scholastic record she had been offered a prestigious academic scholarship from the state's flagship university, LSU, and she had been accepted to Tulane University, one of the South's "Ivy League Schools" in New Orleans.

Prior to the rumors and revelation of her pregnancy, Dee could not walk down the hallway at Walker without hearing multiple congratulations and well-wishes. She had lots of friends, most of whom now shunned her and acted as if she'd shown up to class with the boils of a leper. Peggy Sue was the new homecoming queen. "Great!" Dee thought: Peggy wanted it more in the first place, let her have it.

They were friends but Peggy had become extremely jealous of Dee and turned cold after the homecoming dance. When word got out about Dee's pregnancy—likely from Peggy's best friend who happened to be Jack's sister, Jenna—Peggy Sue was almost giddy and spared no opportunity to give Dee grief, calling her "tramp" or "Rahab" in reference to a prostitute in the Bible.

It was all behind her now, she had a baby on the way. She knew that she would have to grow up fast. She no longer had time for the pettiness and schoolgirl antics of Walker High School. Unfortunately, those petty antics would follow Dee everywhere she went.

As the first resounding clap of thunder rocked the small, predominately wood structure, she found a seat at the end of a pew near the back of the sanctuary. Her cute, little, curly headed brother, known to everyone as Locke, sat down beside her, as he always had, seemingly unaware or at least unconcerned with the scandalous cloud hovering above his beautiful big sister's head. On the other hand, her older brother, Truman, still refused to speak to his only sister, let alone sit with her or acknowledge her existence at the family's church.

Truman, now in his second year at LSU, was adamant that Dolores be sent off somewhere private, like the New Orleans Home for Unwed Mothers to have her "bastard child." She should give it up for adoption, he said. A violent argument erupted between the two when Truman demanded this course of action after Dee broke the news to her family a little over a month prior and the two had not spoken to each other since that night.

The Widow Kelli-Kay's eldest son, David Jr., three years older than Truman, had been home on leave from the Air Force when the Crockett family discussed Dolores's indiscretion and the fate of her would-be illegitimate offspring. As David was good friends with Jimmy-Jack's older brother Frank, he was sure that JJ and Dee would marry, and Jimmy-Jack would do right by his wife and child.

Since Dee hadn't heard from Jimmy-Jack in over a week—and his mother had phoned Kelli-Kay to "assure" her that her own good son would have nothing more to do with any of Dee's "nonsense"—no one in the family really believed he would do the right thing, and Dee was starting to have doubts of her own.

David Jr.—the man of the house since Papa died—would have been a very welcome comfort to Dee as the little church erupted in the overly-emotional singing that was intended to whip the small congregation into a spiritual frenzy. Unfortunately for Dee, however, David Jr. was back on the Dobbins Air Force Base somewhere in a place that she had never heard of prior to David Jr. being stationed there—Marietta, Georgia.

The music, a precursor to the damnation that would rain down, as if Heaven above had poured out its great bowls of wrath, was tame compared to the young and ambitious "Bible Bill" Grantham once he took the podium of his congregation.

Grantham, a graduate of Bob Jones University, had spent a few years moving around through different congregations and denominations, but it was here in Livingston Parish, at the little church in Walker, that Grantham would hone his infectious style and perfect the Old Time Revival that would soon catapult him into the national spotlight and help him build a religious empire.

It was hard to discern the difference in the Crusader Band and the thunderstorm now raging outside when Grantham's equally thunderous voice joined the chorus.

"REPENT, REPENT, REPENT ye workers of wickedness, for the LORD GAWD is a wrathful God."

For over an hour Dee sat mortified as the Right Reverend—who seemingly made eye contact with no one but her—hammered on loose living, "whoring" around, insufficient character, that evil Elvis Presley's immoral music, and last but not least, plain ole fornication; "only by openly confessing YOUR sins, repenting and turning from that big wide road of sin and destruction can YOU be forgiven and saved from YOUR wretchedness."

"Come ye, to the LORD," went the altar call.

It was as if every eye in the congregation, not just the obvious glare of Grantham, was bearing down squarely on her soul. Dee wanted desperately to repent, to be forgiven, to have her broken heart healed right there at the mahogany and granite-topped altar in the front of the old church but she couldn't move—she was mortified, terrified, and at the moment she felt paralyzed. She sat sobbing as a lightning bolt struck the ground just outside the church and everyone inside the building could feel the hair on the back of their neck stand up.

Grantham simultaneously sounded the second altar call. "OBEY the LORD, lest thy eternal soul be damned to everlasting fire!"

When Dee couldn't budge, let alone bring herself forward to the altar, the Reverend Grantham's wife let out a piercing howl that announced to the congregation that she would now, "Prophesy in the name of the LORD."

In a loud shrill voice Sister Grantham declared, "The wicked shall burn in the eternal fire that I have reserved for the Devil and his offspring, and the Devil's own daughter is in our sanctuary this night, she will burn in damnation's fire for her sins . . ."

Dee ran out of the sanctuary and back through the portico as fast as her legs could carry her, soaked as much from her own tears—which would not seem to stop pouring from her nearly bleeding eyes—as from the torrent pouring from the heavens.

She slipped on the rocks and scraped her knee as she neared the end of the gravel where Highway 190 stretched out in front of her. As she looked back at the old church, which seemed to be smoldering with an unholy spirit, she saw Truman dragging a struggling Locke back inside. No one else followed. No one else even cared, she thought. She took off running again, away from the church and away from the direction of her home, though no one saw which direction she ran as the struggle between her brothers now had the attention of the church and her mother. By the time Kelli-Kay did start looking for her, Dee was miles away.

Dee kept running, it kept raining. By the time she looked up she had run through Walker and into Denham Springs. She just kept running, crying, and asking God why, why God, why? She was in fairly good shape—she had been on the Walker track team until her mother showed up for one of the track meets and found her wearing a pair of short pants—so it wasn't impossible for her to run great distances, even through a hammering rain. Nonetheless, two hours had passed when she realized she was crossing the Amite River Bridge that led into Baton Rouge.

She had been to Baton Rouge a few times, most recently on the visit to LSU to discuss the scholarship she had been awarded, which she now had no chance of utilizing. It was the big city to Dee, the capital of Louisiana, and the hub of the southeastern part of the state. To a small-town girl like Dee, it might as well have been New York City.

As she stopped on the middle of the old iron bridge, which was noticeably swaying beneath her feet, she looked at the raging water below. It was dangerously close to the bottom of the bridge and for a brief moment she wondered if it wouldn't be easier to just let the raging waters wash her like a piece of driftwood through the parish and on toward its final destination, Lake Maurepas.

She was jolted as an enormous stout oak crashed into the bridge rocking the entire structure and knocking her down like she'd been hit by one of the Walker Wildcats' all-state linebackers. A limb protruded through the guardrail tearing her saturated dress and leaving a deep gash right across her impregnated belly. As it started to bleed profusely, she realized she had to find shelter rather quickly or her baby might not ever grace this planet.

Running again, now in desperate need of a dry and safe place to be, she had to finish almost another mile before she found La Rouge Motel, guided by the beaming neon "vacancy" sign.

The nice lady who ran the motel—a brand new roadside, which had opened only a month prior—along with her husband, made her way down the stairs from their apartment into the office behind the front counter when she heard the bells—attached to the door frame—announcing the new arrival.

"My lord child, what happened to you, has someone hurt you?"

"No ma'am," Dee said catching her breath from her final sprint, "I'm okay; I just need a shower and a warm bed. I've got five dollars with me, is that enough to pay for a room?"

"Never mind the room, honey; do your parents know where you are?"

"No ma'am. It's really a long story but I'm not welcomed at home right now, I'm afraid."

"Well, come on over here and let me take a look at that cut. We'll figure out where you belong later."

Two

No one at the church thought much of the surge when lightning struck the ground outside. They were entirely focused on Brother Grantham raining damnation down on that misguided sinner so no one realized that the fire, which was about to consume that horrible night and the little wooden church, was already burning inside the walls when they flipped the power switch off after the Sunday Evening Worship Service.

By now the "April showers" had poured more than eight inches of rain onto the saturated ground but the heavy thicket of tall oaks and evergreen pines surrounding the church absorbed a lot of the downpour. As the last car made its way onto the old two-lane blacktop the glow of the spirit blazed into a raging inferno. The rain as well as the saturated exterior may have prolonged the crackling roast but by the time the Denham Springs Volunteer Fire Department's one water truck and four barely trained firemen made it to the scene, the timber-framed, cedar-sided and heart-pine floored structure was all but a memory.

The congregation would argue for years that the lightning was brought on by the wrath of God, to warn that wicked little sinner. Some even speculated that perhaps the scorned Crockett girl returned to set fire to the place herself. But a small silent minority thought the lightning was, indeed, from God—yet it was not meant for the poor child that Grantham chased off into oblivion. Instead, though they would never voice the opinion, they believed the lightning was meant for ole Bible Bill himself.

Far from the disaster the local community and that silent minority thought the fire would be for the reverend and his flock, the fire proved to be the ember that would set his ministry ablaze.

A large tent was set up in the field next to the church ruins and Bible Bill Grantham thumped the Good Book and stroked the spirit with a vigorous zeal and thundering dialect that moved even the most heathen soul. Each service drew more than the last and each altar call brought a steady stream of sinners to repentance. It was an old fashioned, fire-and-brimstone revival like Livingston Parish had never seen.

By the end of that summer, the Walker Church of Christ's Old Time Revival was saving lost souls every night of the week, except Monday. The general ministry and the reconstruction fund were discussed with great need and soul-stirring urgency twice each service. The collection plates were emptied three or four times before they finished each pass in front of every soul present; they were blessed, indeed.

With the rapidly growing treasury chest, the church elders hadn't even thought about the possibility of an insurance claim. But when Grantham walked into Elder Dean Higginbotham's living room with a $300,000 check for the full value of the church's recovery policy—a policy Bible Bill had negotiated with another church member two days after the fire—a minirevival broke out right there at the Higginbotham's house.

Two

The gathering quickly turned into a preconstruction meeting to plan the new church in Walker, which would essentially be a simple rebuild of the old church, perhaps a few upgrades and would cost an estimated $45,000. Another $30,000 would need to go toward the "insurance premium." The rest of the money, along with 80 percent of the revival collections, would be donated to the Old Time Revival Ministry—which had just agreed to a weekly radio broadcast. In fact, Grantham's ministry would soon be sweeping the nation thanks to an appearance Bible Bill was preparing for at the Madison Square Garden, New York City, where he would stir the audience into his trademark spiritual fury before introducing the renowned Reverend Ralph David Abernathy Sr., a leader in the Civil Rights movement.

Grantham's sermon—delivered in a deep southern drawl—on civil rights and the evils of segregation wasn't very popular back in his all-white church in Walker, Louisiana, but the notoriety made him an A-list preacher and gave him a national stage, virtually overnight. Soon he would be delivering his brand of salvation "from God, for Country" to presidents, senators, civil rights leaders, and a devoted national radio and television audience.

By the time Kelli-Kay Crockett would request a meeting with him in 1965, the Reverend William T. Grantham—Bible Bill—was the preeminent and most successful televangelist in the history of the media, his Old Time Revival Tour (OTRT) was selling out twenty-thousand-seat arenas all over the country and construction of the grand new seminary bearing his name had just broken ground near his home town of Hattiesburg, in the flat southern plains of Mississippi, about an hour from New Orleans.

He was a very busy and important man, but he would not hesitate to meet with the Widow Crockett.

Three

The Amite River crested at thirty-four feet and the bridge into Denham Springs was submerged under at least six feet of water. The same massive tree that had struck Dee had lodged itself into the side of the structure, busting loose one end of one of the two riveted iron support arches that straddled either side of the fifty-year-old bridge. It would take the National Guard over a week to repair and reopen the bridge. The flood would also fill La Rouge Motel with local folks looking to escape the rising water in their low-lying homesteads, the National Guard working to restore the bridge, and volunteers helping with the rescue effort. The place was about to be buzzing.

Nora Hutchins, coowner, and general manager, agreed to accept two dollars as a deposit for the room, not knowing how long the flood siege might hold this poor little girl from Livingston Parish hostage. Dee promised that she had more than enough money stashed away—money she had been saving since she started doing odd jobs, babysitting, working at the library, and tutoring since she was twelve—to cover the three dollars per night and would pay in full plus any extras as soon as she could make her way back home. She knew she had at least $400 in the old Hills Bros Coffee tin that she kept in the back of the closet she shared with her mother. It seemed like a small fortune to Dee, but she would soon learn how expensive life in the real world could be.

The child looked like she had been for a midnight swim in Alligator Bayou when Nora first laid eyes on her. She wasn't much younger than her own daughter, Brenda—a sophomore at Louisiana College in Pineville, living on campus and away from her parents for the first time—and though Dee reminded Nora of her college-aged daughter, this one was still just a little girl. Nora found one of Brenda's old outfits that looked like it would fit Dee and insisted she borrow it so Nora could mend and launder the tattered mess she was wearing when she walked into the motel.

After a warm shower and the plate of leftovers that Nora had given her, Dee passed out on top of the bed covers and slept like a baby. She woke up to the buzz outside La Rouge as the National Guard set up its small rescue outpost. There were also at least two dozen pick-up trucks lined up in front of the motel with various types of boats either being pulled behind by or tied onto the vehicles in some way.

Less than 400 yards down the new blacktop called Stevendale Road there was a dip where the street would normally descend a short hill, cross a 350-yard bridge over Steven's Creek, and go on for several miles down toward the river basin. Now the dip was a boat launch along a muddy brown shore with a murky, debris-filled raging current as far as the eye could see. The boats were searching the flooded zone for people from the two small neighborhoods that had been recently built off the new blacktop or further back where the Amite River camps were located. These camps—mostly small, A-framed wood structures built on stilts—were typically down along the Old River Trail, a dirt road at a much lower elevation than Stevendale Road and well below the flood stage level. If those people had not evacuated by now, they might as well be the driftwood.

Nora was busy in the motel office when Dee ventured downstairs to use the phone booth, dreading the phone call she knew she had to make. Dee had never so much as been late for a curfew or gone to the library without her mother's approval. Now she had to face not only the scorn of running out of the church in shame, but also she had virtually disappeared. Dee knew that in addition to being angry her mother would have worried herself sick by now, not knowing where her daughter was.

"I'm okay, Momma . . . I'm in Baton Rouge."

"Baton Rouge . . . how in the world did you get to Baton Rouge, honey?"

"I guess I ran."

"So now my daughter is a runaway too?"

"No ma'am, that wasn't what I was doing, at least not from you, I just had . . . I just had to get away from the church, Momma. It wasn't fair for Brother Grantham to do that to me in front of God and everybody."

"Well, child, you did make your bed, now you have to lay in it."

"I know, Momma, but does the whole congregation have to tuck me in?"

"No, I reckon not, dear. Where are you? I'll come pick you up."

"You can't, not yet anyway. The bridge from Denham Springs is out and it might be days before they fix it."

They agreed that Dolores would call her mother the second the bridge reopened and they would take up her discipline once she got home safely. After they hung up, Kelli-Kay Crockett called the office of La Rouge Motel and thanked Nora for looking after her little girl. She assured Nora that her bill would be paid in full. Mrs. Hutchins promised Kelli-Kay that she would take care of her and complimented what a lovely girl Dee seemed to be.

"God bless you, ma'am!"

"And you, too, Mrs. Crockett."

They would say this to each other twice a day for the next six days.

Dee walked into the LeBlanc Family Diner next door to La Rouge and spent eighty-five cents on a scrambled egg, a plop of grits, a link of andouille sausage, and a couple pieces of toast. It seemed like a lot to her, but the place was packed, and the food was pretty good. She could do better, she thought. She had learned to cook before she was eight years old and breakfast was her specialty.

By the time she got back to La Rouge several boats had returned with survivors from the flood. One family was pulled from their roof top, while another man had climbed a tall tree where he spent the night being bitten at least twice by water moccasins. He did not look very good. An ambulance and a nurse had been sent from the Our Lady of the Lake Sanitarium all the way on the other side of town, near LSU. Dixon Memorial Hospital in Denham Springs would have been a lot closer, but they did not have an ambulance and it did not have a bridge to cross even if they did.

The screech from the siren was one of the most piercing sounds Dee had ever heard. Well, maybe not quite as piercing as the prophesying Sister Grantham, but enough that it made Dee stop and say a silent prayer for a man she had never met. She would never know if that little prayer was answered. She wasn't really sure if God would still hear her prayers, but she hoped that he would.

Dee walked back into the office where Nora and her husband Dick were on the brink of being completely overwhelmed. They were happy to have any assistance when Dee asked how she could help.

Her first task was helping with the laundry and for the next six days Dee got a crash course in the motel business. It was hard work, but she learned a lot about taking care of the guests; the proper way to turn down a bed; and food service, as opposed to just cooking food. There were even a couple of irate customers that she had to deal with.

Dee studied Nora as she negotiated with the National Guard captain who contracted all their meals through the motel, which Nora promptly subcontracted to the LeBlanc family. Dee was put in charge of the menus and making sure Dick and Lucinda, the motel's maid, set the meeting room up properly for their meals. The Guard also rented over half of the rooms at the Inn, most on the first floor, which were the smaller, single-occupancy rooms at a "special government rate" of six dollars per night, ten dollars for the suites on the second floor. This gave Nora an excellent opportunity to explain supply and demand and teach Dee all about market rates and the principle of reasonable and customary.

By the time Mrs. Crockett arrived to collect her child Nora was ready to offer Dee a full-time job as the assistant general manager of the motel. She told Kelli-Kay how much help she'd been and how kind and considerate she was toward the guests, her two employees, the poor people who were trying to endure the flood—really everyone who she came in contact with.

Nora refused to accept payment when Kelli-Kay tried to settle up.

"Not a chance. That girl more than earned her keep."

Nora gave Dee a big hug and told her to come back to visit sometime while Dick handed her a twenty-dollar bill and thanked her for all her hard work.

For the first time in a while Kelli-Kay remembered why she had always been so proud of her little girl.

Four

Dee broke the silence. "Momma."

"Yes, honey?"

"You know how you said that I made my bed."

"Well, I suppose that boy had something to do with it too. But it's your burden to bear, yes."

"I didn't mean for this to happen, Momma, but I'm not ashamed of my baby. I'm going to do what I have to do to raise it right."

"I know you will, honey. But life is hard and you're not ready to raise a family by yourself."

"I won't be by myself, Momma!"

"Well, where is he then?"

"I don't know, but he'll be back. I know it. I know he loves me."

As they made their way thru Denham Springs, Dee told her momma that she wanted her college money, the modest inheritance her father—a WWII Navy Veteran and direct descendant of Davey Crockett, who had died eight years earlier in an oil-rig explosion—left behind for his only daughter. Kelli-Kay initially rejected the notion, but she knew it would be all but impossible for Dee to attend college and raise a child now. She wanted to know what Dolores intended to do with all that money. Kelli-Kay knew it wasn't enough to last forever but it would have put her through college and given her a nice start in life.

"Oh, my goodness, Momma, the church! What happened?"

"Well, some folks are saying you might have burnt it down. I 'spect God did it."

As they passed the ruins of the church and the enormous white tent that was being erected in its stead, Kelli-Kay was noticeably shaken in her unwavering stand for all things Bill Grantham. It wasn't that she was proud of her daughter's situation or that she thought it was okay for her first grandchild to be born out of wedlock. But watching her sweet, beautiful little girl run from the church in terror and spending a week worried sick about her while the hypocrite clique at the church threw stones at her family from their own glass houses was just about all she could take.

The $12,000 was placed in a checking account—along with the $573.75 from Dee's tin coffee can—with Dolores Helen Crockett as the sole account holder. She promised her mother that she would keep a balanced check book and a strict budget. Though she was barely seventeen, Kelli-Kay knew her daughter was capable of balancing a checkbook and living on her own—Dee had been balancing Kelli-Kay's checkbook for nearly four years and was responsible for writing and mailing the checks for the family's monthly bills. Kelli-Kay would sign the checks and would always review the bank statement and check book register with Dolores in an effort to teach the child about managing money but Dee had long since been better with money than her momma.

The duplex was only a mile and a half away from the family homestead, out near Satsuma. Dee had promised above all else that she would not allow unchaperoned boys into her home at any time for any reason. It was a two-family, pier-block wooden structure with knotted cedar siding and a slightly rusting but charming tin roof.

The small community of cute, if slightly rustic structures, had been built by the logging company that stripped the thick forest from Hammond all the way through Livingston Parish to East Baton Rouge in the 1930s making way for the construction of Highway 190 and the small towns that cropped up along the route.

The community manager, Mr. Barlow Arledge and his wife Sara, lived in the other half of Dee's duplex. They were members of the Walker Church of Christ and they, too, had been put off by the branding and banishment of the Crockett girl. The couple had known Dee since the family arrived from Michigan over a decade ago—they knew she was no wicked temptress.

She had obviously made a mistake, but surely a merciful God could make room to forgive the sweet and innocent little girl that was known for the wonderful homemade chicken noodle soup that she delivered to virtually every family in the congregation who had ever had a sick member. Some of those hypocrites faked a cold just to have a bowl of "the healing soup" as it had been nicknamed by the women of the congregation.

Mr. Arledge agreed to put new woven carpet in the two-bedroom home, have the slat and plaster walls painted, and keep a watchful eye over Dee and her coming new arrival for a $150 deposit and $75 per month.

Dee would learn to wait tables at the Walgreens Cafeteria where Kelli-Kay was the first-shift manager. A good waitress could make $40 to $50 per week if she worked hard and had a friendly attitude, two traits Dee had in bushels. They figured she could work for about a month and a half before she would need to take time off to give birth and tend to the baby for "a while."

They pretty much had it all figured out and both Dee and her momma were beginning to think everything was going to work out just fine.

Five

Dee's ankles felt like eggshells crashing against a cast-iron skillet with every step she took. It was late September, the hot summer sun burned through the old tin roof to the point that she could see the heat. She had a brand-new Westinghouse Electro-Matic fan but all it seemed to do was sling the heat at her in sweltering repetitive waves. She held one hand hard-pressed against the small of her back to the point that she felt like she could feel her palm print formed into her skin. It was hotter than a whore in church on Sunday, her belly was as big as one of those giant beach balls she had seen kids playing with in Biloxi, and every inch of her body ached.

If I could get my hands on that Jimmy-Jack right now, she thought, I just might kill him.

She heard Mr. Arledge's voice at about the same time as the knock on the door. "What's your business here, son?"

"I came by to see Dee," came Jack's voice.

"She 'specting you?"

"I wasn't," Dee said as she opened the door. "But I don't 'spect he'll be staying long, Mr. Arledge."

As Barlow started walking away, he gave Jimmy-Jack a look that seemed to communicate the promise of death and dismemberment if the boy so much as shook hands with Dee.

"What are you doing here?"

"I missed you, Dee. I want to make things right."

"It's a little late for that Jack. You deserted me."

"I didn't desert you, Dee. My parents freaked out and made me go to boarding school."

"Well, I had to quit school. You've been home for almost two months, where've you been all this time?"

"I've been trying to figure it out, Dee."

"Were you trying to figure it out at the drive-in with Peggy Sue Atmore last week?"

"I wasn't there with . . ."

Dee closed the door and Barlow, standing about twenty-five yards away, pulled the starter string on his old chainsaw and started cutting branches off the same tree he had trimmed down the day before.

They both knew she would forgive him; Jimmy-Jack just had to give Dee a little time. He knew that she loved him, and he was pretty sure he loved her. He did miss her when he was away and he really didn't care for Peggy Sue that much, though he had taken her to the drive-in and then almost to home base until her mother got home, forcing him to flee through the open window of her bedroom. God forbid Mrs. Atmore find a boy alone, necking no less, with her perfect little angel.

He was also pretty sure that Dee's mother had given her the inheritance money she was supposed to use for college. He knew that Mrs. Crockett would not pay her rent or support her living on her own; it just wasn't her way. She apparently wasn't working at the moment and

Five

his buddy at the used car dealership told him that she had handed him fifteen, crisp one hundred dollar bills for the bubble-gum blue '52 Studebaker resting in the deep gravel in front of her house. Not that he cared about the money, he told himself, but it sure could help them get started if he did marry her.

Kelli-Kay was still steaming at the fact that Dee agreed to marry the little cretin just two weeks after he showed up on her doorstep. She was glad that at least the wedding would take place before the child was born but she also could not stand the fact that Dee was wearing a flowing white dress. She had wanted her daughter to be married in her own white gown but that was now out of the question. Kelli-Kay loved her daughter but she was certainly not a virgin and that is what the white dress is supposed to signify: purity.

When the justice of the peace asked if anyone knew any reason why these two should not be wed, Kelli-Kay thought of about three or four instantly. She knew if she had a little time she could write a book on the reasons why they shouldn't be yoked but she held her peace, like the other twenty-seven witnesses present, and James Jackson Dempsey and Dolores Helen Crockett were pronounced man and wife.

There wasn't a honeymoon, though they agreed to take a trip to Biloxi as soon as the baby was okay to travel. Jack took a job at a butcher shop in Denham Springs, where he would learn the trade, and they prepared as best they could for their firstborn.

Anna Rae Dempsey, born in the middle of the night on Sunday, April 13, 1958, was a tiny, beautiful spring arrival. Her eyes were as big and blue as a cloudless summer sky and from the first time her little dimpled mouth smiled effortlessly at her mother the two were in love.

In the lifetime that would unfold in front of them they would experience good times and bad; they would enjoy magical times and needless suffering; they would hate and love each other as much as they would love and hate each other's choice in men; and they would grow up and raise children, grandchildren, and great-grandchildren together and one day they would be BFFs, but today all Dee could see was hope in a beautiful baby girl.

Six

The following summer Jimmy-Jack and Dee took Anna Rae to Biloxi, Mississippi, for a nice long weekend. They relaxed under the shade of one of the large public sunbrellas on the beach just across from Broadwater Beach Hotel and Resort, where Jack wanted to stay. Dee agreed to go to the resort's upscale restaurant for an evening meal, but she insisted that they stay in one of the cheaper roadsides to keep within their agreed-upon budget for the trip. With taking care of the baby and working all the time there had not been a lot of intimacy in their marriage, but Dee felt the sickness Sunday morning on their way back home.

She did not say anything to Jimmy-Jack right away, they were doing okay but he was having a hard time with the daddy thing.

Where they were both from, most of the parenting, the feeding of an infant, diaper changing, rocking the baby, and such were considered just as much "woman's work" as the birthing. She was okay with that mindset to a point, or at least resigned to it as the way of the world; but Jack hardly wanted to touch the child. He was much more interested in fishing, hunting, football, and spending her money.

Between Jack's mother, Kelli-Kay, and Mrs. Arledge there was always a willing sitter for Anna Rae, so Dee decided to work as much as she could before baby number two came along. At the rate Jack was burning through money they were going to need it. He had a job too and was making a decent living, but it was still her money that made them comfortable.

The duplex was well decorated, they both had nice clothes and Jimmy was driving around in a beautiful, aquamarine '57 Chevrolet 210. He had really wanted the more expensive Bel Air—supposedly for Dee as he swore he would drive the Studebaker—but Dee was not about to spend an extra $500 just so the windows could roll themselves up, even though the Bel Air was really pretty with all the extra chrome and such.

For a couple months she would work six first-shifts and an occasional second-shift or two when one of the other girls could not make it in or didn't show up. She liked working the Café at Walgreens, and was making about ninety dollars per week, which was great money, but her momma nagged her endlessly. She meant well, and she was probably right about Jack's irresponsibility but what was she supposed to do now? He was her husband.

In October, in part to show interest in the things Jack liked and to have a little fun, Dee crafted Chinese-themed Halloween costumes for the family. She and Anna Rae were the cutest geisha girls Livingston Parish had ever seen, even if she was starting to show ever so slightly, and Jack was a purple-and-gold donned Chinese bandit, in honor of the defensive squad that was capturing the attention of the LSU football faithful and the college football loving nation.

The tickets were hard to come by, but Jack called in a favor from a regular customer at the butcher shop and landed three tickets to

Six

the Halloween Night game between #1 LSU and their archrival, the #3 Ole Miss Rebels, at Tiger Stadium. Dee had been to a few Walker High School football games and she loved the atmosphere of a fall Friday night with hundreds of happy fans cheering for their team.

This was something different entirely. She had never seen so much purple or smelled so much bourbon. She had been a little nervous about bringing Anna Rae into a crowd of sixty-seven thousand people but when Billy Cannon broke up the sideline—shedding would-be Rebel tacklers like a bucking Brahma bull shedding skinny cowboys—she was afraid the stadium was going to collapse around them. The crowd, most of them in various Halloween costumes, went absolutely wild and the decibel level never dropped below a completely deafening roar. She literally could not distinguish Jack's voice as he screamed at the top of his lungs standing right next to her.

Anna Rae survived as did the Tigers, thanks to a last-second goal line stand, also led by the man who would cement his legend, and the 1959 Heisman Trophy that night, LSU's #20, William Abb "Billy" Cannon.

The Dempsey family had a great time at the game and would enjoy a nice holiday season, but Jack's spending was getting out of hand. When the January 1960 bank statement arrived, she cried.

Christmas had been wonderful, but Jack bought lavish gifts for all his family, some of whom she had never heard of. And of course, they bought a ton of stuff for Anna Rae, but now her account was out of balance by over $500 and she barely had $1,000 left in the account.

Between her and Jack-Ass, as she started calling him to herself, they were earning over $8,800 per year, which was more than most families—more than Truman was making at his job as a branch manager at Louisiana National Bank (LNB) in Baton Rouge—and they didn't have any loans to repay. But here she was looking at a squandered fortune, just a couple months away from having two children and she suddenly felt like she was on the verge of homelessness.

They had a pretty heated fight over the statement, and they did not speak to each other for over a week. They managed to patch things up and buckled down for a while and he was a little more present after Jimmy-Jack Jr. came along at high noon on Monday, April 18, 1960.

Jimmy-Jack Sr., the nineteen-year-old father of two worked two shifts at the butcher shop most days and had been promoted to assistant manager. He did regret blowing Dee's money, but he worked hard for his money too, while she had inherited most of hers, he told himself.

"Peggy Atmore," Jimmy-Jack said looking up from his display case.

"Hey, Jimmy. I haven't seen you since you hightailed it out of my window."

"Well, I'm still scared of your mother."

"Everybody is."

Peggy got two filet cuts and handed him a piece of folded paper with her phone number on it. He folded it over again and stuck it in his billfold.

Peggy Sue Atmore had become a pretty young lady, she had blossomed quite well, in fact, he thought, but Dee Crockett-Dempsey was by far the most beautiful woman Jimmy-Jack had ever seen. She had been a cute, little, green-eyed girl that he chased around in church when they were kids. In high school she had been asked out by and subsequently rejected virtually every guy that could muster up the courage to ask her for a date.

She had turned him down several times, too, but she had never been to a movie theater so when *The Ten Commandments* starring Charlton Heston was released in 1956, he talked Truman into asking her to go with him and some of their friends. It was also the only way the Widow Crockett would have ever let her out of the house, let alone to go anywhere with a boy.

Six

Now she was about to turn twenty years old, a shapely and tall, stunning brunette with soul-piercing hazel eyes. She had grown two humans in her belly, and quickly lost the excess weight afterward. The reason she made so much money waiting tables was because the construction guys would come into the Walgreens every day just to see her smile. The average tab would be $1.50 and the customary gratuity for adequate service was a quarter but Dee almost always got a crisp new dollar bill and a tip of the hat.

She didn't even realize it either. That's what bothered Jimmy-Jack, she was so meek, humble and, frankly, naive. He wanted to take her to New York City or California where she could be a model, but she wouldn't have any of it. Even if she could bring herself to don a bathing suit in public—thanks to her browbeaten upbringing at the hands of her stiff old mother—she would never believe that she was beautiful or that someone would want her picture in a magazine. But she was, and they would have, there was no question in Jack's mind.

Buddy Holly might be singing about Peggy Sue, he mused to himself, but that's only because he had never seen Dee Crockett!

Seven

Dee didn't know anything about the loan and wouldn't have agreed to it in a million years. Jack Ass, the Jimmy part would pretty much be dropped for good after this episode, marched into the Louisiana National Bank and convinced Truman to loan him $7,500 to open his own butcher shop. He used Dee's Studebaker as collateral and put both of their names on the promissory note. Thanks to the fact that women had fewer rights than blacks in the early sixties and her brother and husband were both Jack Asses, she was now in debt without so much as a mention.

Allowing herself to be as gullible as she was trusting, Dee didn't dig too deep when Jack started enacting his plan for the Satsuma Meat Market. It was a good idea, she thought. She was always complaining that they needed a market a little closer to home and the Jack Ass was pretty good at running the store over in Denham Springs.

She was now pregnant with their third child, though JJ's evil sister was running around telling everyone in town that the child wasn't her brother's. Dee had always been the brunt of a lot of jealous rumors but this one hurt. She was a good mother, a hard worker, and despite the selfishness and fairly regular jack-assery of her husband she was a supportive and faithful wife.

They found a spot on South Pine Street near State Route 190 in Livingston. It was a little further out but other than the general store, that didn't have much for fresh meat or produce, there wasn't any competition. Still, $400 a month seemed high rent for the small storefront, but Jack insisted they would hit it big and the rent would be easy to make. She did most of the decorating, painting, cleaning, and bookkeeping, though her cousin Abby Mae, who lived two blocks south, helped a lot. Even with doing most of the work themselves, by the time they plugged in the little neon sign announcing that they were open for business the Dempseys had spent almost all the $7,500 and Dee still didn't know where it came from. Jack called it his "family money."

Dee, Jack, and the two kids would arrive at the store every morning promptly at 7:00 am. Dee would help the children with a few "chores" and wait for Abby to come for them. Abby would take them for playtime at Aunt Martha's house over on Magnolia Street. Once the kids had gone Dee would check the four double rows of "grocery" shelves to see to it they were stocked neatly and appropriately, arrange the newspapers at the deli counter, and make sure she had proper change in the cash drawer. When the store was ready for business, she would unlock the door and put on a large pot of the healing soup, a pot of chili, or her mother's étouffée—if the crawfish were in season—and start slicing bread, tomatoes, and cucumbers.

With the thinly sliced deli meats Jack provided and fresh baked bread she got from the bakery three stores down, the $1.60 soup and sandwich special at Dee's Deli in the Satsuma Meat Market was a huge hit. She sold out every day. They sold roughly $2,800 a month in groceries, another $3,200 in fresh meats and produce, and the deli did almost $5,000, not counting the tips and there was always a jar full of tips. Yet, after the cost of goods sold, the rent, electricity, water, the high equipment payments, which were over $1,500, they were still only clearing about $390 a month.

She was now just too pregnant to be working two jobs but at least they were scraping by, she thought. The coming hospital and delivery bills wouldn't be easy to pay but if they could just keep the store and deli going until she could get back on her feet, she could start taking some second-shifts at Walgreens to make up the difference.

Truman and his wife Joy came to visit her at the hospital in August of 1963. Russell Dean, an 11 lb, 3 oz baby boy arrived early that Wednesday, the 7th, and was currently snuggled safely in his momma's arms.

In a way his siblings would always appreciate but never fully comprehend, Dee's third child—second son—made her feel safe from the very moment she took him into her arms. They would have a comforting affect on each other from that day forward and Dean would always be Momma's big boy.

Truman, on the other hand, was there not to comfort his little sister or meet his newest nephew; he was there to make a collection call. He waited until Kelli-Kay stepped into the bathroom to freshen up a bit.

"Dee, I know this might not be the best time, but you guys haven't made any payments on your loan and the bank is getting impatient . . ."

"What loan, Truman? What are you talking about?"

"The loan my bank extended to you and JJ to open the market."

"What are you talking about, Truman? I've never borrowed anything in my life!"

"Well, Jimmy-Jack told me about your plans together and he said you were afraid to ask, so I was doing you a favor."

"I wasn't afraid to ask, Truman, I wouldn't ask, how could you loan *me* money without talking to *me*?"

"We'll he is *your* husband, so the loan documents are legally binding."

Kelli-Kay was out of the bathroom and when she returned to the room, she did not like what she was hearing.

"How much money does she owe, Truman?"

"Seven-thousand five-hundred dollars plus the interest and three months of delinquent fees; it's about $8,600 all together and growing."

Dee was sobbing and rocking her baby as she held him tightly in her arms.

"Dolores Helen, did you know about all this?"

Dee couldn't speak. She just kept shaking her head "no" and crying uncontrollably. Kelli-Kay asked Truman and Joy to leave.

"We'll be down to the bank as soon as she's able and we'll figure it out."

"You're not cleaning up another one of her damn messes, Momma!"

"And you are not gonna tell your mother what she will or will not do, young man! And if I remember correctly Dolores and I have been cleaning up after you your whole life so just go on now, we'll come square it up as soon as she's on her feet."

Kelli-Kay tried to take the baby away so Dee could rest, but Dee held on to Big Dean as if she were clinging to life itself. Dean was awake and seemed to be looking into his momma's eyes, but he didn't make a sound. Right now, Momma was doing all the crying.

When Jack Ass—as he was also about to be known to Kelli-Kay—came bopping into the hospital at 7:00 pm Abby was waiting to take the kids over to Aunt Martha's.

"Where's my big ole baby boy?" he wanted to know.

"Did you take out a loan at Truman's bank in my name?" Dee asked abruptly.

"Uh, well, it was for us, Dee, for the kids, for the market, and we're doing so well . . ."

"Doing well? We haven't made a single payment on the loan apparently, we're barely able to pay the rent, and now we have another mouth to feed. How is that doing well?"

"Well, we're getting there and he's your brother, Dee—he's loaded, and he can afford to give his little sister some time to pay back a simple loan."

"It doesn't matter if he's loaded or not loaded. He's responsible for the bank but he doesn't own the place and him being my brother doesn't give you the right to borrow money, especially if you can't pay it back."

"Well, he is loaded, Dee, can't he cut his little sister some slack?"

"Slack? No, you Jack Ass, now, thanks to you, in addition to being the tramp of the family he thinks I'm a beggar who doesn't fulfill her obligations."

"He'll get over it."

"No, he'll get paid. If we have to sell everything we own, he'll get paid."

"You know what," the Jack Ass snapped and angrily opined, "you are a pain in the ass and maybe your brother has a point, maybe you are a tramp! That baby is way too big to be my boy. Maybe you are having an affair like people are saying . . ."

"That'll be just about enough of that!" Kelli-Kay stepped in sternly before her daughter could collect herself from the shocking accusation, "You had no right to do what you did and you've got no call to be saying what you're saying, so you get yourself on out of here this instant before I lose my way with the Lord!"

Jimmy-Jack knew it was time to go and he knew his relationship with Dee was pretty much shot, so he went to their house and packed his things.

The Satsuma Market didn't open the next morning and Jimmy-Jack waited across the street from LNB until he saw Truman climb into a candy-apple red Ford Thunderbird convertible to leave for lunch. Once the little rich boy's car was no longer in sight he walked in and up to the teller where he wrote a counter check to himself for the entire $892 in Dee's checking account.

He also cleaned out the $1,730 savings account, the family's rainy-day fund, that she had been depositing half of her tips into without telling him. He had found the statement a few weeks ago so he had the account number. The account didn't have his name on it but she was his wife and according to the law of the land women had very few rights and property was held by the husband. It wasn't even stealing, legally.

Jimmy-Jack left Dee flat broke, over $15,000 in debt with a stack of unpaid bills and three children to feed. To make matters worse, he took the Chevy and had pledged her Studebaker for collateral. Her name was on the note for the equipment at the market but not on the lease for the building nor any of the stock certificates. She had been thoroughly used by him and would have absolutely nothing to show for all her hard work at the market.

James "Jimmy-Jack" Jackson Dempsey Sr., never sent to or spent a dime on his children and he seemed to ignore their existence, altogether. From the day he left, the entire Crockett family, even Truman's sweet wife Joy, referred to him simply as the Jack Ass.

Exactly two weeks and one day after the divorce was final the Jack Ass married Peggy Sue Atmore and their first child together, Peggy's second, carried to full term, arrived less than six months later.

Eight

❦

Livingston Parish Sheriff Taft W. Faust instructed his secretary to usher Mrs. Crockett and Mrs. Dempsey into his office and offer them a cup of coffee or water if they would like. He allowed Deputy Odom Graves to finish the briefing on the matter at hand and then he joined the two ladies in his office.

"How can I help you today, Mrs. Crockett?"

"Thanks for meeting with us, Sheriff. You remember my daughter, Dolores?"

He vaguely remembered David Crockett's sad-eyed young daughter who rode home from school in his squad car when her father died. But this full-grown, bombshell brunette sitting next to the Widow Crockett was not someone he would have forgotten.

"Ma'am," he said nodding toward Dee, "it's been a while, what can I do for you today?"

"Well, Sheriff, my husband, Jack A . . ." she caught herself, "Jimmy-Jack Dempsey left our family and took all of our . . . my money and my car—she was holding the canceled check she'd used to pay for the '57 Chevy—with him. He had no right . . ."

"I've had a couple of my deputies looking into the situation and there may not be a lot we can do. The car is actually in his name and even though you clearly paid for it," the sheriff said examining the check, "he is still your husband, so your property is his property in the eyes of the law."

"So, you're saying it's okay to steal from your wife and kids and leave them high and dry as far as you are concerned?" Kelli-Kay asked with not a small amount of agitation in her voice.

"I'm not saying that Mrs. Crockett, but the great State of Louisiana is, unfortunately."

"Well, I'm not asking the State for help, Taft, I'm asking you."

"I understand, and I want to help, I really do, he just hasn't technically broken the law here, no matter how much of a Jack Ass we all know him to be." He paused for a minute and opened the folder he had been handed by Deputy Odom, "There is one thing, however; we looked at the loan agreement between Mr. and Mrs. Dempsey and the Louisiana National Bank over in Baton Rouge. Truman, your son I believe, also signed the document." He stated as he then looked at Dolores, "Is that your signature right there, ma'am?"

"Well, it does kind of look like it could be mine, but I swear I've never seen that document before today"

"Yes, ma'am, we compared the signature on this document to the signature on your privilege license as a waitress, which we have here on file, and the two don't match at all so we are pretty confident we could make a bank fraud charge stick against your husband. But you need to understand, we'd be asking the DA over in East Baton Rouge to indict your brother Truman as well."

"Why Truman?" Kelli-Kay asked in a solemn, quiet tone.

Eight

"Someone forged Miss Dolores's signature and the teller at the bank notarized all three signatures which has to be done simultaneously and in person, so she'll be arrested too."

Dee didn't know what to say and Kelli-Kay was unable to speak. The sheriff broke the silence.

"If you ask me, the whole lot of 'em is crooked," he said referring to bankers in general. "But I don't know if your brother actually realized what your husband was up to. If you want to press charges, I'll go after 'em all and you'll have to testify against your husband and your brother."

"If y'all want to take a day or two and think about it, I understand. I will continue my investigation for now, unless you say otherwise," he said more as a courtesy than a question.

"We better talk about this, Momma."

"I reckon, child. Sheriff, don't let us keep you from your business."

"No, ma'am, I'll be in touch."

Sheriff Faust was a shrewd lawman and a pragmatic politician who would serve Livingston Parish for twenty-eight years, but he was also a devoted father and believed in a man caring for his own. Child support enforcement laws wouldn't be enacted in Louisiana for more than a decade, but to Sheriff Faust a bigger low-life didn't exist but a man who would steal from his family—and it was stealing whether the great State saw it that way or not—and leave 'em with no means of support.

"How can I help you, Sheriff?"

"You Truman Crockett?"

"I am. Please come on into my office, can I get you anything?"

"Well, I was wondering if you could produce a documented power of attorney that allowed you and that low life brother-in-law of yours to forge your sister's signature on this here loan agreement?"

"I'm sorry, Sheriff. I don't understand what you are getting at."

"Well, it's pretty simple, Mr. Crockett, your sister wasn't here in the bank when that teller lady out there, Emma Parker, it says right here, notarized this here document that has your signature, Mr. Dempsey's signature, and the name of your sister that was obviously signed by someone other than her.

"Now, I'm not entirely sure that your sister is going to press charges. Her and your momma left my office about an hour ago to ponder. What I am sure of, is that if this is your signature and your sister's here is fake, which we both know is a fact, well y'all gonna need to find another line of work after you spend a little time in a jail cell."

"It wasn't what it might look like, Sheriff. I was trying to help my sister, I never thought JJ would do what he did, but it was a legitimate business loan that I thought my sister wanted."

"A judge might buy that, and he might not send you to prison but you'd be done as a banker either way, don't you think?"

"What are you suggesting, Sheriff?"

"I'm not suggesting anything, Mr. Crockett. I don't pretend to know how you bankers operate but I suspect forging signatures on loan documents is one of those things that might tend to disqualify one from such a profession," the surly lawman said slowly and menacingly, "But I can tell you this, as an elected official I'd be some kind of perturbed if I knew a nice young citizen like your sister was walking about in my parish because she lost her car in some scam. Of course, I couldn't do much about it if the folks what took her car were in another parish . . ." He paused for effect. "Lessen, of course those same folks was to drive up Highway 190, right past my office, every other Sunday to go a visiting, I 'spect I'd want to keep an eye on folks like that, yep, I'd keep a real close eye . . ."

"I get it, Sheriff, but I promise it was a legitimate business loan and it has to be paid back to the bank."

Eight

"Well, that's between you and your kinfolk and I reckon y'all need to figure it out, but I sure would hate to see that girl a walking, that's what I'm saying, unless your sister decides to press charges, then I 'spect I'll have a little more to say . . ."

There wasn't much he could do with the other Jack Ass—other than take him gator baiting out on Bayou Manchac—if Dee didn't press charges. He knew she wouldn't send her brother to jail or be responsible for him losing his job; after all, he, too, had mouths to feed. The sheriff was pretty sure his visit motivated the banker to figure out a way to waive the collateral requirement of the loan. He wanted to do more, but he had to uphold the law, even when he didn't agree with it.

Nine

Truman *noted a clerical error* on the documentation and signed a waiver of the collateral requirement in the delinquent loan extended to Mr. and Mrs. Dempsey. Since he was the loan officer his annual bonus would be impacted by the bad debt and one or two more decisions like this loan and his lending authority would be downgraded if not revoked.

He explained to his mother and sister that he had only been trying to help Dolores and her family, JJ had him believe that the whole business plan was Dee's idea but she was afraid to ask for help, and she didn't think she would have been taken seriously.

"Truman, I'm tired of this discussion, you've been hateful to me for years and every chance you have to put me down, you take. I don't believe for a second you wanted to help me, and you don't believe for a second that I would have allowed you to make a loan on my behalf. For whatever reason you believed in the Jack Ass but y'all needed my name on the documents because I've had money in this bank for years and I pay my bills. And after one of you Jack Asses forged my signature and ruined my credibility YOU allowed that crook to walk into YOUR bank, while I was laid up in the hospital, and steal every last dime I had to my name."

"I . . . I was out to lunch, Dee; I didn't even know he was here."

"What kind of bank allows someone to write a check to himself; from an account that doesn't even have his name on it?"

"Well, he is your husband so that gives him the right in the State of Louisiana."

"So basically, I have no rights, stealing is okay as long as you steal from a woman and her children?"

"Listen, Dee, the money is gone I can't get it back but I'm going to pay back the loan, you won't have to worry about that."

"Oh, no you will not! You are not holding that over my head. Here's my first payment and I will pay however much I can every month until it's paid off but you might as well go ahead and close my accounts at the bank, not that it matters but I will no longer be a customer."

The payment was only sixty dollars but that was all she could come up with after working eight shifts in five days. She still had three kids to feed, she was behind on the rent, and now she had hospital bills to pay.

Kelli-Kay was disgusted by it all. She'd raised her children better than this. She was mad at Dolores for letting that worthless boy get her pregnant in the first place, so she had to marry him, and what a Jack Ass he turned out to be!

She had three beautiful grandbabies and she loved them dearly but my goodness, she thought: "How in the world is this poor girl going to raise them all by herself?"

And Truman, there was no excuse for it, she was inclined to let him face the sheriff come what may, but Dolores wouldn't do it. She said she wasn't going to put Joy and their two babies through what she was going through. Still, Kelli-Kay didn't like it and she didn't raise the

Nine

boy and put him through college so he could learn to be sly. Maybe he was only trying to help Dolores, but you don't sign someone else's name to obligation without ever discussing it, whether some stupid law that should have been abolished with slavery, said it was okay or not.

It would be a while before Kelli-Kay would forgive and or speak to her son, she wanted him to pay off Dolores's debt and be done with it, but she knew Dolores wouldn't have it. She was too independent and headstrong for that; she would see it as charity at this point and charity she didn't need.

Dee would, however, allow the children's grandmother to help her watch over them, which Kelli-Kay would have to do a lot from now on. Dolores would be working an average of two shifts a day, six days a week pretty much from that day forward.

Dee tried to work a first- and third-shift every day but Sunday. This allowed her some time with the kids in the afternoons when she could have supper with them, play, help with homework and tell them how much she loved them before lying down on the couch to sleep for a couple of hours before going back to work. Kelli-Kay or Abby would normally keep the kids at night or stay over at Dee's place to keep an eye on them. Anna Rae was starting to be a big help as she was learning to cook and clean with Kelli-Kay, just like her mom had.

Dee worked hard over the next three years to get their life back on track. She sent at least seventy-five dollars per month to LNB; she paid the rent, the light bill, the phone bill, bought groceries, shoes, clothes, and toys for the kids, put gas in the old Studebaker, and occasionally put a few dollars in her old Hills Bros Coffee can in the back of her closet.

She only saw the Jack Ass three times in that three years; once in the courtroom when he was lying through his teeth to the judge, once when he took the kids for a weekend and tried to "give" Anna Rae and Jr. to his sister, Jenna; and once when he came into the Walgreens asking for her recipe for the healing soup and/or Momma's étouffée, it seemed his regulars at the market were becoming not so regular with Dee's smiling face gone and none of her famous soup on the menu.

She would have stopped to give him directions to hell, where she promptly told him to go, but the Café was busy, and she had tables to tend. He never even asked about his children—in the forty years that would pass between then and his death, aside from paying seventy-five dollars a month per court order, which he did for less than a year, he never lifted a finger for his kids—at least not the three that he'd fathered with Dee—and he didn't leave a tip when he left the Café. Jack Ass!

The Satsuma Meat Market would fold less than ten months after Dee's departure.

Dee had a regular following at the Walgreens' Café; she was still a knockout, slap-you-in-the-face, desirable young lady, even if she did feel fifty. She had turned down too many "date" offers to count and at least a half-dozen marriage proposals. It wasn't that she wouldn't want a man's company and she had wanted desperately for her first marriage to work out but she just didn't have time to date and she had three kids and an ex-husband already at the ripe old age of twenty-three. What decent man in his right mind would have her?

In the summer of 1964, a man named Joe started showing up at the Walgreen's coffee counter every morning at about 7:15 where he would eat two fried eggs, grits, a strip of bacon, and drink three or four cups of coffee while he watched Dee. After a week he asked Dee to join him for a minute; he had a proposal.

"Listen, Mister," she pretty much had a canned response to the "proposals" at this point. "I appreciate that you think you are interested in me but I'm not the dating type, I've got three kids, an ex-husband, and a momma," she said nodding over to the front counter where Kelli-Kay nodded back with scornful disapproval, "who don't take kindly to her waitresses dating the customers, so can I get you another cup?"

Nine

"Well, Dee, I'm happily married, but if I'd met you five years ago nothing you just said would have scared me away. You might not be the dating type but you are definitely a keeper; and that's not the kind of proposal I had in mind," he paused. "I want you to come work for me."

Joe Alesce was a successful businessman in Baton Rouge with an iconic restaurant, The Pastime Lounge, and two other very busy bars. His crown jewel was the Star Mist Lounge near LSU. It was an upscale joint that served a modest, happy-hour selection of finger foods and specialty cocktails to the courthouse and city government crowd; those who liked to frequent the campus area but were not into the college wildlife. The bar was open on Saturdays, too, when it got a little "livelier" with the college crowd, especially during football season, but nothing too rowdy he promised.

"I'm willing to train you to be my prime-time bartender, you'd be my star."

"Okay, I'm listening, but why me, Mister?"

"Well, because you're gorgeous for starters, you treat your customers well, and you don't let the hound dogs bother you. How much do you make in a shift here?"

"I earn eight dollars from Walgreens and about twenty-eight to thirty dollars in tips per shift and I usually work at least ten to twelve shifts a week."

"So you're bringing home about $420 a week, that's damn good money for a twenty-something-year-old girl out here in the boondocks but it sounds like you work too much, and I'm talking about the big leagues here, honey."

"My girls make $75 to $80 a shift on the weekend, girl like you, on a Saturday night; you'd take home $100 easy, $150 during football season and I'd be willing to pay you a $450 starting bonus to hold you over until the tips start rolling in."

Dee wanted to start that night, but Kelli-Kay wasn't having it.

"Baton Rouge; Tiger Town; at some honky-tonk? Have you lost your mind, child?"

"It's not a honky-tonk, Momma; it's a swanky place, with a piano bar, where all the lawyers go."

"Lawyers, is that supposed to make me feel better? They're worse than bankers!"

"Don't worry, I'll tell the bouncers not to let Truman and his crowd through the door."

They laughed.

Kelli-Kay knew it was a losing argument, but she had to say her piece. They talked it over for a day or two and Dee accepted the offer.

Ten

Brenda Hutchins was the general manager of the Star Mist; she was a few years older than Dee and very attractive in her own right. She had a business degree from Louisiana College and had agreed to tend bar for a year, or until Mr. Alesce could find a suitable girl for the happy hour/night shift, if he would give her the chance to prove herself as a manager. She was awesome, she was good at the management job, a great barmaid, honest, dependable, and though she wasn't much bigger than a whisper she didn't take stuff from anyone, including Joe.

There was something familiar about the way she looked and the way she carried herself. Dee knew they had never met but her name was familiar, she just couldn't put her finger on it.

Brenda taught Dee how to pour, mix, and mingle; it was about working the bar, working the crowd, and staying sober.

"Be sweet, seem available, and always laugh at their jokes, no matter how stupid, and if they want to buy you a drink, let them. Repeat after me, scotch and water . . . mostly water!" She said as she put her index finger over her lips to let Dee know that she was in on the secret.

"What if the boys get too friendly or want more than a drink?"

"Just raise your hand up, Big Ray or one of the doormen will take care of you, but the guys that come in here behave themselves, most of the time, they just want to flirt with a pretty girl and act like big shots . . ."

She studied the bartender's guide Brenda loaned her and memorized the Star Mist menu. For two weeks she came in two hours early to help, and observe, the first-shift bar maid named Lilly—who she swore looked like a reincarnated Marilyn Monroe—and then she bar-backed for Brenda during happy hour. The place was busy, and Dee was having a blast. All the suits—mostly lawyers, clerks, and secretaries from the Court House and Huey P. Long Capitol, which were both about five minutes away—started streaming in about 4:30 every weekday and by 5:30 there was a line a half-block long to get in the front door.

Brenda didn't hesitate to turn a table or a stool that wasn't producing; "You bored, honey?" she would ask after a second pass at an empty glass. "If you've had too much to drink, I can get you a cup of coffee and a cab but the real estate around here is pretty expensive so can I get a paying customer in that stool?"

They usually just smiled and had one more for the road. Occasionally they would get offended and make a fuss.

"Listen, little girl," one hot shot said, "do you know who I am, I'm the assistant district attorney for this here parish and this is a free country, so I'll sit here as long as I damn well please."

"You see that nice-looking man standing in line at the door, the one standing right in front of Judge Grafia, that's our new Congressman, Edwin Edwards, and both are waiting for a seat. I'd be willing to bet neither one of them have ever heard of you either, so buy a drink, buy some food, or move on, honey."

Ten

"Listen bit . . ."

"Problem, sir?" asked Big Ray, placing his enormous, firm hand on the hotshot's shoulder and one more for the road suddenly seemed reasonable.

Congressman Edwards liked to sit at the bar—partially to be front and center and partially to watch the girls work—he liked to boast that he was going to name one of them new freeways after Brenda (and the new girl) when he became governor, a promise he wouldn't keep but he did become the governor in 1972, 1984, and 1992—and then a convicted felon—His stool at the bar always produced huge revenue for the bar, big tips for Brenda and Dee, and a lot of political capital for Eddie—Edwin Edwards was a Star Mist fixture during his rise to power in Louisiana.

Dee's first solo shift as the head bartender of the Star Mist Lounge was on a Saturday Night in the fall of 1964, a Football Saturday Night in Baton Rouge. It was kind of like taking a kid fresh out of boot camp, pinning four stars on his collar, and sending him off to win the Great War.

LSU played rival Texas A&M in front of 69,000 screaming Cajuns shortly after the sun set in the western sky over Death Valley, as Tiger Stadium is known. To Dee, it seemed like every single purple-and-gold clad one of them came through the bar and she didn't know so much alcohol could be consumed by human beings. Of course, these aren't your normal human species, they are Fighting Tiger Fans.

The Star Mist opened at 10:00 am on football Saturdays with a menu consisting of jambalaya, shrimp creole, crab or crawfish boil depending on the market, and Joe Alesce's famous hush puppies. They served twenty-ounce Papa Doble, strawberry or hurricane daiquiris in something called a Styrofoam cup, and the bar was wide open.

When LSU won, as they would this night, the drinks would flow like the mighty Mississippi, the kitchen crew couldn't make enough hush puppies, and the tip jar would be filled three or four times. If the Tigers lost, the Tiger fans would drown their sorrows and the drinks would flow like the mighty Mississippi, the kitchen crew couldn't make enough hush puppies, and the tip jar would be filled three or four times.

In victory or defeat, celebration or sorrow, the Tiger fans would come out in droves, drink like fishes, and cuss, and swear that they or an underdeveloped baboon could outcoach whatever poor slob happened to be the head man on any particular Saturday.

Dee had never worked harder, laughed louder, or smiled more. She didn't really do a lot of flirting like some of the other girls, but she had a good rapport with the patrons, let them buy her drinks—scotch and water, water, water—she laughed at dumb jokes, repeated any good one's she'd heard, and she poured as well as any barkeep in the parish.

After her first shift, and after she had tipped the bar-backs, bus boys, and kitchen staff Dee would take home $168 in tips—that was five shifts at Walgreens—and even though she was worn out, she could get a good night's sleep, spend time with her kids after they got home from church on Sunday, and not need to be back at work until Monday evening. She loved her new job and as she tucked the wad of cash into her bra she thought, "Geaux Tigers!"

Eleven

*B*renda had been dating Rick O'Bannon for over a year when they decided to drive to Biloxi and get married. Brenda asked Dee to go along, as her maid of honor. They weren't eloping per se, as her parents and his mother were meeting them in Biloxi for the small wedding, they just didn't have time for a big production, and they wanted to go ahead and get hitched. Apparently in Mississippi you could get a marriage license out of a gumball machine, or something to that effect, so they all met at the Harrison County justice of the peace in Biloxi, Mississippi.

"I knew your name was familiar, you're Miss Nora's daughter!" Dee said excitedly when Dick and Nora Hutchins walked into the justice's ceremony hall.

"You know my mother?" Brenda asked, very surprised.

"Yes, Brenda, she knows me and your old pops," said Nora putting her arm around Dee. "This is the little girl we told you about from the storm back in '57, she's all grown up now but this is our little Storm Angel!"

"Well, now she's my little Scotch Angel!" quipped Brenda.

They all laughed. It was a nice reunion and a happy occasion. Rick and Brenda O'Bannon were a cute and happy couple; Dee was a tad bit jealous but very happy for her dear friend.

Rick's best man and drinking buddy from college, was none other than the eldest son of the now world-famous Bible Bill Grantham, Elvin P. Grantham, they called him "Elvis" due in part to his name, his sideburns, and, of course, the enormous popularity of a certain King of Rock "N" Roll. His dad and most of the church crowd were not amused by the nickname.

Elvin was a brash, inherently wealthy twenty-two-year old that was used to having whatever and whomever he wanted. He was barely a teenager the night Dee ran out of the Walker Church of Christ and he claimed to not remember her but said he did remember the night the good Lord took the old church and "called Papa to his greater ministry."

Dee really didn't like him any more than his father, but he sure took a shine to Dee.

Rick and Brenda would beg her to double-date with him and occasionally they'd guilt her into a Sunday afternoon picnic with the four of them or an evening movie. Dee would spend most of those "dates" telling Elvis to keep his hands to himself.

At the same time her mother was nagging her about going back to church: "Your children wonder why they go to church every Sunday, but you won't darken the doorstep, Dee. If you want the kids to love God, the love for the Lord must first be on your heart . . ."

"I know, Mother, but I just can't do it, after what that hypocrite Grantham did to me, and now his heathen son is chasing me around like a whipped puppy dog that can't take no for an answer; they're phony, the whole lot of 'em and I want no part of that."

"I know how you feel, honey, Brother Grantham really let me down too, but that doesn't change how I feel about God, you have to understand men aren't perfect, none of us are, but Jesus loves you, Dee."

"I'm not so sure he does, Momma, but I'll think about going with the kids every now and then."

Kelli-Kay asked Bro. Rex Johnson, the current pastor at the Walker Church of Christ, and an occasional guest speaker on the Old Time Revival Tour, to arrange a meeting with Bible Bill Grantham at his upcoming Revival. She'd read that the OTRT would be "saving souls in the springtime" at the John M. Parker Agricultural Coliseum at LSU.

"Thanks for coming in, Sister Crockett; it's always a blessing to see you."

"You as well, Pastor, were you able to contact Bro. Grantham for me?"

"Well, I haven't heard back from his assistant yet, so I don't know, he's awful busy in the work, sister, I don't know if we'll be able to arrange the meeting or not."

"Did you tell them it was me wanting to speak with him?"

"Well, not specifically, Sister Crockett, I'm not sure that'd matter much, no offense meant."

"None taken, but he'll see me, just tell them I'm the one asking."

The phone in his office rang about twenty minutes after he'd left a message for the Reverend Grantham. "I'm happy to do it, Rex, anything I can do for such a pillar of the church as Sister Crockett. Did she say what's on her mind?"

"No, just said she wanted you to help her make something right."

"She wants me to meet with Dolores," He said rather timidly.

"Who's Dolores?"

"Her daughter," he explained. "I was pretty hard on her one night during service and she ran out of the church in tears, dang near died in a massive storm, same one that took the old church. They couldn't find the kid for a week and she hasn't been to church since."

"Wow, what'd she do?"

"Got herself pregnant, or I should say that Dempsey boy get her pregnant, but she was a good kid and a real asset to the church, she was also a good Christian, who made a mistake, and I lit her up like the Devil incarnate, don't even know why I did it actually, humiliated the whole family. I tried to apologize to Sister Crockett, didn't do much good. She told me she was in the church to please God, not me and she reckoned she'd keep on worshipping him, not me. She kept coming to church but stopped tithing and she never really spoke to me again. My last service, before you took over, I told her if she ever felt like it would make a difference that I would make a personal apology to Dolores and try to make it right."

"Well, seems like she's ready."

Twelve

"*I said I'd go back to church with you, Momma,* I didn't say anything about going to one of that shyster's shady TV tent shows."

"He wants to talk to you, Dee; I reckon he wants to apologize for the way he done."

"I don't need his apology, Momma, and I really don't need his tear-jerking damnation either."

"Just go with me, honey, hear what the man has to say, it won't hurt and you don't have to ever see him again if you don't want to."

"Okay, Momma, it's against my better judgment but I'll go this once."

It was a mildly warm Sunday evening in southern Louisiana, the light wind blowing through the magnolia and live oak trees made the ubiquitous Spanish moss seem to point in the direction of the John M. Parker Agricultural Coliseum—the "Cow Palace" as it was called—located near the Southeast corner of the campus, where the OTRT was finishing a week of capacity crowded, soul stirring, old-time profitability religion.

When the young lady at the box office looked over the "will call" list she handed Kelli-Kay and Dolores badges that indicated they were VISs (Very Important Souls). As they walked into the coliseum, Elvin walked up; "Hi Dee, Dad told me you were coming tonight; I was kind of surprised but praise Jesus, I'm happy to see you"

"Good to see you too, Elvis, you remember my momma?"

"Of course, Sister Crockett, fine to see you as well."

"Hello, Elvin. Are you the one's been chasing Dee around?"

"Well," he said as he and Dee looked at each other slightly embarrassed, "I guess that would be me, but she doesn't seem very interested in being caught, Sister Crockett."

"A girl has to make sure a hunter wants a real catch, son, not just another trophy."

"Daddy taught me that you never hunt unless you need to eat, Ma'am."

After the awkward hunting analogies were over Elvin, who Dee noted was acting like a gentleman—not a side of him she'd seen a lot of—asked the two ladies to join him down in the front of the arena.

"I've saved us seats right up front by the stage and after the service Dad would like us to meet in his dressing room/office, said something about a mea culpa, and said he'd like to offer a private blessing."

Dee was a little overwhelmed, she hadn't been in a church since she ran out of the one in Walker, the hypocrite and the self-proclaimed prophesier's son was all but stalking her—though she was strangely comforted by his presence at the moment—and this seemed more like a rock concert than a spiritual revival.

"Okay, Elvis, we're all yours, but don't get any ideas, were just here to save my soul!" she said laughing sarcastically.

"Jesus loves his angels, Dee; I think you're going to be fine."

Elvin worked the crowd like an old-school politician; he was polished, smooth, in his element. He was Bible Bill's boy so to the seventeen thousand folks in the arena that night he was royalty.

Twelve

"Brother So & So, I hope the Good Lord is blessing your path, let me introduce you to my very dear friend Dee Crockett and her lovely mother, Sister Kelli-Kay Crockett."

"Sister Such & Such, I want you to meet one of the Lord's angel's, this is Miss Dee Crockett."

Dee felt special and she was actually starting to think Elvin might not be such a bad guy, after all. He made her feel welcomed, special, and excited to be there. The fact that his father had made it known that he wanted to apologize had her thinking that it was a good idea to come after all. The icing on the cake was when they got to their seats, right next to Sister Grantham.

"Mother, you remember Sister Crockett, and my good friend Dee?"

"Indeed, Kelli-Kay," they nodded to each other.

"Dolores," she stated without hesitation or a hint of phoniness, 'I've prayed for you and about you many times since the last time I saw you. I've asked for forgiveness if our family scorned you in any-way . . . if I scorned you in anyway, I'm hoping you'll have the heart to forgive me."

She stepped to Dee and embraced her before she could move away. For a second Dee tensed up but Sister Grantham warmly squeezed her like a mother squeezing a sick child and Dee felt her pain from all those years ago fall right to the floor. She returned the hug and the two broke out in tears. It was very genuine on both of their part and Dee forgave Sister Grantham and Brother Grantham—by exten-sion—right then and there.

Thirteen

The Crusader Band—*a virtual orchestra now*—splashed into a rendition of "How Great thou Art" followed by "Amazing Grace" and Dee, hands raised to the heavens, was in the midst of her own spiritual revival.

The Reverend Rex Johnson gave a very warm and encouraging discourse about God's mercy and forgiveness—a brief outline prepared and provided by Bible Bill—to set the mood for the good reverend's soul-stirring sermon on The Prodigal Son, the suffering of Lot, redemption, and the glorious coming of the Lord Jesus, when all tears and sorrows would be gone forever. As Johnson was preaching, Elvin gently placed his hand over Dee's and for the first time she didn't pull away, she held hands with him as the service continued, she thought she might actually like this guy.

The elder Grantham had always felt bad about chasing the poor child from the church and truth be told, he was looking forward to cleansing his conscience of that blazing night—he had convinced himself that setting matters straight with the Widow Crockett and her daughter, even though the girl did bear a child out of wedlock, would absolve him of that whole steaming episode; her flight, the fire, shady insurance deal, and anything else he might have done.

As he took the stage to "Revive Us Again" he thundered into the microphone beginning in Latin "Confíteor Deo omnipoténti."

"I confess to almighty God."

And as he got just a few seconds into his intro he looked down at the front row and saw his only son, the heir to his religious throne, the man he was grooming to expand the empire to even greater heights and the newly installed director of operations of OTRT *holding hands* with that, with that, with that little immoral tramp! The mother of three children and barely more than a baby herself, daughter of a hell-raiser, raised by a mean old widow, the girl that had already ruined her life, well he'd be damned if she was going to ruin Elvin's. Whatever mea culpa Bible Bill had planned quickly faded from his mind.

"I confess to the almighty God, that ye must repent of your wickedness!" he thundered, looking right at Dee—and Elvin this time—and as if moved by a spirit, certainly not a holy one, he launched into his old sermon, the same one he'd delivered back in Walker on the night of the fateful storm.

"REPENT, REPENT, REPENT ye workers of wickedness, for the LORD GAWD is a wrathful God . . ."

As he went on Kelli-Kay was contemplating whether the Good Lord would forgive her if she climbed up on that stage and choked "a man of GAWD" in front of the whole blasted world; at about the same time Dee decided she'd had enough. No longer sobbing, the brief tears of joy washed away and with nothing but pain in her heart, Dee got up and walked out.

She also had a lot of sorrow—sorrow for her own past sins, which were once again front and center, sorrow for her poor mother who wanted so badly to put her faith in this man and sorrow for Elvis (even Sister Grantham) for being related to this shyster; but mostly she felt sorrow for all the good people that were taken in by the charlatan and his hypocritical act—and if she thought it would have made her feel better she would have slapped her own mother for talking her into putting herself where she had sworn she'd never be again. There would not be a third time, that much she knew.

Elvin looked at his father with a perplexed and angry glare as he followed Dee out of the auditorium and even Sister Grantham, who was genuinely sorry about what they had done to the child, was shocked. She tried to reach out to Kelli-Kay as she stormed out of the hall and Brother Grantham preached his way to other side of the stage as she got to her feet, just in case.

"Dee, wait up!"

"Just go back to your world, Elvis, I'm the sinner, I'm the tramp. Your family would never let you be with someone like me!"

"It's not their say first off, and I don't know what got into my dad, I swear he brought you here to apologize, he said he wanted to make it right. I just don't get it."

"Well, instead of an apology he damns my soul again with the same judgmental, hateful words he crushed me with when I was a little girl. It'll never happen again, though, I can promise you that!"

"I'm so sorry, Dee, please don't take it out on me, I don't know what to say for my dad, but he doesn't speak for me."

"I just need to go, Elvis; I just can't be here anymore. I have to go!"

"Let's go, child." Kelli-Kay demanded as she took Dee's arm and they walked away not looking back. "Elvin, let her be now and get on back to your people, we're done here."

Fourteen

By 1965 *the US involvement* in the War in Vietnam was heating up under President Lyndon B. Johnson. Along with his National Security Council, a three-staged bombing operation, known as Rolling Thunder, was deliberated and commenced, in part, as retaliation to the attack of the US Marine barracks at Pleiku.

The CAO (Casualty Assistance Officer) and the First Lieutenant who served with Lieutenant Michael C. Crockett—Dee's sweet baby brother, Locke—were not at liberty to give more details, other than he was KIA—killed in action—somewhere in North Vietnam during that operation.

The notification came just three days after Dee and Kelli-Kay walked out of the Old Time Revival and at this point Dee just went numb. She drank scotch, without the benefit of much water, and cried without the benefit of a pause while she and Kelli-Kay planned the memorial service and notified family members.

When the discussion got to who would conduct the service a brief dispute broke out as Truman all but demanded that the Reverend Grantham be asked to conduct the funeral.

"It would give Locke a wonderful send off and the nation would hear of his sacrifice, it doesn't matter if he hurt Dee's feelings or not."

David Jr. was a little put off by Truman's suggestion. "Assuming for a minute that I was okay with the way he treats our sister, which I absolutely am not, I also don't want him turning our little brother's memorial into a circus."

"It wouldn't be a circus; he is a very well-respected man of . . ."

"He's lost my respect and he will not be eulogizing my son, end of the discussion," stated Kelli-Kay.

As if the family, and specifically Dee hadn't suffered enough, another bombshell was about to drop. Sheriff Deputy Odom Graves knocked at the door.

"Deputy?"

"Mr. Crockett," Deputy Graves said tipping his hat to David Jr. "I'm awful sorry to be bothering you good folks at such a bad time but I'm afraid I have some legal papers I need to serve on Miss Dolores."

"Could it wait Odom?" David replied not trying to hide his irritation.

"Well, there's a time limit and it seems the attorney couldn't get it to our office no sooner. The sheriff asked the judge personally for an extension, but he said we had to follow the law, I really am sorry David, and I'm so sorry for your loss."

"I'll give 'em to her."

"I'm real sorry again, David, I've got to hand 'em to her personal."

"Well, if this isn't some Mickey Mouse manure, hold on."

Deputy Graves served Dee with a lawsuit in which Jimmy-Jack Sr. was suing for custody of the two eldest children and claiming that he was not the father of Big Dean. He claimed that Dee had been an unfaithful and unsupportive wife and had been derelict in paying their bills, creating financial hardship for the family.

Dee refused to read the nonsense until after the funeral.

Rex Johnson conducted a private prayer meeting with the family and a few invited church members and close friends. He expressed great admiration for the soldiers who were sacrificing their lives half-way around the world and he recounted some of the stories he'd heard of Locke and the rest of the Crockett children. He spoke specifically of Dee and her "meals on wheels" and the famous "healing soup" he hoped to taste someday and said what a great asset Kelli-Kay and all of her kids had been to the church.

He talked about a plan and some great mystery and though he seemed like a nice man, Dee thought, the more he talked the further away from God she felt.

At the graveside, Locke's base commander, from before his deployment to Vietnam, said a few words of appreciation on behalf of the United States of America, as he said, a grateful nation. He ordered three rounds fired from the seven-man honor guard and Dee felt what was left of her faith fall to the leaf-covered ground with all twenty-one empty shell casings.

In the back of the crowd, Elvin Grantham watched Dee and her three kids and surveyed the graveside crowd. He felt terrible for Dee and her family and for the very first time in his life he wasn't entirely proud of being Bible Bill's boy.

"Dee," he said approaching slowly, after the service was completed, "I am so sorry for your loss and I just wanted you to know that I'm here for you any way I can be."

"Thank you, Elvis," she replied softly, almost broken, "you didn't have to come."

"Of course I did, Dee, despite what a jackass my father might be you are my friend and I need you to know that I'm here and that I care."

"Thanks, Elvis, that means a lot actually. I'll call you in a week or so when I can breathe"

"Call me if you can't breathe too, Dee, I want to be there for you," he said as he moved on to say a few words to Sister Crockett and Dee thought: Who knew the jerk could be so sweet?

It had been a week since the funeral and Dee had taken some time off of work but she really needed a drink. She'd been with her family since they received the news and despite Truman feigning love and concern for her she was sick of talking to them. She asked Kelli-Kay if she'd watch over the kids and called Elvin.

"Hey, Dee, how are you feeling?"

"Well, no offense but I'm feeling like I'm tired of that question and I need a drink."

"I'll pick you up in a half hour."

"No funny business, Elvis, I just want to get out of here for a while and get a drink."

"I swear Dee, perfect gentleman."

"You'd better be," she quipped. She liked gentleman Elvin a lot; maybe he's just been growing up, she thought.

He took her to Arlington Perrodin's restaurant on Twelfth Street in Baton Rouge. Perrodin would become one of the first nationally known Cajun cuisine chefs and Didee's, in 1965, was one of the best restaurants in town.

Dee had the Shrimp Creole, which she thought was even better than the infamous Creole they served at the Star Mist; Elvin had the baked King Duck, the dish Didee's was famous for, and shared a few delicious bites with Dee.

They enjoyed a great meal, Dee had a couple of drinks, told a few happy stories about Locke, cried a little, and Elvin was a perfect gentleman. He drove her home before midnight, walked her up to her momma's door, gave her a hug, kissed her on the cheek, and left. It was hard to take her mind off of Locke but she was glad she'd called Elvin. She might do that again sometime, she thought.

Even though she really wasn't ready to deal with it, she had to read the lawsuit. Among other complete fabrications the Jack Ass claimed that Dee was an alcoholic who frequented bars and had multiple boyfriens. The document alluded to pictorial evidence to corroborate these claims. Another interesting note in the document, the Jack Ass asserted he could provide a better environment for the kids with the aid of his sister, Jenna—the same one he had previously tried to "give" the children to.

"He's not taking my kids!" she said to her mother as she finished reading the document.

"No, I reckon we can't let that happen," Kelli-Kay replied. "Truman gave me the number of one of his lawyer friends; you'll need to call him."

"Truman's not interested in helping me, Momma . . ."

"Well, I told Truman that if you lost my grandbabies to that Jack Ass, forgive my language, I was going to hold him personally responsible so he better make sure this attorney fella is a good one, I reckon he is, so go ahead and call him."

She called and then met with Mr. Anthony Savagio, Esquire, Truman's college drinking buddy and a pretty good lawyer.

Fifteen

❦

Over the next month or so Dee and Elvin would see each other occasionally, usually on Sunday when she and Brenda were off of work and the foursome could run down to Biloxi or New Orleans for the day or catch a movie over in Hammond, Louisiana. Dee would always insist on Brenda picking her up and the two of them would meet the boys wherever. She still didn't know what the Jack Ass had for "pictorial evidence" but she didn't want them to add to it.

Dee was caught in an emotional hurricane, she was actually falling for Elvin, which still surprised her. She felt guilty for having any sense of happiness in the wake of Locke's death and she was terrified that somehow the Jack Ass and his hateful sister were going to steal her kids with their lying and conniving. In retrospect she shouldn't have started drinking on the trip to Biloxi but by the time they crossed the long bridge over Bay St. Louis she was gassed.

On the way back home Monday morning she thought she might be pregnant.

She didn't tell anyone for a couple weeks, but she knew she was, once again, unmarried and with child. She had only seen Elvin once since Biloxi, he had been traveling with OTRT and his job was going very well. He did call her—long distance—every day and she enjoyed the reports of his travels.

Elvin's father, Bible Bill, didn't approve of their dating. Kelli-Kay didn't approve of their dating; she wasn't sure she approved herself and her lawyer warned her that an illegitimate pregnancy could and likely would be used effectively against her in court.

She wasn't showing yet, but she knew she had to do something quickly, she asked Elvin if he would be home soon. "We need to talk."

"Okay, Dee, I'm coming home this weekend, I was planning to surprise you at the Star Mist Friday night, but we can plan to talk over breakfast on Saturday," he said with an assuming chuckle.

"I'll see you Friday, Elvis, but you need to behave yourself."

She also talked to Brenda. "You can't tell a soul, Brenda, if it gets out, I'll lose Anna Rae and Jr., I can't let that happen."

"That's not gonna happen, Dee. There is no way a judge is going to take them away from you, you're a good mother and that Jack Ass-ex of yours could barely pick them out of a lineup, some father . . ."

"I don't know, he claims I'm an alcoholic tramp and well, I'm pregnant, unmarried and oh, I work in a bar."

"Yea, you do sound like a real hussy," Brenda joked.

"Well thank you, Mrs. O'Bannon, you've trained me well."

"I don't know about that, I made Rick marry me before we got knocked up, maybe you and Elvis just need to run to Biloxi this weekend!"

"Did you just say that you're pregnant too?"

"Yep," they laughed, poor ole Joe, his two superstar bar girls were both about to blow up with babies in their bellies and he didn't have a clue.

Fifteen

"We'll work it out, Dee, even if I have to send Big Ray down to Denham Springs to convince your ex that he'd be better off without the kids."

"There's an idea, he might need to go talk to Jenna too!"

She met Elvin for breakfast at a little diner out on Airline Highway. Elvin had begged her to let him take her home—to his hotel suite—the night before but she said she had to go home to her kids.

"We need to get married, Elvis, and soon," she blurted.

"Well, that's a little forward, Dee, can't say I haven't thought about it but I'm not sure about the timing."

"I'm pregnant!" She said in a panicked whisper as she leaned forward making sure no one else could hear her.

Elvin rested back in his seat, deflated. "Are you sure?"

"I know; I've been here before."

"But how, we only . . . Biloxi . . . it was . . . oh my god, Dad will kill me, I'll be ruined . . ."

"If we just go get married, like tomorrow, no one will ever have to know I was pregnant before."

"Dee, I love you, I've wanted to marry you since the day I met you, but my Dad will disinherit me and I'll lose my job, everything . . ."

"Screw your father, Elvis, he's a hypocrite and he can't run your life!"

"Give me some time to figure it out, Dee, are you working tonight?"

"Yes," she said, agitated.

"Okay, I'll come see you tonight, we'll talk, promise."

Saturday night came and went, no Elvin. She tried to call him on Sunday, no Elvin.

By the time she left the Star Mist on the night of October 23, 1965—a good football Saturday night that witnessed LSU defeat South Carolina 21–7 at Death Valley—she hadn't heard from Elvin in over two months. She was starting to show, though she had learned to dress in a way to hide it well. She and Brenda had been shopping together and were helping to cover for each other—it wasn't as big a deal for Brenda as the general manager—but they were both getting pretty darn close to the point of being obvious.

Dee rolled away from campus with chants of "L S U—L S U—L S U" still ringing through the moist autumn night. There was a light drizzle of rain as she moved through East Baton Rouge into the nearly deserted suburbs in the 1958 Chevy Bel Air she'd purchased a few weeks earlier—It wasn't new, but it was a year newer and a lot prettier than the one Jack Ass had stolen from her—she roared past Stevendale Road and saw Nora's office light on at La Rouge; checking in a late arrival no doubt.

She thought back to the week she'd stayed at the motel when she was just a scared little girl on the run. Who knew she'd become so close with Nora's family, with Brenda—her best friend, the best friend she had ever had. They would be lifelong friends, she opined to herself.

As she breezed across the Amite River Bridge, she adjusted her rear view as an old Ford pickup truck sped past her, she was cruising at sixty so this guy was flying, she thought. As she refocused on the road directly in front of her a deer shot onto the roadway and into her path. She swerved to the right, only grazing the animal but it caused her to hit the soft shoulder of the road. As the shoulder pulled her into the canal her back tires hydroplaned on the wet asphalt and she hit the twenty-four-inch thick, steel-reinforced concrete culvert downhill and head on, at roughly sixty-six miles per hour.

Sixteen

K elli-Kay wasn't sure if she was angry or worried. It wasn't like Dee not to show up when expected or to call if there was a problem. She phoned Brenda who hadn't heard from her since she left work the night before, and she was instantly worried. "We'll find her Mrs. Crockett, I'm sure she's okay. We'll call you as soon as we can."

She and Rick jumped in his powder blue Ford Mustang and started making the drive from their apartment to the Star Mist and then followed what should have been Dee's route home to Livingston Parish. "This is just too far for her to drive every night," Brenda said. "I've been telling her to move forever."

"I'm sure she's fine, Brenda, maybe Elvis showed up and took her to Biloxi after all?"

"Don't talk to me about that phony, holy-boy friend of yours; I'm still deciding if I'm going to kill him or you!"

"Settle down, hot stuff, it's not my fault he's too scared of his rich hypocrite daddy to step up."

"Well, I hope you know he'll never be welcome in my house, with his little Mickey Mouse, holy rolling, two-faced . . . ."

"Hey, looks like a wreck ahead."

Dee's car had been pulled from the canal by a large crane truck—apparently a tow truck and two wenches failed to dislodge the wreckage; it was an amalgamation of twisted chrome, mashed metal, shattered glass, and blood. It had taken over an hour for two state troopers and three volunteer firemen to cut Dee loose from what had once been a fine automobile. There was a lot of blood, Brenda became weak at the knees, and nearly fainted.

"The driver was taken to the Emergency Ward at the Baton Rouge General Hospital; you had better hurry if'n she's a loved one," they were informed by the trooper that was still on the scene.

Given the time she left the Star Mist, it was estimated that Dee crashed around 2:10 am; she was not found until approximately 7:25 am when a bakery driver was turning around in the driveway next to the culvert. Dee lay unconscious; still bleeding, with clots forming—with gaping wounds all over her upper torso, neck, and face—for more than five hours.

As soon as the emergency staff at BRGH was able to stop the bleeding, clean and dress her wounds, and get her vitals reasonably stabilized she was rushed in a fly car, escorted by a state trooper to the Trauma Center in New Orleans at Charity Hospital. At the time Charity Hospital was the only Level I Trauma Center south of the Cook County Hospital in Chicago, Illinois, in the Eastern United States, though it had a reputation for the quality and speed of care akin to standing in a government breadline on Christmas morning.

Brenda and Rick made it to the Emergency Ward entrance just as Dee was being loaded into the fly car.

"Is she going to be okay, Doctor?" Rick asked as they ran up to the vehicle.

Sixteen

"She's alive but we need to get her to the trauma ward in New Orleans as soon as possible, we're just not equipped to deal with her wounds here."

"Please sir, can I ride with her? She is my sister!" Brenda pleaded.

"Of course, ma'am, just give me room to work."

"Rick, call Mrs. Crockett and Momma and let them know where we are. I'll see you in New Orleans!"

"I Love You, take care of her!"

"I will, love you too!"

Brenda held Dee's nearly lifeless hand all the way to New Orleans, crying and praying the entire way. She had never seen such carnage. Her dear friend, her gorgeous, lovely friend, her sister, was barely recognizable. Her skin was either pale or bruised and almost blue or wrapped in blood-soaked bandages.

She was deathly afraid of the answer, but Brenda brought herself to ask; "Is she going to make it?"

"She's not in good shape, ma'am" said the intern assigned to fly car duty, Dr. Billy Fleming. "We'll take good care of her and patch her up but there's no way to know if there is any permanent damage until we get her to New Orleans."

"She's pregnant, Doc, is there any way to check on the baby?"

"The baby's heart is still beating, and the pulse seems to be normal, I've been keeping an eye on that since we got her in at Baton Rouge General. I'm guessing she's in the second trimester, do you happen to know?"

"She's about four months along," said Brenda. "Please don't let anything happen to them."

"I'll do my best!"

After more than seven hours of surgery, which included 3.5 liters of blood transfusion; skin grafting from her inner thigh to cover the virtual loss of her chin and the implanting of a set of chromium-plated pins to set her right femur and upper humerus, Dee was in serious but stable condition and for the next six weeks she would remain in a level three state of comatose.

"We don't perceive there to be any lasting brain damage but there is no way to be certain at this point," the chief surgeon explained to Brenda, Rick, and Joy—Truman's wife—who were all in the waiting room when the team of blood-soaked doctors and nurses began to emerge from the operating room. "Her vitals are stable, and her brain seems to be getting sufficient oxygen, she just has a severely bruised frontal cortex and that's going to take some time to heal."

"What about the baby?" Rick blurted out to Joy's surprise and Brenda's annoyed piercing gaze.

"The baby seems fine; I think they are both fighters and with a little luck and a lot of rest and care they should both survive."

Brenda silently thanked God. She really wasn't that big on religion but she'd seen the wreckage and she knew that it would have to be a miracle for anyone to have survived that crash.

"Miss Joy," Brenda said pulling her aside, "I know you must understand the situation with Dee and the custody battle, she didn't want anyone to know about the baby!"

"I can imagine," Joy replied empathetically. "Believe me; we will support Dee and her children in any way possible."

By this time Kelli-Kay had arrived with the children, Truman was there with Joy and their two children. David Jr. was embroiled in an argument with his Air Traffic Control supervisor over catching the next flight to New Orleans, but his wife and their newborn baby girl, Cindy Ella, were already in the air.

Nora Hutchins was there, she'd left Dick in charge of the motel—which she would later joke was the second major "car wreck" of the day—and they were all crowded into a small waiting area when Brenda and Joy came in to deliver the prognosis they'd received from the chief surgeon. No mention was made of the baby they could discuss that later.

"So, my mommy's going to be okay?" asked a still terrified and hopeful Anna Rae.

"Yes, sugar, we're going to need to pray with her a lot and take care of her, but she's going to be okay, praise the Lord," said Kelli-Kay consolingly, hoping and praying that she was right.

"I've got to warn you all, she looks really bad; I know they've patched her up some, but she was barely recognizable when she got here." Brenda informed them before they were allowed to go into her room two at a time to "check" on her.

Seventeen

They couldn't tell how bad it really was as most of her face and upper body were wrapped in bandages. She had at least three bags of different types of fluids and/or medicine flowing into her veins via something the nurse referred to as intravenous therapy and there was a machine connected to her called an electrocardiogram along with other monitors, probes, and electrodes.

To Kelli-Kay—the daughter of a Choctaw Indian Woman and Evangelical Christian, who had given birth to all four of her children at home with the aid of a midwife and who'd never been to a movie theater nor did she own a television set—her near mortally wounded daughter looked like something from out of this world.

Kelli-Kay was deeply troubled and scared to death that she was going to lose her little girl. It was magnified by the fact that she knew something was wrong with herself. She had started forgetting things, like where she was and what the kids' names were, and she occasionally had brief lapses of cognizance.

She knew it was more than just her getting older, though she had been around for many moons now. She remembered her mother, a full-blooded Choctaw, suffering "Abeka Ahaksi"—the forgetting sickness—and becoming violently disoriented before finally deteriorating to a barely recognizable, barely human corpse. Though she was in the early stages, she knew her days were numbered, and she wasn't going to be able to help much with the kids or anything else before too long.

She would spend a lot of time and miles over the next three months traveling up and down Highway 90 and traversing the new Interstate, I-10, between New Orleans and Livingston Parish. She prayed and talked to God a lot on those trips.

"Lord, my Dolores is a good girl, she's made her mistakes, with a little help no less, but it seems to be she's the only one that has to deal with those mistakes. I reckon I've been hard on her at times and I've made my mistakes too, but I've always been a good Christian woman and I really need you to take care of my baby girl, Lord. Please help her and her babies."

Kelli-Kay now knew about the pregnancy, and she had spent a lot of time discussing matters with Brenda and Rick and with Joy and Truman. They were all in agreement that it was best not to discuss the baby outside of the five of them and they went to some lengths to keep her "condition" a secret. Brenda commandeered a handful of pillows from the hospital's linen storage and she fluffed them all around Dee on the hospital bed, which had moving rails. They kept them upright and laid a sheet or blanket over Dee during any visiting hours.

The nurses had all been asked to keep any details about Dee's condition(s) private and not to discuss with anyone other than Dee's mother or siblings, which included Brenda. Even though HIPAA laws were still decades away, the nursing staff was used to being discreet and they were happy to oblige. If the lady's family didn't want anyone knowing her business, then they wouldn't learn it by nosing around the nursing station in the Critical Care Ward.

Jenna Dempsey thought nothing of the mountain of comfort Dee seemed to be buried under when she stopped by "to offer support and prayers" and deliver Christmas presents to the kids. What she really wanted was to know if Dee was going to recover. Jimmy-Jack's attorney had assured them that he would be awarded legal custody if Dee was incapacitated long-term or certainly if she was deceased.

"Ma'am, we don't discuss a patient's condition with anyone but immediate family, you'll have to ask one of them."

"Oh, I'm her sister-in-law, we are very close."

"That's nice dear but your name is not on this here list so I really can't help you."

"I can help, Miss, what do you need to know?" Brenda asked from the doorway of the small waiting area across from the nursing station, where the Crockett family had celebrated Christmas the day before.

"And who might you be?" Jenna asked.

"I'm Dee's sister, and you are?"

"Well, I . . . I'm her sister-in-law but Dee doesn't have a sister," she said, perplexed.

"According to that list right there she does, and if you are Jack's sister then you know they're divorced as well as I do so you're not exactly her sister-in-law, and y'all were never close, no offense."

"First off, we call him Jimmy-Jack and I just need to know if Dee is going to make it," she said shortly getting to the point.

"Well, we call him Jack Ass but I was trying to be nice and you can bet your sweet bottom Dee's going to be fine so if you're here hoping she won't make it so you and your Jack Ass brother can swipe her kids you can just carry yourself on back to Denham Springs, we don't need you here."

"I'll second that," Kelli-Kay said as she walked toward them, on her way back from the ladies' room.

"Mrs. Crockett . . . . I, uh, we just want to help with the kids, we don't mean no harm," Jenna said, trying to feign humility.

"We don't need your help, Jenna, and we both know what you want. Well, it's not going to happen while I'm still kicking and breathing so just get on back home now," Kelli-Kay said in her very convincing way. Jenna knew she was in a losing battle with the Widow Crockett, so she left.

Two days later Dee was starting to show signs of arousal. She opened her eyes numerous times and seemed to be somewhat responsive. After several hours of nonverbal responses and going in and out of consciousness Dee tightened her grip on Brenda, who was at her bedside when she opened her eyes. When Brenda leaned forward Dee softly said, "Baby?"

Brenda burst into tears and happily said, "The baby is going to be fine and you are going to be fine, thank God!"

Over the next few days, which included ringing in the new year, 1966, the Crockett family, joined at times by Dick and Nora Hutchins and Rick and Brenda O'Bannon, counted their blessings together with Dee and her three children. They felt as if she'd returned from the dead and most of them, and most of the medical staff that cared for her, believed that it was a miracle she and the baby had survived the horrific crash.

Nonetheless, as the bandages were removed, and the stitches healed it became obvious that Dee would carry some of her scars for the rest of her life. She now had a five-inch scar with stitch marks outlining her chin and a similar line marking her left eyebrow. Neither altered her general appearance or changed her innate beauty, per se, but with the new scars and the fact that she would soon deliver her fourth child she would begin to notice that she no longer turned heads quite like she had before.

Seventeen

"Dee, we need to talk about this child and how we are going to deal with Jack's family; you know they'll use this to bury you in court and they really want to take Annie Rae and Jr. away."

"I know, Momma, I don't know what to do, it's not like I can keep the baby hidden and I guess the preacherman's son turned out to be just what I thought he was from the get go, a hound dog hypocrite . . ."

Rick had shared with them that Elvin was denying that he'd been with Dee and the baby must be someone else's. What he didn't share was that Rick and Elvin were no longer friends since he had decked Elvin, in front of his mom and dad, when he confronted them with doing the right thing by Dee and the baby. Elvin lying to his face while saying he would pray for the poor confused Dee was apparently all Rick could stand.

Bible Bill's attorney sent Rick and Brenda a threatening letter regarding "slander and libelous" and warned that he would disclose Dolores's illegitimate pregnancy to her ex-husband's attorney if they made any further attempts to link Elvin to the pregnancy. Dolores would soon receive a very similar letter.

"I'm sorry, honey, I feel so bad about dragging you to that revival and pushing them Granthams on you, I just thought they practiced what they preach."

"It's not your fault, Momma, I'm a big girl and it's not like I don't know where they come from," she said rubbing her impregnated belly.

"I know, honey, but they just keep coming on you and the men that help you make 'em keep turning out to be horse's asses."

"Momma, watch your bad mouth!" she said smiling.

"Sorry, dear; Lord please forgive me!"

Truman floated the idea of placing the baby with his church's adoption service—he had converted to Catholicism and was attending mass at the Our Lady of Mercy Church out on Marquette Avenue—he knew that they would accept a private and/or secret adoption and he was willing to facilitate the process.

"Process, you want to process my baby?" Dee snapped.

"Dee, I don't want to argue with you, you're having another baby, without a husband, and if you keep it, you're going to lose the kids you already have. I'm willing to help so just let me."

"You only want to 'help' because you don't want another scandal."

"What does it matter, Dee, just decide if you are going to keep the baby or not."

Over the next two weeks, as she recovered at the hospital back in Walker—where she'd been transferred, after she stabilized in New Orleans—she agonized over what to do. She was convinced that the Jack Ass and his fanciful lawyer would roast her in court if they found out she had another baby out of wedlock.

Anthony Savagio, Dee's attorney, convinced the Judge to agree to an extension due to the tragic accident his client had been involved in. Even at the motion hearing Jimmy-Jack's attorney trashed Dee and made her out to be a loose-living, hard-drinking boozer—who'd probably lost control of her vehicle because she was drunk—without a shred of evidence, other than the fact that she worked in a bar and there were numerous rumors of her ill-repute—all started, of course, by Jenna and the new Mrs. Dempsey, Peggy Sue.

Mr. Savagio argued that the children were safe with the mother's family where they had access to her during recovery; Jimmy-Jack could continue to enjoy visitation privileges—which he had ignored to that point. The judge concurred and the custody hearing was scheduled for March 1, 1966, at 9:00 am assuming the former Mrs. Dempsey was well enough to appear in court.

Eighteen

Dee's water broke in the early morning hours of Friday, Jan. 28th 1966. The beautiful baby girl was born after eleven-and-a-half hours of labor and handed to Dee, by the midwife, after the umbilical cord was cut and she had been cleaned and swaddled in a soft, pink blanket with little poodles stitched into the fabric.

"She has your eyes, honey; she is gorgeous!" Kelli-Kay said in a wishful tone.

"I know Momma, how can I give her up? Am I doing the right thing?"

"I don't know, honey, I shudder to think what would happen if that danged lawyer gets wind of it, and frankly I don't know how we're going to afford another mouth to feed but I guess we'd manage either way."

She had changed her mind several times already and Truman was no longer allowed to visit as the two of them had nearly come to blows at least twice. Nevertheless, he and Joy had worked with Catholic

Child Services who selected a family from Gonzalez, Louisiana—the Boudreaux—to place the child with.

Due to the accident recovery and the fact that the baby had arrived a few weeks ahead of schedule the baby would remain in the hospital, under observation in the Special Care Baby Unit—Incubator Ward—for three weeks. Dee, after nearly four months of intensive care and recovery, would finally be released on the same day as her new baby girl, Dana Kelli.

In the three weeks leading up to their release Dee met with a Catholic nun, Sister Mary Elba, concerning the possible adoption, almost daily. She agreed, recanted, and agreed again several times. The sister assured her the selected family was a good, upper-middle-class Christian family who had successfully adopted a young boy eighteen months earlier. The church monitored them, and all the adoptive families, and she was sure Dana would have a good home and a good life.

Dee told herself that the child had a better chance with this Catholic couple, though she didn't know much about their faith—just that they had enormous, gothic-looking cathedrals and the people seemed to worship their pope—but at least she wouldn't be raised on Bible Bill and OTRT hypocrisy.

The sister told Dee that Dana would keep her name and without Dee's knowledge—not that she would have objected—it was written into the adoption agreement that the adoptive family (who was not actually of the Catholic faith) would raise her in the Catholic Church, come what may. The agreement also mandated secrecy and the identity of the birth mother as well as that of the adoptive family was to be permanently sealed.

Sister Mary Elba brought in an assistant to notarize the document and Kelli-Kay held Dee's free hand while she signed in blue ink and tears of sorrow. They both kissed the child goodbye and the sister took Dana Kelli to her new family who was waiting at the main entrance of the hospital. They would sign the same document, with the same blue ink pen and tears of joy.

With the aid of a walking cane—which she would need for at least another six weeks—Dee left the hospital about two hours after Dana through the same entrance and climbed into her old Studebaker, with her mother driving—something Kelli-Kay would only be able to do for about another year—and they went home to Momma's house on Route 1 in Walker.

Outside of the two of them, Truman, Joy, Rick, and Brenda—and of course the Granthams, no one else knew about the baby. Anna Rae had asked several times why Mommy's belly was so big and when Kelli-Kay had asked her what she wanted for Christmas she said a baby sister. Dee and Kelli-Kay felt bad about deceiving the poor child, but she was as sharp as a tack and had a memory like a cemetery— everything was etched in granite—they had to help her forget.

On the drive home they agreed that Dana was in a better place and would be well cared for—they didn't know where that was geo-graphically but they assumed it was somewhere on the Gulf since the father was an engineer at a refinery—and they promised each other to never talk about it again. They would almost keep that promise.

Nineteen

"**T**he *Honorable Judge Frederick Stephen Ellis* is now presiding," Deputy Odom stated in a loud, firm voice as he called the court to order in the custody hearing regarding the children of James Jackson Dempsey and the former Mrs. Dempsey, Dolores Helen Crockett.

During his opening statement, Arden T. Caldwell, a surly and arrogant old-school litigator ravished Dee's character, based entirely on rumor and innuendo and all but called her a railroad whore. He speculated the children's maltreatment and neglect and claimed that Dee was an alcoholic who drank on the job and virtually any time she could get her hands on a cheap bottle of scotch. He told the court that Dee had purposely gotten pregnant back in 1957 in an elaborate scheme to trap his client into marriage.

He insinuated that Dee had caused the recent collapse of Mr. Dempsey's quite reputable business establishment and Dee was pretty sure he was getting ready to implicate her in the Kennedy Assassination, or at least claim that she was sleeping with Lee Harvey Oswald, it was sickening.

Directly behind her she could feel the atomic crescendo heightening in Kelli-Kay's legendary temper—a hereditary gift from her Choctaw mother—with every new allegation and scurrilous accusation. Dee was afraid her mother was going to break into a native warrior ritual and scalp a few Dempseys and their "worthless loudmouth" lawyer right there in the old courthouse.

Thankfully, David Jr. had come to town and was sitting next to Kelli-Kay with a firm, calming hand on her knee as the accusations were flying. David had spoken with Mr. Savagio at length concerning the case and they were both confident that the Dempseys had no legal grounds to stand on and after Caldwell finished his disgusting showboating the complaint would fall apart.

Savagio was prepared to defend all of the allegations, if necessary, and was sure that the facts and evidence were on his side. More than that, they had both read a copy of the friend of the court brief that had been filed with the clerk by one Sheriff Taft W. Faust. Their strategy was to read the unsolicited report into the court record as a rebuttal to Caldwell's opening lunacy and then petition the court for Summary Judgment.

In the "Dempsey Brief" Sheriff Faust detailed his investigation into the bank fraud allegedly perpetrated upon LNB and the former Mrs. Dempsey. The bank and the banker were not in his jurisdiction and the former Mrs. Dempsey had elected not to press charges so the case had not been referred to the EBR DA. However, he detailed the evidence he had collected, including the forged documents.

He had sent the documents to the forensic crime lab in New Orleans and the NOPD report was attached concluding that it was 99 percent certain that Mr. Dempsey's and the former Mrs. Dempsey's signatures were signed by the same hand. Mr. Dempsey's signature had been subsequently matched 100 percent to his driver's license and the document.

Nineteen

Moreover, Faust, out of concern for the subject children, due to the allegations raised by Mr. Dempsey, conducted an investigation into each of the charges leveled in the complaint that his office had served on the former Mrs. Dempsey and his report eviscerated, in detail, virtually all of those allegations. He even traced the source of most of the rumors.

Caldwell feebly objected at one point.

"Overruled."

By the time Savagio finished reading the brief the Dempseys were wondering if they shouldn't dart for the exits.

"Your Honor, if it pleases the court, Mrs. Crockett is prepared to defend her reputation against the frivolous charges alleged by her former husband in this complaint. However, in light of the detailed report submitted to the court by our fine sheriff I'd like to move for summary judgment and ask the court to dismiss this case with prejudice."

"Mr. Caldwell?"

"Your Honor, we feel it is highly unusual; and frankly prejudicial for the sheriff to interject himself into a case like this and we object to the entire brief."

"Can you cite to the Court any case, law, or precedence finding it unusual or inappropriate for a duly elected and installed law enforcement official to investigate alleged and actual crimes within his constitutional jurisdiction?"

"Um, well, your honor, I might need some time to research that," said Caldwell, embarrassed.

"I suppose you'll want to appeal my decision then; good luck with that," deadpanned the judge.

The case was dismissed with prejudice and Dee maintained full custody of all three of the Dempsey children. The judge's order required Jimmy-Jack to pay seventy-five dollars per month; twenty-five dollars for each of his children. Further, due to Mr. Dempsey's failure to return the children without law enforcement intervention the one time he had exercised his visitation as outlined in the divorce settlement, the judge mandated that Jimmy-Jack notify the sheriff's office if the children were going to be in anyone's care, other than his own during future visitations and all visitations had to be prescheduled with the former Mrs. Dempsey.

Dee felt the weight of the world lift, she could breathe again, and she was beginning to regain her strength and mobilization. She knew she would receive limited help from the Jack Ass, despite the judge's order and she wasn't comfortable living with her mom. It was time to get back to work; she had mouths to feed and bills to pay, including the massive ones that were pouring in from the hospital(s).

Dee and Brenda decided she would remain on medical break until Monday before taking her first shift back at the Star Mist on March 6, 1966. Joe had visited Dee a couple of times when she was in a coma and once after she regained consciousness. He, too, fell for the cover created by Brenda and Dee's family and never realized that she had been pregnant.

He was privately concerned that she would not recover from her facial wounds and had been quietly looking for a new prime-time bartender, while Marilyn Monroe (Lilly) filled in for Dee. Brenda had been out for nearly a month as well. She gave birth to Richard Michael a week after Dee delivered Dana; so, Lilly, Joe, and another daytime bartender had been working doubles and losing customers for several months.

Joe was very concerned about his prized establishment, both of his bars and his restaurant were profitable, but he was feeling the pinch at Star Mist in the absence of his two rock-star bar girls. He needed them both back and beautiful, tending bar and bringing in the boys.

Dee had lost her baby fat fairly quickly after her first three children and had been on a diet since she walked out of the hospital, however, she was having a hard time getting back to her normal weight this time. The doctors had intravenously nourished her with a lot of proteins and calories to try to keep the baby healthy and to keep her from losing any weight during her comatose state, and pregnancy. When she walked into the Star Mist on Monday, she was still about eighteen pounds heavy.

She also had a slight limp but was not dependent on the cane, this part she was forcing. She had carefully applied her make-up, with a little extra base to cover her freshly healed scars and at first glance she looked pretty good, Joe thought. She could lose a little weight but overall, Joe felt a lot better when she walked in that evening.

"Dee, we are so happy to see you, sweetie. We missed you so much and were worried we'd lost you there for a little while!" Joe said, nearly running to her as she walked in.

"I'm happy to be back too, Joe, but if you keeping bear hugging me like this I might break!" she laughed and he let go.

"Sorry, I'm just so happy to see you!"

Brenda came out of the kitchen. "Well, look who it is, where've you been, slacker, in a coma or something?"

"Something like that, what about you? I hear you've been making babies."

"He's not a baby, the little screamer is a milk-suckling demon, can't sleep, wants to eat ALL the time. If he keeps it up my boobs are gonna be as big as yours!" They all laughed.

Monday was normally a slow night, but a few regulars had heard Dee was coming back to work, so they stopped by to see her. One of the semi-regulars during the AFL (American Football League) off-season was former LSU football great, Billy Cannon, and he normally drew a crowd. Billy was in town that week and met his buddy Beck at the bar.

Pretty soon there were two dozen people crowded around listening to Billy recount his exploits as a professional footballer and relive his glory days at LSU; the group also listened intently and sympathetically as Dee, the hot-to-trot (or hot-to-limp) barmaid shared her back-to-life experience after slamming her car into the culvert the last time she'd left the bar.

She had a pretty good shift, Billy left her a $100 bill and she took in another $100 or so from her take of the tip jar—which was phenomenal for a Monday Night shift—but by 11:00 pm she couldn't walk. Charlotte, one of the waitresses, and Danny, the bar, back picked up the slack behind the bar and Dee spent the last two hours that night sitting on the customer side of the bar coaching Charlotte through drink pours.

Danny went out to Dee's car and brought in her cane, which she used to limp out of the bar after they closed that night. Over the next few nights Dee would use her cane as little as possible, much less than she needed to but much more than she wanted to. She was dreading Friday and Saturday nights; she wasn't sure she could make it through those shifts. By the end of each shift, so far, Dee's feet felt like she was walking on hot coals with sledgehammers slamming into her ankles. Her hip was sore and swelling and her limp was getting worse. She needed more time to heal.

Twenty

Billy Cannon made one more visit to the Star Mist, it was the off
season but Billy was scheduled to return to Oakland, where his
Head Coach and General Manager, Al Davis was set to accept the
appointment as Commissioner of the American Football League and
Davis wanted his team (and the AFL's) biggest star at his side for the
announcement. Beck wanted to get to know Dee a little better and
who could be a better wing man than "Legend" so he talked his friend
into a night on the town before he headed out to California.

It was a rather warm and humid Friday night and the college
crowd was in a rowdy mood. Beck and Legend walked in around
10:30 pm and a crowd instantly formed around Billy as he started
answering the usual questions, signing a few autographs, and reliving
the "Hallowed Run" of '59.

Beck—6 ft. 5 in. 285 lb former football player with a solid phy-
sique—could have been a bodyguard and most people thought that to
be his role in the relationship. Truth was that Billy could take care of

himself and Beck was just a drinking buddy he'd known since he was being recruited out of Istrouma High School in Baton Rouge. Neither of the two men, however, corrected any possible misconceptions as they were both okay with the general public thinking Beck was Billy's muscle.

Beck leaned over the bar and ordered top-shelf bourbon (an up shot) for himself, same for the Legend, and whatever Dee was drinking.

"Sorry, Mister, I'm still trying to heal up from a bad car accident so I'm laying off the libations for a while," Dee said as she started pouring a couple of Old Crows.

"I can appreciate that; I heard your story last week when we were here. So glad you made it."

"Thanks, Mister, you want to run a tab?"

"Yea, I'm sure it'll get some use, you know how Billy is . . . ?"

"Yes, I do, he's a legend around here for more than just football." They laughed.

Beck was no match for Billy Cannon when it came to the magnitude of his stories, or the storytelling, but he was pretty good with the crowd himself. Beck was the type that never met a stranger and if you knew him, he was one of your best friends. He was also the guy, for whatever reason, that bravery-in-a-bottle guys wanted to test their raging testosterone against.

It virtually never failed when Beck was out on the town—whether Legend was in company or not—that some bloated-ego drunk wanted to start trouble and Beck, inexplicably, seemed to attract them like flies to honey. He was also fairly adept at picking up on the would-be troublemakers' bad vibes before anyone else knew what was happening.

Once when Beck and another friend, DJ, had gone to a bar in New Orleans that was broadcasting (via radio) the Muhammad Ali vs. Sonny Liston Heavyweight Championship, an off-duty, muscle-bound firefighter sitting at a table with five of his muscle-bound firefighting buddies and two cute blonds—whom they were all trying desperately to impress—stared Beck down as they approached an empty table next to the firefighters.

Beck, who was wearing his Ole Miss hat—he had spent a brief stint on the team prior to joining the Navy—saw the stare down but purposely didn't make eye contact. He was instantly cognizant the guy was looking for an opportunity to start something and he preferred to avoid trouble when he could.

As Beck ordered a drink and started to turn his head back toward the conversation he was engaged in with his buddy the firefighter leaned over and said, "What are you looking at you, Rebel prick?"

"Nothing buddy, I'm just minding my business and looking forward to a good bourbon; why don't you do that too and we can all enjoy the boxing match," he said sitting back in his chair. Beck's rule of thumb was: Avoid trouble if possible, but if violence was imminent hit first, strike hard, and end it quick.

"Why don't you stop worrying about what I enjoy Mr. Inbred Rebel?" the punk said as he got up out of his seat and moved toward Beck. As he reared back to take a swing at a sitting target Beck came to his feet with his right hook simultaneously cracking the guy's jaw. He reached out and caught the guy's shirt with his left hand, breaking his fall, and set him unconsciously back into his chair where he slumped over the table, out cold.

As all of the punk's buddies and DJ jumped to their feet in defensive postures, Beck said, "Y'all might have us out numbered but I promise you at least two or three of you are going to have a broken jaw just like your pal here—you can tend to him and let us enjoy the fight or we can see if anybody else has a glass jaw?"

They quickly talked themselves out of vengeance and carted their friend out of the bar, presumably to locate the nearest hospital. The blonds refused to leave with the immature firefighters and were soon laughing over drinks with Beck and DJ.

Dee poured up shot number four for Beck and the Legend and a round for the twenty or so people surrounding them at the bar. By now Dee was relying on the cane and her hip was killing her. She asked four hippy guys at the other end of the bar what they were drinking. "It's on the house, guys, compliments of Mr. Cannon, what are you having?"

"I already told you lady, we're not drinking tonight, just waiting for some friends," the one with several tattoos said.

"Well, no offense, sir; but you guys have been here for over an hour and haven't ordered anything. We need those stools to produce revenue for the bar so if you're just waiting you may need to stand outside."

"Forget it, lady, we're going to sit right here until we are good and ready to leave."

"Listen guys, I can call Big Ray over here to escort you out, you can order something, or you can just leave, why don't we do it easy?"

"No, you listen, you gimpy little bit . . ."

"Stop giving the lady a hard time, buddy. She's just doing her job," Beck stepped in.

"And why don't you mind your business, big fella? You don't scare me and neither does Big Ray, your dumb jock friend down there or anybody else in this crappy joint for that matter," he said flicking a switchblade from his pocket.

"Guys, stop it, we don't need any trouble," Dee said frantically.

Beck never said another word; he just stood there waiting for the punk or one of his crew to make a move. Big Ray rushed into the fray and saw the knife just as the tattooed thug slashed at him. Beck threw his arm in front of Ray and took a gash to his right bicep, while smashing the guy with a powerful left jab. An all-out brawl ensued with Big Ray, Beck, and a Star Mist regular going blow for blow (and dodging a blade or two) with the four punks and two more of their buddies that showed up just as the brouhaha got started.

Twenty

Billy set his drink down calmly and made his way to the fight where he walloped one of the guys just as the arriving police sirens started ringing outside. It wouldn't be hard to break up the fight as Big Ray, Beck, and the regular with the Legend's contributive blows had pretty much demolished the crew; but the aftermath would be immense if the press got wind of Billy Cannon out boozing and brawling in Tiger Town.

Beck pushed Billy toward the kitchen door and looked at Dee, "Please, get him out of here for me, would ya, doll?"

"Come on, Legend," Dee said impatiently pushing the swinging door open with her cane. He would disappear out the back door and Dee would never see the Legend in person again.

Based on Dee and Big Ray's account to the lead officer, the BRPD arrested three of the six men in the fight and left Beck and the other three with a misdemeanor summons. One of the guys arrested kept crying about being beaten up by Billy Cannon. No one at the bar, other than the six punks, would admit he was even there—at least not to the police. They would, of course, tell their story to anyone who would listen, after the fact, adding to the many tales of the wild times of Billy Cannon.

After the police had gone Dee insisted that Beck go to the hospital to get his arm—which was currently wrapped in a blood-soaked kitchen towel—checked out. "That's going to need stitches."

"Well, I reckon Legend took off in my car so if I'm going to the hospital, you'll have to take me."

"I've got to clean this place up and close the bar; I can call a cab to take you."

"You can go ahead, if you want to Ms. Dee," said Danny the bar back. "Charlotte and I can close up and you're in no shape to be cleaning any way."

"You see, no excuses, one of your patron's needs you to keep from bleeding to death, you're not going to let that happen to me, are you?"

"Oh, for Pete's sake, come on!"

Twenty-One

During the drive to the hospital and in the three-and-a-half hours they spent at the hospital—mostly waiting for someone to suture Beck's laceration that would require seven stitches—Beck and Dee had a great conversation and started getting to know each other. Dee was always shy about herself, but she opened up enough to let Beck know that she was divorced and raising three young children on her own.

Beck, not shy at all, told her story after story of his exploits. He told the sanitized versions to Dee—whom he perceived, despite the fact that she worked in a bar and was a little young to have three children, to be a "good girl"—and left out the fact that he, too, was previously married and had two little girls of his own, living in Florida.

He told her about his family in Carroll County, Mississippi, and his life there as one of the town of North Carrolton's superhero football players—High School Football in the South, particularly in those days, was the end all to be all—and he enjoyed all the perks of being the biggest fish in that little pond.

It was different at Ole Miss—a much bigger pond than good ole J.Z. George School (K–12) in Carrolton—but he didn't stick around long enough to catch on or become a bigger fish. He accepted his scholarship, made it through one spring training and sat on the bench for most of his freshman season before leaving school to join the Navy.

He'd spent time in Korea on the USS Purdy—a destroyer—during the conflict, and was in the Pacific Theater, Marshall Islands, when the first hydrogen bomb was detonated in '52.

He had seen a little action, fired the 40 mm cannon shot that brought down an enemy aircraft, which crashed into a Korean warship and sank it. He had literally sailed around the world twice and eyewitnessed a nuclear explosion.

When he returned to civilian life he moved to Memphis, Tennessee, and took a job at a machine shop—M.B. Parker's—where he had to train this weird little kid right out of high school that was supposed to be some kind of singing prodigy. Beck thought the kid was soft; everybody else called him "King"—Elvis Presley.

"You're pulling my leg," Dee said, "you didn't know the King!"

"Swear it, and I kick myself every day I was so hard on him," Beck said shaking his head and smiling. "He barely lasted a month and by the end of that summer he was all over the radio and within a year he was the biggest thing on the planet. Color me stupid!"

"How'd you get hooked up with Legend—some friend by the way; took off in your car, left you to pay the tab and face the police, bleeding to boot . . . ?"

"He knew I'd be all right and he can't afford to stick around to face the heat when that kind of stuff happens," he said as if it happened frequently. "Besides, I got to have you come to my rescue!"

"Yea, that's right, I'm the hero . . ." she said laughing.

Beck went on to tell her about his attempt to break into football coaching. He had a friend he'd met through the military, Alvin "Muscle

Boy" Roy that got him an interview with Istrouma High School Coach Jim "Big Fuzzy" Brown in the spring of 1954. Brown would allow Roy to start the first weight-training program associated with high school (or any level) and would quickly turn Istrouma into what would be recognized as one of the first high school "Football Factories" and a competitive dynasty—Brown couldn't offer Beck a paid position due the school board's limitations but if he would volunteer for a year or two, and did a good job, Brown said he would either get him on the payroll or help him find a paying gig with another school.

Beck picked up odd construction jobs to pay rent and went after his dream. He assisted Roy with the weight-training program—Beck was a Roy disciple himself—and he worked with the defensive line and served as the team's scouting liaison. As the SL he was responsible for meeting with college coaches that wanted to scout any Istrouma players—there would be a lot of them—and occasionally he would drive recruits or accompany them with their families to visit prospective universities.

In 1955, senior tailback Billy Cannon rewrote the state's record books by scoring 33 touchdowns and averaging more than 100 yards per game rushing. In the State Championship he led the Warriors to a 40–6 demolishing of Fair Park by scoring 3 touchdowns and rushing for 178 yards.

Every scout in the country was after Cannon and Beck became the kid's personal gatekeeper. He joined Cannon and his father, who had difficulty traveling due to a prolonged workplace injury, for the first couple of scouting trips and once the Cannons knew Beck had Billy's best interest at heart it was pretty much just Billy and Beck—and occasionally one or two of the other Istrouma players being recruited—every weekend, visiting college campuses.

Each Friday night, under the lights at Memorial Stadium, or some other high school venue, Billy would run all over the opposing defense—or terrorize their offense as an All-State defensive back—and lead the Warriors to a victory; typically by the fourth quarter he'd be resting on the bench, victory well in hand, discussing which college campus he and Beck would conquer over the weekend.

College Station and Austin, Texas; Norman, Oklahoma; Oxford and Starkville, Mississippi; Auburn and Tuscaloosa, Alabama; Athens, Georgia; Knoxville and Memphis, Tennessee; Gainesville, Florida; Clemson, South Carolina; Lincoln, Nebraska; they had even flown out to California and visited USC. There were probably a few he'd forgotten and a few not worth mentioning.

Beck looked out for Billy and kept him out of trouble, They weren't above going out on the town, accepting a little charm and hospitality, and Beck would allow Billy to knock back a few bourbons with him, but Beck always kept Billy and the prospective coaches, fans, and co-eds in check.

Billy was the star, but Beck was the operator. He made all the visits happen and kept the piranhas from biting at the budding star. College football recruiting wasn't yet what it would become but the big-time programs rolled out the red carpet and Billy was the most sought-after high school senior in the nation that year.

Several schools approached Beck and offered him serious cash and prizes if he could steer Cannon to their program. Beck always laughed it off and told them that he was pretty sure Billy was going to make the decision that was best for him and Beck was cool with that.

The offer of cash was pretty much the kiss of death for any particular school's chances of landing the star athlete—Billy wanted no part of any pay-for-play programs—but Beck was always fairly sure the kid was going to wind up at LSU come what may—his family loved the university and his older brother was already on the football and basketball teams.

It came down to the revered Paul "Bear" Bryant at Texas A&M and LSU's second-year head coach, Paul Dietzel, who had yet to have a winning season. Beck admitted that he tried to get Billy to consider Ole Miss and his former coach, Johnny Vaught—who had a much better track record and a more well-established program than either Bryant or Dietzel at that point—but Vaught would only allow Cannon to play Football (no Track and Field) so Billy said "go to hell Ole Miss" and Beck left it alone.

Cannon was all set to sign with Bryant. From the phone in Alvin Roy's office, with Beck and a local businessman present, who was pleading with Billy to sign with LSU, he called the coach's office at A&M to make his decision official. One of Bryant's assistants answered the call and asked Cannon to let him in on the big decision. Billy wanted to save the good news for Coach Bryant, and he was also a bit of a jokester so he told the assistant he would wait and "break it" to Coach Bryant.

"Look Billy," the assistant said, not joking, "we need you here, man, if someone else is offering you money we can offer more. Money, a car, you name it, we'll take good care of you, buddy."

"I'm not interested in money or cars, sir, I was interested in playing for Coach Bryant. Just tell him I made my decision though, thanks." Billy hung up and the call was made to Paul Dietzel.

A reporter in College Station, bitter at the loss of the prized recruit, wrote an article accusing Cannon and his "recruiting agent," one Becket T. Hayden, of auctioning Cannon's services and collecting cash from boosters at many of their recruiting stops. It ran beside a grainy photo of Beck and a then seventeen-year-old Cannon drinking a "shooter" at a College Station bar.

LSU, the NCAA, and the SEC largely ignored the article as there was no evidence of the accusations and to most of the general public in those days a seventeen-year-old having a drink—eighteen was the legal age—simply wasn't a big deal. It never became a big story, but it cost Beck his coaching position at Istrouma once the East Baton Rouge School Board got wind of the allegations and that basically ended his involvement in football.

Billy, however, stayed in touch with Beck and made sure he had two tickets to every LSU home football game. He offered Beck a job as his "personal manager" once he signed the big contract with Houston after he had been drafted as the overall #1 pick for both the NFL and the AFL. Beck didn't know what a 'personal manager' was supposed to do and by then he was doing fairly well as an iron-and-steel subcontractor so he declined; but they stayed in touch and went out drinking whenever Billy was in town.

By the time Beck finished telling Dee his tales they had agreed to go on a date and the next chapter in their lives had begun.

Twenty-Two

The Boudreaux couldn't have been happier with the beautiful baby girl, who they had renamed Elisabeth Anne. The promise not to change her name was never conveyed to the Boudreaux and it was not in the adoption agreement, but they had agreed to raise the child as a Catholic; believing that the request was made by the birth mother, so she was christened just days after joining the Boudreaux family.

John Boudreaux was not a particular fan of Catholicism as a born-and-bred Southern Baptist, but they had worked with Catholic Child Services to adopt the child and agreed to raise her a Catholic so to a man who believed that his word was his bond, there wasn't much thought of doing it any other way.

Julie had never seen the inside of a Catholic Church, but Sister Mary Elba had arranged for a private Mass for the christening of young Elisabeth Anne, by Father Frey. The church was a stunning classic, if not gothic, cathedral with a large, open auditorium flanked by six 12' trefoil, stained-glass tracery windows with an inset oriel bay between each of the traceries. The raised stage behind the large marble altar and untold number of candles and candle stands was backdropped by two 24' tall white brick walls centered with what appeared to be an expensive, red Dupioni silk, full-length curtain and several floor-to-coffered ceiling white Doric Roman columns.

There were more statues and archaic artwork than she'd ever seen in one place and the ceremony was a bit ritualistic for her liking, but she had agreed to it and like her husband she would keep her word.

Joy Crockett made her way quietly into the back of the sanctuary and witnessed the baptism seated behind a small gathering of the Boudreaux's family and friends. She shed a few tears and prayed silently that the little girl would have a good life. She surmised that the Boudreaux's seemed to be a decent bunch, but she didn't really want to have any contact with them; she was just there to say a silent farewell.

Julie Boudreaux noticed Joy toward the end of the ceremony and started to make way toward her. As she reached the aisle Joy was exiting Sister Mary Elba stepped in front of Julie and gave her a big hug and welcomed her to "the Catholic Family," even if it was by extension.

"Thank you for everything, Sister, we are so happy to have Elisabeth and you have been so helpful in the process."

"Well, I have no doubt that you'll give her a good home and that's our mission."

"We will do our best. Hey, do you know who that woman was that was sitting here during the ceremony?"—Joy had hurried to and out of the main vestibule doors.

"Well, she is a friend of Child Services; she helped me locate a family in need, Elisabeth's family, actually. She just wanted to witness the christening; I hope it's okay?"

"Yes, I suppose so; could I meet her? I would like to thank her."

"I'm not sure if that's a good idea. This is a confidential arrangement and she might be a connection that doesn't need to be made, I will express your gratitude personally if you'd like me to?"

"Yes, I would like that, we'd like that," Julie said placing her arm around her husband who had just walked up holding their newly christened baby girl. "Thank her for all of us!"

"I will, Julie, may God bless your family."

Elisabeth would be a well-cared for little girl that came into a family with a brother a year older—who had also been adopted—and two more siblings would come along over the next six years, via natural childbirth, something Julie and John Boudreaux had been told was medically impossible.

They would raise all four children as equals, being careful not to show bias to their biological children over the adopted ones—though they were all raised to understand that the eldest two had been adopted, so as to avoid any notion of secrecy within the family. It didn't help that none of the family knew anything about the biological families of Elisabeth and Paul; so many questions, mostly Elisabeth's questions, could not be answered.

Paul wouldn't show much curiosity about his biological family, deep down he felt somewhat rejected; but he had a family that he loved, and he would build a contented life around them. Ultimately, he decided he didn't care about his biological family, if they didn't want him then he didn't want them, and he determined he was better off for it.

It wasn't that simple for Elisabeth; she, too, loved her family and they loved and provided well for her. She never felt that she was alienated from them or that she wasn't part of the Boudreaux family, but she always felt there was something she was missing.

As a little girl she would name her dolls and stuffed animals, twice. One name she'd give them that she would use in front of her family;

but when she was playing by herself, she had secret names for them, her "sister and brother" names.

As she grew up, she would imagine herself a member of just about every new family she met. She would curiously question all of her friends and schoolmates about their heritage, their siblings, and family members. She would vicariously adopt several families along the way, though, for the most part, none of them ever knew it.

She also imagined a thousand stories about her birth mother and the family she longed to know. She made up stories ranging from her being pulled from a wrecked, burning car that her birth parents died in simultaneously to her having been kidnapped as an infant and sold to her upper-middle-class family to be a child slave—though she admittedly wasn't very good at cleaning her own room, which was her only regular chore.

Once she heard a story of a young, beautiful woman—Jane Clement—that had disappeared on Easter Sunday, in Baton Rouge, in the midsixties. The woman had a son and daughter around the same age as Elisabeth and Paul. One of the rumors* swirling around the disappearance was that Clement's estranged ex-husband had wrapped her in a missing bedsheet and buried her under a levee that was being repaired at the time on River Road.

From that story Elisabeth surmised that her biological father was in prison—for killing her biological mother—and the Boudreaux's were their refugee campkeepers. When she was a teen-aged girl her favorite song was Tom Petty's "Refugee."—*Who knows? Maybe you were kidnapped, tied up, taken away, and held for ransom. It doesn't really matter to me, baby, everybody's got to fight to be free, I said you don't have to live like a refugee.*

Elisabeth also had the unique experience of being "raised Catholic" in a Southern Baptist home and this added to her nagging sense of displacement. She wanted to know where she came from; she needed to know; she had to know.

While her siblings attended the same public schools as virtually all the kids in their community, she was sent off to private school at the local Catholic parish. She endured Catechism classes and wore ugly uniforms throughout grade school.

She studied Latin, some Arabic, the King's English, and the history of Catholicism, which in many ways was—or at least overlapped—World History, for the last 1,800 years or so anyway. She did enjoy her education and it would prepare her well for higher education and it also provided a resourceful, intelligent, and insatiably curious teenager access to the inner workings of the local Catholic organization, including ultimately, Catholic Child Services.

It should be noted, Jane Clement's ex-husband was never named by the police as a suspect in his wife's disappearance, nor was he charged in any way. Moreover, he raised their two children as a single father and never remarried.

Twenty-Three

By her third week back at the Star Mist Dee was officially dating Beck Hayden and he was becoming a regular. Dee warned him to keep his hands off and not to act jealous if any of the other guys acted flirty with her. "It's kind of part of the gig, the big shots want to flirt with pretty girls, and Joe wants us to seem available."

"No problem, Dee, I can behave."

She had still been limping—using the cane whenever necessary—and though she had lost most of her baby weight, she had also lost—if only temporarily—a small part of her appeal. Especially with the muscle-bound brute hanging around and watching her like a hawk.

"We've got to replace her, Brenda, she's just not cutting it anymore," Joe Alesce said in a private meeting with his general manager.

"You can't be serious, Joe!" Brenda retorted. "She's still recovering from her accident, she'll be fine. And besides, our numbers are back up from when she and I were both out. Just give us a little time; we'll get it back to normal."

"I can't wait, Brenda; we've been losing money for the last four months and I can't afford to just hope she'll fully recover."

"Joe, you can't do this to her," Brenda said raising her voice. "She has been the best bartender you've ever had and you know it. She's also the most dependable, hardest-working woman I've ever met and she's got three kids, for Pete's sake. If you cast her aside because she had an accident it's going to hurt your business a lot more than having you and ditzy Dolly bartending did the last few months while she and I were laid up in hospital beds."

"I'm sorry, Brenda, I've already made the decision and hired the girl, Alexis; you'll need to start training her tomorrow. She's young and very pretty and she's a fairly decent waitress," he stated firmly. "I can break it to Dee when she comes in for tonight's shift, but I wanted to give you the option to do it yourself."

"So that's it then, she doesn't have a job anymore, just like that? We are going to fire her because she got into a car wreck and you've found some 'halfway decent' prettier girl?"

"It's not like, that Brenda, but what can Dee do? She can't wait tables like she is and I've already got a manager."

"Not anymore you don't, you son-of-a-bitch. I'll break it to Dee, but you can consider this my resignation."

"Hold on now, Brenda, don't do anything you are going to regret."

"I'll tell you what I regret, I regret helping you build this place into what it is, but I will not regret telling you to go to hell, so you go to hell," and out of the back office she walked.

As she made it to the front door Dee was walking in to get ready for her shift.

"Come on, Dee, let's go, we're out of here."

"What do you mean; I have to get ready for my shift."

"Sorry kid, Joe went and found himself another girl. He thinks all those customers him and his Marilyn Monroe look-a-like lost are gone forever so he went out and found him another younger model!"

"I don't understand, am I fired, what did I do?"

"You didn't do anything, honey, but it doesn't matter Joe made up his mind, and so did I!"

"So, what, you're quitting, you can't do that, what about your family?"

"Doesn't matter, we'll find work." She grabbed Dee's arm and they headed out of the Star Mist for the last time as Bob Dylan's new hit song—"Rainy Day Women #12 & 35"—blared *Everybody must get Stoned!"* from the jukebox.

"This place was going to pot anyway!" Brenda quipped as Dylan's nasally voice faded behind them.

"Brenda, I've got mouths to feed and I'm already broke thanks to the accident and my ex-Jack Ass, what am I going to do?"

"We're going to find new jobs and we'll be fine; I promise," Brenda said confidently. "Actually you remember my mom's friend, Mr. Leland, you met him at our Christmas party a couple years ago, at La Rouge?"

"I guess so, why?"

"Well, he runs the Prince Murat Hotel over on Nicholson Drive, and they are looking for a banquet manager. He asked me if I would consider taking the job a couple of weeks ago, I could get us both on there, I'm sure."

"Would I be able to make the kind of money I was making here Brenda? I'm really in a tight spot and I can't afford a pay cut."

"I don't know, let me go talk to him and we'll see what we can do."

Shortly after they left the Star Mist and before she could talk to Beck, he walked in through the front door, already buzzing from his previous watering hole. He had already knocked back a couple of whiskey sours when Joe Alesce sat down beside him and tried to explain why he had fired Dee.

Beck didn't take the news very well and Big Ray knew he was no match for Beck, he'd seen him in action. After Beck slapped Joe across the face, Ray tried to reason with him, but he was pretty angry and was sure Joe would look better with fewer teeth. Joe was cowering behind the bar and behind Big Ray and the two cooks when the police arrived and convinced Beck to leave peacefully. Joe said he would not press charges for the smack to the face or the two broken barstools if Beck promised not to return. He promised he would not, but he did warn Joe that Baton Rouge was too small a town to hide but a big enough city to disappear.

Joe would always regret losing Brenda and Dee, and he would never truly replace them, but he would also look over his shoulder for years. He was pretty sure Beck wasn't the idle-threat type.

Dee never knew about the incident, until she ran into Big Ray a few years later. Ray said Joe had it coming for the way he treated her but of all the guys he had bounced from the Star Mist over the years Beck was the one he was glad he didn't have to tangle with.

"That guy's a monster!"

By the time that conversation took place in December 1969, she was beginning to agree with him. But by then she had two more kids and another one on the way.

Twenty-Four

Brenda would take the job at the Prince Murat Hotel and Dee would work as a banquet waitress and bartender, though she typically would not earn as much per shift as she did at the Star Mist. The schedule was flexible though and Brenda pretty much let her pick up whatever shifts she wanted.

She also began working a couple of nights a week at the Fleur De Lis Cocktail Lounge on Government Street and before long a lot of the regulars from the Star Mist made their way to the little, pink, Roman pizza parlor and Dee's shifts were buzzing.

Dee and Beck got serious and started talking about getting married. Dee wouldn't sleep with Beck, though not for a lack of his trying. But she wasn't about to go through another adoption and if he was worth having, he'd be happy to wait.

What Beck didn't tell Dee, something she wouldn't learn for many years, was that he had been previously married and was not legally divorced from his first wife, Belinda. She lived in Florida—where she was raising their two daughters—and had no interest in Beck's whereabouts. From the day he left her, she prayed that she'd never see him again.

Beck had snapped on her and she knew his Jeckle-and-Hyde personality—he was the kind, gentle giant with a magnetic, gregarious personality by nature but an angry, violent lunatic by liquor. The liquored-up lunatic was not something you wanted to deal with more than once. Three times was far more than enough for Belinda.

He wasn't yet a completely out-of-control alcoholic—though he had certainly lost control a few times in his life—but he was well on his way. He had failed to complete or compete in college, his military career though memorable had been mediocre, his coaching career ended before it really got started, and he had moved from job to job many times without realizing much success after high school, where he had been the cock of the walk. One of his brothers was a decorated war veteran, who would have a hometown holiday named after him—In Carrolton, Mississippi, they call it Michael Hayden Day, the rest of us call it Veterans Day—another brother was a business owner and Mississippi State Senator and his cousin Trent was working for a Congressmen in Washington, DC—he would eventually be the US Senate Majority Leader—growing up they all looked up to Beck.

Beck convinced Dee that a friend of his, who worked at the State Capitol Building, was a justice of the peace who could marry them without a lot of hoopla. He called in a favor of the friend and they met in the Capitol Rotunda. Justice Martin, as Beck introduced him, escorted Beck, Dee, and Kelli-Kay through the long hallway where Governor Huey P. Long had been assassinated in 1935 and up to a small, locked conference room, which he declared upon entry, had once been used by the Kingfish himself (Long) and this very room had been the location of his last political meeting, just minutes before being gunned down.

He offered a brief homily and quoted scripture for effect, he asked Beck and Dee to repeat their vows, and declared them husband and wife. He had them sign an official Marriage License Certificate, which would never be filed with the state, and twenty minutes after they entered the historic conference chamber the four of them walked back through the rotunda and Martin congratulated the happy couple.

As he shook hands with Beck he leaned in and quietly said, "You owe me, big guy!"

"Thanks, Justice, you're the best."

The family would move into a small house in the community managed by Mr. and Mrs. Arledge where they were very happy for a time. Micah Ray, their first child together—Dee's fifth born—would be conceived in that house and brought into the world at the Dixon Memorial Hospital—on July 4, 1967—The same hospital where Dee had said goodbye to Dana Kelli less than a year and a half earlier.

The older children really loved Beck and were happy to have him in the family, he was their big hero. For Big Dean, and then Baby Micah he was like a jungle gym they could climb on. He was the father figure they needed, and they were the family he wanted.

Between 1967, when Micah Ray was born, until May of 1970 when Frank James, the seventh and final child, arrived—with Tonya Lynn, born sixth, coming in June of 1968—they became the Brady Bunch, before there was a Brady Bunch, and it worked. Beck was striving, and finally succeeding in his contracting business and Dee worked whenever she could, in between childbearing and began preparing for a career by completing a correspondence course in hospitality and food and beverage management.

In 1973 Brenda accepted the position of general manager of the historic Capitol House Hotel on Lafayette Street. Dee was subsequently offered Brenda's former post—food and beverage director—at the Prince Murat, which she accepted. She worked hard and guided a brisk catering and banquet business, which led to solid growth and profits for the hotel.

In 1975 she convinced ownership to invest in several large, projector-style, closed-circuit television screens that were installed in the ballroom and lounge area where LSU football games would be viewed by up to seven hundred people every Saturday night during the fall with Sundays drawing five hundred or so for the New Orleans Saints and other NFL games. Napoleon's at the Prince would become Baton Rouge's first major sports bar and Dee was the driving force.

Beck had landed the contract to lay the foundation for a sixty-four-lane bowling alley on Airline Highway and later for the new tower at the Medical Center off O'Neal Lane, along with many other smaller projects. He found himself with a growing business and an expanding payroll and when things were good, they were very good; but when things were slow or tight financially it was stressful and Beck's copping mechanism—the proverbial bottle—was getting deeper and deeper.

For Christmas in 1975 Beck and Dee went house hunting and they found a beautiful five-bedroom house on Profit Avenue in the new development, Old Jefferson Community, off Antioch Road. He also bought her a slightly used but very nice Buick Riviera—The Rockford Files Edition—and there was barely enough room in the den, under the beautifully lit Christmas tree, for all the gifts for the children. Life was good.

Twenty-Five

Life was good for what now seems* like a fleeting moment but it was in that house on Profit Avenue that things would spiral out of control and they would all meet the monster; the other side of the gregarious hero, the man Frankie called "Big Dad." He became angry, dangerous, violent, unreasonable, unpredictable, and at times completely terrifying; but only when he had been drinking, which was to say, most of the time.

One day Frankie, not quite six years old, was playing at the end of the street on a dirt pile at the entrance to one of the home lots still under construction—the children had been forbidden from playing on the construction sites but Frankie's five-year old brain had forgotten the command—and as he played with his Tonka Trucks he slid into the mud puddle near the bottom of the pile. The mud puddle turned out to be a very deep, thick muck and was basically what you would call "quick mud," like quicksand just thicker. Frankie began to sink and could not pull himself free, the more he struggled the deeper he sank.

Micah, who was riding his bicycle nearby, heard the frantic screams of his sinking little brother and came to his rescue. By trying to pull Frankie out he got himself stuck and within seconds they were both sinking and both screaming. Big Dean came running over and he and a friend would pull both boys—now shoeless and covered in mud up to their necks—from the life-sucking sediment.

By now everyone in the house was running toward the construction site. Dee thanked God they were okay, but she made it clear that they would be punished for disobedience.

"But, Mom," Micah said, "I wasn't playing I just got stuck trying to help Frankie."

"We'll talk about it when your father comes home," Dee said turning the waterspout on to hose the two boys down. She wasn't expecting Beck to show up drunk on a Wednesday but show up drunk he did.

Tonya Lynn met him at the door. "Daddy, Daddy, guess what happened today?"

"I'm sorry, Daddy," Frankie said. "I forgot."

"You're not going to forget when I tan your hide," he growled ordering Frankie to "go find a switch." This was a special kind of torment. Birch and Willow trees are known to have thin flexible branches that make a switching sound when used as a lash for corporal punishment. When ordered to "go get a switch" in the Hayden family you were charged with selecting the best instrument of pain you could locate—If you brought back one that was too thin to leave a welt when lashed or too thick to make the dreaded lashing sound, then Big Dad would beat you with that one, or his belt, on the way out to select a more appropriate implement of discipline.

"And you!" he said to Micah. "Did you forget?"

"No, Daddy, I was just trying to pull Frankie out of the mud and we both got stuck."

"Well, what are you going to do for shoes now to go to school tomorrow?" he asked.

"I'll wear my earth shoes, Daddy," Micah said referring to his suede and rubber-soled shoes that were all the rage at the time.

"Earth shoes?" Beck snapped, thinking the child was being sarcastic, "Earth shoes?" He raged again as he smacked his terrified son across the mouth and snatched him up with one hand while pulling his belt off with the other. "I'll beat your little Earth ass and we'll see if you still want to be a wise guy."

Dee tried to calm Beck down and explain that Micah was referring to a type of shoe, not being a smart aleck but the genie was out of the bottle and Beck was already two bottles in. He went on a horrible rage, belting Micah repeatedly with his forty-eight-inch-long leather strap. When Frankie hid in a closet out of sheer terror he was dragged out and strapped several times for good measure before the switch was employed and Dee was slapped to the ground at least twice while trying to intervene.

By the time JJ flew into Beck—a man that towered over and outweighed the scrawny sixteen-year old by almost two hundred pounds—swinging with all his might, the den of the family home looked like downtown Tokyo, and Godzilla was smashing the hapless victims with no end in sight. JJ's blows were about as effective as a pellet gun in taking down Godzilla, but they would serve to put Beck and JJ on a collision course that would nearly end one of them.

Eventually Godzilla grew tired of the one-sided battle and went to the dinner table to eat supper—that was set out before his tirade began—alone. Dee tended to her sons' wounds and tried to make sense of what had just occurred. After shoveling down his dinner the still fuming tower of terror retired to his La-Z-Boy and passed out with a drink in one hand and a Viceroy cigarette in the other.

Another day, not long after the first Godzilla sighting, Beck showed up in a 1972 Chevy pickup truck. The truck was jet black with hot orange and yellow flames painted on its hood and flared fenders. It had custom chrome rims, racing tires, and an open flatbed—with poly finished wood planks lag-bolted to the frame to form its bed-deck. Beck tried to explain to his irritated wife that he needed it for work and Micah and Frankie were sure it was the coolest thing they had ever seen.

As Dee stormed into the house all of the kids—including a couple from the neighborhood—wanted to go for a ride so Beck, who was feeling pretty good—too good actually—started piling kids into the cab and onto the flatbed of the truck. As he whipped out of the driveway, two of the kids on the bed, including Frankie, flew off the side and rolled heels over head through the front yard.

Hearing the commotion Dee ran back out of the house, "Are you crazy, Beck? You cannot ride kids on the back of a flatbed, what are you thinking?" she said checking Frankie for cuts and bruises.

"Settle down, woman, the kids are fine, they just need to learn to hang on better."

The verbal sparring ensued while most of the neighborhood kids ran off and more than a few of the neighbors witnessed the first backhand Beck delivered across Dee's face through their living room windows. Now blooming into a psychotic rage, he demanded that all of his boys line up on the bed of the truck so he could "teach" them a lesson.

"Beck, no, you can't do this," Dee said trying to wrestle the keys away from him.

He batted her to the ground again, and demanded the boys get on the back of the truck and told Tonya to climb into the cab—Anna Rae wasn't at home. As JJ helped Frankie onto the wood deck he suddenly paused, looked at Beck, and charged at the monster making a perfect waist tackle—like all the boys were taught by their respective football coaches, and Beck himself—Beck fell to the pavement and was stunned by the take down. Without hesitating, JJ sprang to his feet and bolted across the yard.

Beck picked himself up, screaming "I'm going to kill you, you little coward. Get back here and ride with your brothers." Determined to make whatever his stupid point was, he climbed back into the driver seat as a sobbing and hysterical Dee placed her outstretched hands on the hood of the truck.

"I'm not going to let you kill my babies, Beck," she said, as he started the powerful big block V8 and the 350ci engine rumbled through its open tail pipes.

"Swear to God I'll run you down if you don't move, woman," Beck snarled as he noticed JJ emerging from the garage with his hard maple Louisville Slugger. Before Beck could get himself out of the vehicle JJ made it across the yard and in a fluid motion—that looked like a penalty shot with a hockey stick—he exploded the passenger side headlamp on the pretty, black hot rod. His second swing removed the side view mirror and left a gaping wound in the door, where the mirror had been mounted.

"I'm going to kill him!" Beck bellowed as the entire family rushed to get between him and JJ who had assumed his most aggressive batting stance—with his back foot firmly planted—in the middle of the front yard. "Come and get me you miserable drunk!" JJ shouted as the sheriff deputies started pouring down the street just in time to save one or maybe both from certain destruction.

One of the deputies loaded Beck into the back of a squad car. The snarling drunk warned the young corporal that he was a close friend of Al Amiss—East Baton Rouge Parish Sheriff, J. Al Amiss III—and after a call in to the sheriff, the deputy informed Beck that he would be taken in to the drunk-tank at the East Baton Rouge Parish Prison, where he could "sleep it off" but he would not be charged.

In fact, rather than charge him with any crimes, such as the obvious battery he had committed on his wife and at least two of his children, the child endangerment or the terroristic threats he hurled at JJ in front of the deputies, the lieutenant—who also knew Beck from his days at Istrouma—asked him if he wanted JJ charged with property damage and assault.

"Hell yes, I do," said Beck. "Look what the little, long-haired punk did to my new truck."

Dee protested mightily "How can you arrest a sixteen year old for trying to protect his family and you won't even charge this monster for beating his wife and kids?" she demanded.

"Well, ma'am, we don't have any witnesses that he hit you, other than your own family—he said without knocking on a single neighbor's door—but you all verified that your son tackled the man and then attacked him with a baseball bat, which he was still wielding when we arrived. I'm sorry, ma'am, but I'm afraid we're going to have to arrest him."

Twenty-Six

JJ *was brought into the juvenile detention center*—near Ryan Airport— through a large electronic gate that stood eleven feet high and had razor wire coiled for another three feet across the top. The gate created an entrance into what looked like a blond-stone and cream-colored brick fortress with no visible windows or doors on the outer building envelope. It was only once you reached one of the inner courtyards that you could locate the heavy iron doors with eight-inch peephole windows, which seemed as impenetrable as the massive doors themselves—due to the criss-crossed rebar inside the thick glass.

JJ—handcuffed and in shackles—was escorted into the intake hall where an ominous sign stated "No Talking" and he was latched onto a bench next to a muscular black kid, with a huge afro, who called himself "Nipsy."

They sat there "not talking" to each other quietly for over an hour and a half when a processing officer appeared and ordered the two boys to strip naked, place their belongings in a clear bag he provided, and step into the large, open shower area that was adjacent the intake corridor.

The officer briefly sprayed them from a lukewarm, high-pressured hose. "Now scrub this into your hair and all over your body for two minutes," he said handing each one of them a small prescription bottle of RID Lice Shampoo. Once they had scrubbed to the officer's satisfaction, he turned the hose on full blast. JJ felt like he was a building fire being doused when the chemical shampoo blasted through his eye sockets. Once all of the shampoo, residue, and what must have been his outer layer of skin had been pressure-washed from his body a new officer pressed a stack of clothing and a pair of canvas loafers into his arms, noticeably missing was a towel.

"Get dressed!" Officer Howard ordered.

The boys were then escorted through the automated locking doors that led down a long corridor to another set of automated doors where a voice from the overhead speaker said "Identify?" as they approached.

"Howard, adding two."

The loud buzz and simultaneous clicking popped the door open.

"After you, gentlemen," Officer Howard said waving the boys through the big steel passageway.

They proceeded through one of the three recreation rooms where twenty-five or so mostly rough-looking young men sat watching TV or stood playing ping-pong and all scowled as the "fresh meat" walked through.

"Hey, white boy," one of the inmates bellowed through his gold teeth. "We gonna be friends, yeah," he said quite menacingly. Another one called out to Nipsy, "What up, Oaks, you know I still owe you one, right?" he declared menacingly—apparently the two had a history of some sort.

New detainees were placed on lockdown for their first day at the center. Once escorted through the rec room the boys were placed in their cells for at least twenty-four hours. Their meals, if you could classify them as such, were brought to the cell and the sixty-square-foot, cinder-block-and-steel room was inconveniently equipped with all other essentials.

Once the other detainees were returned to their cells the newbies would be heckled, harassed, threatened, and generally promised a hard time. Nipsy was from the Glen Oaks neighborhood and four or five of the other guys on the cell row were members of the infamous "Southside Wrecking Crew." Apparently, they had all been in some battles on the streets—as the nonincarcerated world was referred to "on the inside."

JJ hadn't responded to any of the taunts hurled his way and basically just kept his mouth shut but when all the other boys had gone to breakfast the next morning, he called out to Nipsy.

"Hey man, those guys seem like they really want to hurt you, are you going to be okay?"

"I can handle myself and they know my boys are deep on Block Three, if they mess with me, they'll get theirs out on the yard," he said pretty confidently. "Why, you got my back or something, white boy?"

"Well, you know, we got pressure-washed together," he joked. "And it didn't sound like you had a lot of friends here—not sure I'd be any help to you but, yeah, I've got your back if it comes to that."

They talked a little bit to pass the time when the others were out of their cells but neither one said a whole lot when the cells were full. After dinner that evening their doors buzzed and popped open and they were told to join the Block One population in the rec room.

Reluctantly, JJ walked into the large, open room and found an empty chair by one of the steel-caged windows and sat with his back against the wall. A few gave him hard looks and he couldn't help but notice that there wasn't another white face on his block.

Nipsy bounced out right behind JJ and made sure he strutted by the Southside boys that had been threatening him when he was locked in his cell. He strode across the large room, in the same direction JJ had walked, but stopped at one of the card tables that had one empty chair. "Who you down with, G?" he asked one of the guys at the table—the biggest and meanest looking from JJ's perspective.

"Zion City bro, you?"

"Glen Oaks all day long, we cool?"

"Yup!" They shook hands and bumped their fists and Nipsy sat down where he could look right at the Southside Boys.

"Hey, white boy, what you doing here?" barked the leader of the Southside crew; they called him Silky.

"I'm just minding my own business, man."

"What, you too good to talk with us colored folk?" Silky chided.

"Didn't say that," said JJ.

"Well, what are you saying, white boy, are you gonna tell me why you here or what?"

"He's here because he's here, Silk, and he's down with Glen Oaks, so you might want to back up off him," said Nipsy standing up, and instantly the Zion City (Smurfs) crew, which turned out to be about a third of the block—stood up to back Nipsy. The Southside crew was as shocked as JJ, but they all stood up too and JJ was pretty sure they were all just going to fight over who got to kill the fresh meat white boy.

A siren went off and about eight guards, wielding nightsticks, quickly appeared as the main door to the cell row buzz popped.

"Let's go everybody, to your cells, you're all on lockdown for the rest of the night," ordered Officer Howard, and the detainees all filed into the cramped block corridors as the guards pushed them hurriedly into their individual cells. They were required to do a verbal roll count—wherein the detainee in each cell called out his cell's number in descending order, starting at twenty-eight. There were fourteen cells on each row and at present only three cells were vacant on Block One.

136

JJ would make his court appearance the next morning at 10:00 am but not before he got to experience the yard. After breakfast—which was the fifth meal in a row JJ couldn't bring himself to eat—all three blocks were let out into a yard that took up the back half of the detention property. There was a volleyball and a basketball court, both on cement slabs right in the middle of the acre or so of grass and weeds wrapped all around by two secured fence lines.

The inner fence was twelve feet high and had six strands of barbed wire running through a V channel at the top of the fence. Between the two fence lines there was approximately twenty feet of space with a well-worn track in the middle. The outer fence line was a couple of feet shorter and had the same V channel with barbed wire but had the added feature of a double-coiled shinny and apparently very sharp razor wire.

As the seventy or so detainees made their way out into the yard the noise rose to the level of a busy train station. A section of the raised freeway—The MLK Freeway—stretched past the far corner of the yard with traffic passing overhead, along with the close proximity of the Metropolitan Airport made it all but impossible for the guards to monitor anything but body language.

JJ wasn't scared, per se, but he also wasn't stupid. There was now a grand total of five white faces and the other four were at present sitting on a bench roughly twenty feet from the closest guard and far away from the various congregating crews. He knew the Southside Crew wouldn't mind smacking him around and even though Nipsy backed him up yesterday, he didn't really want to put himself in the middle of a notorious gang like the Zion City Smurfs—the Crips and Bloods weren't nearly as well known in Louisiana as the Smurfs and the South side Wrecking Crew at the time.

"White Boy," called Nipsy, "come meet my crew."

"Yo, y'all look out for this hippie-looking white dude, he's got heart," Nipsy told his Glen Oaks boys and the rest of the Zion City crew. He told them how JJ promised to watch his back when he thought they were outnumbered. "Y'all should have seen the grin on his face when all the Smurfs stood up with me, Silky Reed looked like he wanted to run back to his cage, but this white boy never flinched."

As Nipsy was telling his story the guards came out and called JJ and six other detainees to get ready for court. "No offense, Nipsy, I hope I don't see you again, but thanks for standing up for me, you're a good dude."

"You too, white boy, peace out!"

JJ was led into the courtroom where his mom and Aunt Brenda were waiting with a man who would be introduced as his attorney, Anthony Savagio.

"Your Honor," Savagio said to Judge Grafia, "we move to have these charges dropped. As you can see from the brief I supplied to your clerk, the defendant has provided signed affidavits from four impartial witnesses that establish that not only was Mr. Hayden the aggressor, but also the defendant's actions may well have saved the lives of his three younger brothers."

After a sound argument from Tony and not much of a hard sell on the part of the Assistant DA, the judge granted the dismissal motion. He also issued a temporary restraining order, removing Beck from the home until Family Services could complete their abuse investigation.

On the way home Dee promised a somber JJ—who had already resolved himself to leaving home—that Beck would be moving out.

Twenty-Seven

Ossie Brown was elected district attorney in 1972 and would serve East Baton Rouge Parish through 1984. A Democrat, who would chair the first Child Abuse Prevention Committee for the NDAA—National District Attorney Association—Brown was known to be tough on predators and an advocate for victims, particularly child and spousal abuse victims.

He was also friends with and a political ally of Sheriff Al Amiss—who was good friends with Beck dating back in his days at Istrouma High—and the two elected leaders would occasionally play poker with Beck at Billy Cannon's private poker nights.

When the Family Services investigation report landed on Brown's desk, he picked up the phone immediately to call Sheriff Amiss.

"Al, I need to sit down with you as soon as possible, the report on Beck Hayden's alleged family abuse is frightening," Brown surmised.

"Now hold on, Ossie, you know Beck as well as I do. He might get a little difficult when he drinks too much, but that wife of his is exaggerating these abuse allegations."

"I don't know, Al, I've had one of my best dicks looking into it, and he's pretty adamant that the kids and the wife are in grave danger."

"I'll stop by tomorrow and we can figure out how to deal with it," Amiss promised.

"Okay, Sheriff, I'll see you tomorrow."

Amiss talked to a sober Beck the next morning and was convinced, yet again, that his good friend's wife was exaggerating greatly the degree of physicality involved in their disagreements.

"I'm telling you, Al, she's crazy and she's trying to turn my kids against me. You know I love my kids, hell I love her kids, even that little hippie boy," Beck said making his case. "I tell you what though; you ought to have somebody keeping an eye on that little hoodlum, look what he did to my truck and no telling what kind of drugs and such he's getting into."

"I hear you, Beck; I'm going make this thing go away with the DA, I just need you to stay out of trouble. Okay?"

"No problem, Al, and you can tell that welcher Ossie Brown he still owes me four hundred dollars from the last time he was at Legend's game."

Al Amiss would convince Brown to close the file on the investigation and over the next several years Amiss would basically thwart any efforts by Dee to seek the help of law enforcement, which she finally gave up—the police would only be called if a neighbor or the hospital did so. At first Amiss believed Beck, but even once he realized that Beck was just a child- and wife-beating drunk, he still wouldn't allow him to be prosecuted. Beck was part of the inner circle and he knew where the bodies were buried, or you might say, since they shared river camps on the Amite and Manchac Bayou, he knew where the gators had been fed.

Twenty-Seven

From the midseventies until 1983, when Amiss died in office, Dee would live in fear, fight for dear life, and work multiple jobs to support the family—she was fired from a couple when Beck would show up and make a scene—and move more than twenty times due to a vicious cycle of fight, then flight, and then a promise of "Oh, honey, you know I'll make it right."

Between the six children, at some point, they attended virtually every school in Baton Rouge, and two in Gonzales, and one in Mississippi.

The cycle was pretty consistent; Beck would get paid from a contract; pay his helpers—who knew to be close by when he went to the bank to cash the check, and if Dee or Anna Rae where able to catch him before he got to the bar, he would give them bill money, and then a two- or three-day binge would ensue.

At some point during the binge he would come home to express disapproval of his disappointing family, "coach" his boys, who should have no excuses for not being NFL superstars by that point, because it was in their damn blood. He would rage on his wife, who was trying to turn all his friends against him, and just generally try to straighten them all out.

The straightening would lead to physically bashing and at some point deputies would show up—called by a neighbor—and encourage Beck to sleep it off or take him to the parish drunk tank where he would sober up and be released. During the sleep-off, Dee and the kids would stuff a few travel bags, load what they could into and on top of the old wood-panel station wagon and go find a place to hide out for a few days while Dee found them a new place to live.

One day, while seven-year-old Frankie was playing in the front yard of the house they had just moved into on Eastgate Drive, Beck drove up in his flaming flatbed. "Hey Dad, are you going to beat us up and make Mommy move again, we just got here."

"Is that what your Momma tells you, Boy?"

"No, Dad, I just like it here and when you get mad, we have to move."

"Well I'm not mad, Son; I just want to talk to your momma."

"Come inside, Frankie. Beck you need to leave us alone, you can't control yourself and you are going to kill someone," Dee said as she was trying to close the door.

"I'm coming in, Dee. You are not going to keep from my kids."

She knew it was futile, so she opened the door. Supper was nearly ready, so Dee told Tonya to set the table and include a plate for her daddy. As they sat down, Beck immediately started drilling the kids on school, football, them not being as good as he was and warning them not to believe their "damn momma" about whatever horrible things she may have said about him.

"Damn it, Beck!" Dee said slamming her plate down, causing a crack to run through the plate. "Do you have to browbeat the kids every time you talk to them?"

"Browbeating them, huh?" he said rising to his feet. "And you want to break dishes, huh?"

Beck picked up his plate, with food still on it, and smashed it against the table. "See, I can break a dish too, watch this." He said picking up Frankie's plate of food. Smash!

Dee never flinched; she just told the kids to go to their room and stood motionless while Beck went into the kitchen, opened the cabinets, and proceeded to smash every single dish in the house.

Smash! Smash! Smash! Smash!

"How's that, bitch? you want to break another dish?"

Smash! Smash! Smash! Smash!

Brenda had picked up Big Dean—already a 6 ft. 2 in., 220 lb., thirteen-year-old—from football practice and the two walked into what looked like a fine china factory after a typhoon. Dean, normally the quiet one, was not in the mood to watch Godzilla attack his family again so he marched up to his mother and grabbed her hand.

Twenty-Seven

"Come on, Mom, we're leaving."

"You're not going anywhere, fat boy!" chided Beck.

At the same time, Frankie started trying to clean up the dishes, hoping to keep the family from erupting again and he cut his knee—a deep gash—on a shard of jagged porcelain. Dee picked Frankie up and Beck tried to take him from her arms as Brenda hurried out to her car.

"I'm taking Frankie to the hospital, Beck, just let us go."

Beck jerked Frankie out of Dee's arms, "He's not a baby, woman, just put a band-aid on it!"

"No, Beck, he's going to the hospital!"

"What do you want to do, Frankie? Go to the hospital with your whining damn momma, or hang out here and watch some TV with your ole Big Dad?"

Frankie meekly said he wanted to go with his momma and to everyone's dismay, Beck—the nearly 340 pound gorilla—with a closed fist, walloped Frankie right in the side of the head. There was a brief pause that seemed like suspended animation as they all watched the 65 lb child slam into the wall, losing consciousness, with blood now gushing from his ear and knee, and then all hell broke loose. Dee was screaming in lamentation as she started scooping her lifeless child into her arms while Big Dean, with Micah right behind him, charged Beck like the blitzing linebackers he wanted them to be and they were all swinging wildly.

Brenda, who had returned from her car just in time to see Beck level his youngest son, pulled back the hammer on her .44 caliber nickel-plated Smith & Wesson revolver. BLAM! BLAM!

The melee halted as she put two bullets through the popcorn-stippled ceiling two-and-a-half feet above Beck's head.

"I swear to God, Beck Hayden, I actually want to put a bullet in your heart and I damn well know how to do it—back up and sit down or I will end your miserable life right here and now!"

Beck knew she wasn't playing around so with his hands in the air he backed up and sat down in one of the dining room chairs, after he shook the shards of broken dishes from the seat.

"Dee, go get in my car with Frankie, the rest of you kids go get in your mom's car, right now, Anna Rae, you're driving, follow me, let's go," Brenda said commanding the scene and everyone listened.

They were turning onto Sherwood Forest Blvd, headed toward the Lady of the Lake Regional Medical Center (LOTLRMC) when several EBRSO squad cars screamed into the neighborhood, responding to the reports of shots fired.

Twenty-Eight

At the hospital they learned that Frankie's eardrum was ruptured and the damage was likely permanent. The laceration on his knee received four stitches and his ear was cleaned with iodine, stuffed with cotton balls, and wrapped in gauze. His knee was bandaged as well. When the medical staff was finished, he looked like a wounded soldier returning from war.

The sheriff's deputies arrived about ten minutes after Corporal Patricia Tauzin and Lieutenant Pat Bonanno of the East Baton Rouge Police Department (EBRPD)—the hospital was within the EBRPD's jurisdiction and they had been called by the attending physician upon seeing the child's brutal wounds.

The house was in the sheriff's jurisdiction, and the alleged crime(s) occurred at that location.

Corporal Tauzin, one of the first ranking female officers in the EBRPD, didn't care in which jurisdiction the crime occurred, there was a seven-year-old boy brutally assaulted. She was adamant that the perpetrator was going to jail, period.

"Can you confirm that EBRSO has apprehended one male, Caucasian, Beckett T. Hayden?" Corporal Tauzin asked.

"Copy that, Corporal. Hayden is 10–26 Parish Prison as we speak," replied Deputy Barlow.

"Mind if I ask what he's being charged with?" Bonanno queried.

"Does it matter?" Barlow retorted flatly.

"I'd say it does, Deputy," said Tauzin.

"Listen here, ma'am, I don't know how you PD types feel, but I for one don't appreciate nonjurisdictional LEOs telling me how to do my job in my own parish," Barlow stated.

Tauzin started to go ballistic on the cocky, young sheriff's deputy but her partner—recognizing her trigger—firmly placed his hand on her forearm. "Thanks, Barlow, we know how you feel," Bonanno assured.

"Thanks, I meant no offense. So, did you guys arrest O'Bannon, you know she discharged a weapon?"

"Now I know you wouldn't want to be telling other LEOs how to do their job, would you Barlow?" Bonanno quipped.

Barlow laughed, "I guess not, Lieutenant. We'll let y'all handle this end. Good night, ma'am." He tipped his wide-brim trooper hat toward Tauzin.

"No way am I dropping this, Pat. They better charge him appropriately," Tauzin said after Barlow and his partner disappeared behind the elevator doors.

"I'm with you 100 percent, Trish, we just need to go at it through the DA. You know EBRSO, no chance they cooperate with us."

"Ten-four. You up for a drive-by? Eastgate is on our way back downtown."

At the Beckett home they found a hesitant Anna Rae at home—cleaning and packing. "Can I help you, officers?"

Twenty-Eight

"We were hoping to ask you a few questions about the domestic dispute that happened here about an hour and a half ago, were you here at the time?"

"I got home just about the time we ran out of dishes for him to break."

Anna invited the officers in where they could surmise the scene for themselves. Tauzin questioned Anna Rae about the alleged altercation, previous disputes, and if she had personally witnessed the blow to young Frankie.

"Punched the little guy right in the head, most horrible thing I've ever seen. It was a good thing Aunt Brenda was here or my brothers and Beck would have killed each other after he did that."

While the questioning proceeded, Bonanno snapped countless Polaroids—he was already in possession of the ones taken of Frankie at the hospital, both before and after he was treated—placed a few shards of bloodied porcelain in a plastic bag and announced to Tauzin he was satisfied.

"Here's my business card, young lady, you call me if I can help you in any way or if you think of anything else, let us know," Tauzin said handing Anna Rae the card.

"Actually, I do have a question, if it's okay?"

"Shoot."

"Well, I'm sorry but I don't understand why nothing ever happens to this man. He has been arrested too many times to count. I know he's friends with Al Amiss, but he has just about killed all of us at one time or another, and now look what he did here tonight," she said somberly, waiving her hand across the bloody mosaic scene.

"I'm sure," Anna Rae added, "he was provoked, you know, the sweet tea wasn't sweet enough or the saltshaker was almost empty or something unacceptable like that. He'll swear it was totally called for and the good sheriff will let him sleep it off again, without charges, and then it starts all over again."

"How often does this kind of thing happen?" Bonanno quizzed.

"A couple times a month, unless he's not busy at work, then it's once or twice a week."

"How long has this been going on?"

"Well, it really started getting bad when I was about twelve," the eighteen-year-old responded.

"To answer your question, Miss Hayden," Tauzin began shaking her head.

"Dempsey," Anna Rae corrected.

"I'm sorry, to answer your question, Miss Dempsey, I don't know why it keeps happening, but I intend to find out."

"I would appreciate that very much, Officer Tauzin, and thanks for your card, I'm sure I'll need it."

Tauzin and Bonanno doubled back to the Lady of the Lake to review the hospital's records for any members of the Hayden–Dempsey Bunch. The files were astounding. Each member of the family, save Tonya, had been to this particular hospital at least once. The mother, the former Miss Dee Crockett-Dempsey had been treated the most; multiple nose breaks, cuts above the eyebrow, twice with broken ribs, she had been stabbed with a bamboo stick at some point, and like her youngest son, her right eardrum had been destroyed. There were Polaroids in a few of the files and the hospital had one of those fancy new Xerox 9200 color copiers—like the one from the 1975 Super Bowl commercial, featuring Jack Eagle as a "freed from decades of scribing" monk—so Tauzin made copies of everything.

The file on the mother was frightful and sobering, but little Frankie's file—only spanning a few years, as the kid was barely seven years old—was downright infuriating. In addition to having his eardrum busted—causing a faint ringing in his ear that would accompany him to infinity—the child had been in for so many broken bones, fractures, sprains, and a jaw wiring that it was amazing the little guy could still walk and talk. To be fair, Frankie's style of play also had a self-inflicting quality to it. What they claimed to have been a bicycle fall produced multiple gashes on his head and between two fingers that required over twenty-five stitches in all. Another time he played leapfrog from the deck railing outside of the old press box at Memorial Stadium; he successfully landed across the six-foot divide—to the amazement of the crowd of young spectators, who were watching Frankie and not the "Toys for Tots Bowl" football game on the field below—but when Frankie assumed the victorious Superman stance his back foot slipped off of the narrow edge of the cold, gray concrete ledge and his body plummeted to the ground thirty-eight feet below.

"I remember this kid, I was at the Tots Bowl when this happened, the city made them tear down the old press box afterward," Bonanno recollected. "I also remember the dad, massive guy, 6 ft. 6 in. maybe, and stout, probably goes about three hundred and it wasn't fat. I remember mostly because he was screaming at the coaches, the refs, and his kid (Micah) who was the best player in the game, before the little one fell, the guy was obnoxious. Then when the accident occurred, he was more worried about the football game than his nearly mortally wounded kid. Made some stupid comment about the kid being tough enough to wait until the game was over to go to the hospital, we didn't give him the choice."

"Sounds like a real piece of work, this Beckett Hayden," Tauzin surmised.

"Agreed, let's go pay him a visit at Parish."

Twenty-Nine

When *Tauzin and Bonanno made their way* to the interview room where they expected to find Beckett T. Hayden, they were greeted by Deputy Barlow.

"I thought we agreed you two were going to keep your nose out of my business?"

"Of course, Barlow, we aren't here pertaining to tonight's altercation," assured Bonnano. "We need to question Mr. Hayden regarding the violation of several city ordinances; violations which occurred within the established limits of Baton Rouge proper on 23 August 1975."

"What are you talking about?"

"Well, Barlow, that's EBRPD business, but it involves disturbing the peace, criminal negligence, and child endangerment."

"Listen guys, this ole boy Hayden, he has some mighty powerful friends and you really don't need to start trying to trump up charges against him, unless you'ns don't care about your careers."

"No offense, Barlow, but we're sworn to protect and serve the people, not the politicians of Baton Rouge, so if you don't mind, we'll continue our investigation," interjected Tauzin.

"Suit yourselves, don't say I didn't warn you," cautioned Barlow.

"Fair enough," Bonanno said holding the door open for Barlow to exit.

Beck was led into the interview room where he found Tauzin, an attractive and deceptively soft appearing EBRPD officer, sitting alone with a thin file folder on the table in front of her. Bonanno, her partner, was watching on the other side of the two-way mirror with Deputy Mike Thibodeaux, an EBRSO investigator serving as an observer, on direct report to Sheriff Al Amiss.

"Beckett T. Hayden?"

"And who might you be, little lady?" Beck had a natural charisma and confidence with the ladies, which had virtually never failed him. When he saw a good-looking female "traffic cop" sitting there his guard was immediately down and he turned on the charm.

"Well, big guy," she said playing along. "I'm with BRPD and we got a call from the hospital when your son was checked in but really that's the sheriff's business. I just need to follow up from another matter the hospital brought to our attention, no big deal, really."

"What's the matter? Is Frankie okay? You know that boy's crazy momma makes such a big deal out of every little scratch, like it's some fatal wound or something," said the still slightly slurring Beck.

"The boy is fine," she said fuming inside—she really wanted to pistol whip the big brute and smash both his eardrums, one each for his wife and child—but she continued calm and unalarming. "And I think the issue we need to clear up from the hospital may be a misunderstanding," she said opening the file folder that contained an admittance form dated 8/23/75 for one Frank Hayden and some Polaroids—there were some taken of the boy shortly after his fall from the press box at Memorial Stadium and several from various other "incidents" mixed in.

"Your son fell from the press box over at Memorial Stadium last August, correct?"

"Yea, crazy little bastard thought he was Superman."

"So, you didn't have anything to do with these injuries?"

"Of course not, I was sitting there watching the game. I didn't even know they were playing in the press box."

"Sounds right, a witness said you were giving that boneheaded coach what for."

"That's right. That dumb ass Coach Dickey wouldn't know a game plan if it kicked him in the balls!"

"I know, my nephew played for him, I think I could do better and I'm a girl," she said sheepishly.

"You look like a woman to me, a fine one at that!" Beck said, as if he was sitting at the bar hitting on an LSU coed.

"Settle down now, big fella. I've got to finish up this file so I can go home, it's been a long shift." She pointed to the picture of Frankie's swollen and bloodied upper torso—the fall had fractured his collar bone, broken his right arm in three places, and cracked two ribs. "Was all of this caused by the fall?"

"Yep, when that boy gets himself hurt, he does it up right."

"I'll say. That was a hell-of-a-fall. You must have been pissed, having to miss the rest of the game because the little hellion couldn't stay out of trouble?" she questioned.

"Yea, kid's always getting into something, his damn momma let's him run wild, that's the problem."

"Is that why you smack her around?" Tauzin asked nonchalantly.

"Hey, come on, I don't smack her around. I mean we've had some arguments and she can give as good as she gets but I ain't no wife beater!"

"I hear you, Mr. Hayden, but you know she says otherwise."

"Well, she's a lying whore."

"Okay, calm down. I just have to ask." Tauzin got back to the photos. "How long did Frankie have to wear this awful cast?" she asked pointing to the gauze-and-plaster cast that started midbicep, kept his elbow bent, and went all the way down his arm, past his wrist, and wrapped around the palm of his hand. It came equipped with a brace that held his arm up, above chest level.

"I don't know three months I think."

"Poor kid; had to wear that awful thing, broken ribs, broken nose, horrible."

"Yeah, it was pretty bad, don't think he broke his nose, though, but it was still pretty bad."

"Oh," she said pointing to a picture of Frankie with two black eyes and a swollen and reddened nose. "When did this happen?"

"Oh, that was a few months later, the kid smarted off to me, I guess I don't know my own strength," he chuckled.

"So, you smacked the kid?" she asked curtly.

"Well, yeah, I did, but he had it coming!" Beck explained as Bonanno walked in holding a much thicker file folder.

"This is my partner, Lieutenant Patrick Bonanno," Tauzin said, as if she were making an introduction at a dinner party.

"Mr. Hayden," Bonanno greeted him harshly. "I'm going to cut the crap, unlike my partner here," he said maintaining the good cop/bad cop routine. "I see right through you, you're a bully, a wife beater, a child beater, and a basic low life." He slammed the thicker folder open and started spreading out pictures of his bruised, beaten, bloodied, and generally battered family.

"Hey, wait a minute, Bonzo, I ain't no wife beater and I ain't no low life and what's this got to do with my son falling at the stadium?"

Twenty-Nine

"Well, that pretty much just proves that you are a worthless and negligent parent," Tauzin chimed in. "And you will be charged for it, but you've also just admitted to breaking your son's nose, which is aggravated assault and it also means you lied to the EBRSO, because you claimed your son had fallen off of a swing, so that adds an obstruction of justice charge, and we are going to ask the DA to charge you with serial abuse."

"Now wait just a damn minute here," Beck said rising to his feet, shoving the table into Tauzin. "You don't know who you are messing with!" Beck protested as Bonanno clubbed him with his nightstick and swept his feet from under him.

As Bonanno and Deputy Thibodaux—who had raced in to help subdue the detainee once Beck erupted—slapped the cuffs on Beck, Bonanno said, "I know exactly who you and your friends are, you big piece of garbage, and I'm sure they'll be happy to be your pen pal when you get up to Angola."—*he said referring to the Louisiana State Penitentiary, in Feliciana Parish.*

"And you can add assaulting a police officer to the list of charges!" Tauzin said, straightening the table back to the center of the room.

Thirty

Ossie Brown met Sheriff Amiss at his office in the new Scotlandville Substation—a project they had both lobbied for and a foundation contract that Beck Hayden had signed over beers and whiskey shooters, because he won it with a full house, Aces up, at one of Legend's poker nights—to discuss the latest developments in the Hayden Family abuse case.

"Look, Al, we can't cover for this guy anymore," said an anxious DA. "He's a serial abuser and frankly there is no denying it."

"I get it, Ossie, I don't really like it either and I'd prefer to put him under the jail at this point. Maybe if we can get the Kleinpeter project approved we can lay him under his foundation, but you and I both know if he starts running his mouth a lot of good people are going to be hurt, including us."

"Well, that may be so," Brown retorted. "Or maybe he's just another belligerent drunk, want-to-be big shot running his imagination, but this thing with his family is real and it is getting a lot of heat. EBRPD brought it to the mayor-president's office and Woody—Woodrow Wilson Dumas—is breathing down my neck, and frankly I ran on protecting abuse victims, if it came out that I'm connected to this guy and we let him get away with this . . . ." He said dropping the two-and-a-half-inch thick case file on Amiss's desk.

"Listen," Amiss said pushing the file away from him. "I'm the one in the middle of a tough election and this is just the sort of thing Breaux—sheriff and mayor-president candidate Jack Breaux—would love to get his hands on, and Woody has a few skeletons in his closet too Ossie, so we all need to be careful here. The bottom line is we need this to go away quietly."

Amiss continued, "I've got an opportunity for Beck to do some work over in St. John's Parish, there's a lot of municipal work getting ready to let out and the new sheriff—Lloyd Johnson—owes me a few favors. Charge him, cut some kind of probation deal, and I'll make him leave the parish."

"EBRPD is not going to like that, and even if I can get a judge to agree to it, the only way it works is a suspended sentence; he violates or even shows his face in Baton Rouge and he goes straight to Angola, no exceptions."

"Hayden, let's go, the warden wants to see you," said the ward officer standing at Beck's cell as it buzzed open. He was led through the maze of cell blocks and locked corridors to a secured control area outside of the executive offices where he was handcuffed and shackled before being led into the warden's office where Sheriff Al Amiss sat by himself waiting for Beck.

"Al, am I glad to see you, buddy, these ole boys have had me stuffed in a cell on lockdown for three days now. I've got to get out of here."

"Beck, you are killing me. You know we are friends and I've always looked out for you but this thing with your family, it's bad and you need some kind of help, buddy."

Thirty

"Hold on now, Al, you know my wife is crazy, she exaggerates all that 'abuse' nonsense," Beck affirmed.

"I wanted to believe that, Beck," Amiss said spreading out photos one by one of his injured and beaten family members. "I really did, but you've been getting belligerent drunk and smashing these kids and your poor wife for years, and I'm just damned ashamed to say, I let you do it."

"Come on now, Al, it's not like that," Beck pleaded feebly.

"Damn it, Beck, it is just like that!" he snapped, "Look at your little boy here," he said pointing to Frankie's two black eyes and busted nose. "You broke two of Micah's fingers, according to this note from the hospital, because he dropped a damn pass in a BREC league football game. It's damn little league, Beck, little league!"

Beck lowered his head, "I, I don't know what to say, man, I don't even know what's wrong with me."

"You're a damn drunk, that's what's wrong with you!"

"I'll stop drinking, I swear it, Al, just help me out here, please."

"Here's what's going to happen, Beck," Amiss declared. "You are going to sit in this jail until your preliminary hearing which has been put off for a couple of weeks; an assistant DA is going to offer you a plea deal that includes a fine and a five-year suspended sentence; you will take the deal. When you walk out of here you will have forty-eight hours to pack up your personal belongings and your tools and equipment and you are going to LaPlace, Louisiana."

"What, where . . ."

"Shut up Beck and listen, you are getting a fresh start; we have a mutual friend there who has set aside a couple of foundation contracts on some big municipal work that is going to let out in about a month. The sheriff there is also a friend but he's a no-nonsense, hard-nosed lawman. If you go down there drinking and acting a fool, he's going to nail your ass and you can't come back here. The conditions of your release will be that you do not set foot in Baton Rouge for the length of your sentence. If you do, or if you so much as raise your voice toward one of your kids or your wife then you serve your entire sentence."

"I, I don't know what to say, Al . . ."

"You say goodbye, you say you will keep your mouth shut about any of our friends, and you go get sober and leave your damn family alone!"

"Okay, Al, I wouldn't ever say anything about anything anyway, you know me better than that."

"I know, Beck, but you've got a lot of people nervous."

The judge accepted the plea deal, much to the dismay of—now Sergeant—Tauzin, and Beck walked out of Parish Prison on April 22, 1977, into a torrential downpour—three days in—that would flood much of the Comite and Amite river basin, including the small warehouse where Beck kept most of his tools and equipment all the way out on Greenwell Springs Road.

"I really need a favor, Legend," Beck said over the phone to his old friend Billy Cannon. "Al has me set up for some big jobs in LaPlace, but all my tools are underwater, most of them ruined—I need a loan."

"Beck, I told you last time, I'm not loaning you any more money, I don't even know how much you owe me."

"I've got a couple of contracts, Billy, I'll pay you back, first draw; I swear it. I've got to go, or they are going to send me to Angola, man, you've got to help me, Billy, please, I swear I'll make it right."

"Fine, I'll do it this one last time, Beck, but you better make it right and you had better get yourself straightened out."

When Beck got to the Cannon home on Sherwood Forest Boulevard, Billy loaned Beck $3,000 but told his friend not to ever come back to his home. Heartbroken—Billy was as much a hero to Beck as he was to the rest of Louisiana—Beck drove out to his miniwarehouse and tied down the few things he could salvage by wading through the knee-deep water and dragging them up the drive to the part of Greenwell Springs that wasn't underwater.

The next morning, he drove down Eastgate Road, to the little house that no longer had any dishes, and noticed a sheriff deputy's squad car sitting in front of the neighbor's house. As he pulled up in front of the home Deputy Barlow flipped on the rotating blue lights on the top of his vehicle and stepped out of the car in his raingear, with his nightstick in hand.

"You have a restraining order against you, Beck. Sheriff told me to take you in personally if you tried to go in here."

"I don't want any trouble, Barlow, I'm getting ready to leave town like the sheriff told me, I just need to say goodbye to my family and leave her with a few dollars he said holding up the bankroll he had in his pocket," the humbled behemoth pleaded, standing soaking wet in the driving downpour.

"Stand over there, under the carport. I'll ask Miss Dee if she wants to talk to you," Barlow ordered.

"I'll talk to him," Dee said as she stood in the doorway—still with a visible scratch on her cheek from one of the flying shards of porcelain—"What do you want Beck?"

"I just want to say goodbye Dee. I'm going to work in LaPlace, and I can't come back to Baton Rouge. I'd like to say goodbye to the kids if you'll let me?"

"If you promise you'll just say goodbye and not browbeat them or tell them I'm stupid or anything like that."

"You know I don't mean those things, Dee; I just get crazy when I drink too much."

"Well, you need to stop drinking all together," Dee said, mastering the obvious.

Beck would try to say goodbye to four of the kids—Anna Rae, eighteen and JJ, who turned seventeen four days prior, had moved out to live with the Evans family; a family that had survived a similar plight with the late Denis Evans, another brutal boozer—Tonya being the only one apparently interested in talking to or hugging her Big Daddy. Frankie sat in Beck's La-Z-Boy, with his ear still under a protective patch, and watched cartoons at the highest volume his mother could stand. When Dee turned the volume knob down and said that their father would like to talk to them, Micah and Dean quietly got up and went to their room while Frankie just turned his head and sank a little further into the big recliner.

Beck handed Dee $800 and told her that he would send more once he could start getting draws for the work in LaPlace. "I'm going to quit drinking, Dee, I promise."

"I hope so, Beck, I really hope so, but it is time for you to go."

Deputy Barlow waited for Beck under the carport with the heavy rain seemingly pouring in all directions, including sideways so the covered structure offered little protection.

"Your best bet is to get on I-12 up at Sherwood and head back up toward North Baton Rouge then double back on I-10. Airline Highway is washed out at several intersections along the way."

"Okay, thanks for the advice."

"I've got one more piece of advice for you, Mr. Hayden, and this is direct from the sheriff," he stated sternly. "Stay out of East Baton Rouge Parish. Al can no longer protect you, if you show up around here you are going to spend the rest of your sentence in Angola, and we will be keeping an eye on your family so don't think you can sneak back in here and bother them."

"I got it, Barlow. Al doesn't have to worry about me, I'm out of here."

Beck rolled out of Baton Rouge, in his flaming flatbed, loaded with a duffel bag of his clothing, a spiral notebook that contained all of his job notes and contact information, a few tools and equipment tied onto the bed, a couple thousand dollars in his pocket, and a heavy heart from the wreckage he was leaving behind.

Thirty

He decided that day as he traversed a rain-soaked and flooded southern Louisiana highway—the Amite River would crest at its highest level ever recorded to that point, 40.08 ft.—that he would stop drinking and make something of his business.

He wanted to be a better father, though he would barely see his children for the next several years, and a better husband, lo a better man, though it was hard for him to understand or appreciate the damage he had already done. To his family he was a monster and some of the scars he'd left them with would never heal.

End Part I

PART II

What the Monster Left Behind

Thirty-One

In June of 1977 Dolores Hayden, Dee, accepted the position of general manager of the cocktail lounge at the Baton Rouge Hilton—off College Drive in Baton Rouge, Louisiana. The lounge, Orleans—viewed as just another guest's amenity to the fledgling management at the time—was not very profitable. The LeBlanc family who owned the hotel—mostly lawyers, politically well-connected, and Baton Rouge old money—however, had another plan in mind for the well-equipped and perfectly located cocktail joint.

Jules LeBlanc knew of Dee through connections to the Prince Murat—she had served him more than a few drinks back in the Star Mist days also—and he wanted her to work the same kind of transformational magic at his lounge as she had for Napoleon's at the Prince.

The Hilton—a bright white EIFS (Commercial Stucco) and shimmering glass structure towering above the densely populated Corporate Square, a first of its kind—in Louisiana—planned mixed-use urban real estate development—was the closest thing Baton Rouge had to a five-star hotel, and it was pretty close.

Orleans—under Dee's leadership—would become the latest hot spot; it was close enough to campus to draw upper-class college kids—if she was sure of one thing, it was that LSU students and fans loved to drink and didn't mind spending money—close enough to downtown to draw the government crowd—it was the Star Mist, only bigger, brighter, and busier—and located in the busiest corporate center in the state.

The Hilton was the stay-over point for most of the celebrities, entertainers, visiting collegiate sport teams, dignitaries, and elite visitors passing through Baton Rouge, and most of them wound up spending at least part of their visit at Orleans. This helped draw the local social press and a huge party crowd; the place was always happening, and profits soared.

For the first time in a long while Dee felt like she could breathe; Anna Rae, nineteen now, was engaged to a nice young Marine, Michael Bouillon, even if he was a bit of a raging Cajun. He was an intelligent, hardworking man who really loved Anna Rae so Dee liked him, the whole family liked him—except Beck. She was also attending classes at Spencer Business College, studying to become a paralegal and working as a bartender at Orleans, and like Dee from the Star Mist days, Anna Rae was the star.

JJ, barely seventeen, refused to come home, even after Beck was gone. He had struck out on his own and he would make his own way in the world. He was working at a machine shop and learning to weld. Dee had taught all her children to work hard and they were smart kids. JJ, who started calling himself James, could take care of himself and would prove to do so quite well over the years—eventually earning two degrees, including an MBA from Tulane and rising to the highest levels of the Energy Industry—but right now he was just a skinny kid trying to catch a break.

Thirty-One

The younger children all seemed to be doing fine, though she had no clue of what was happening in a small home just a few doors down from their little haven, which would soon open up another dark chapter in the family's history and add to Dee's many sorrows.

She would receive another shock first though. As she took the children out to Livingston Parish to visit her aging mother, she got her first real look at Abeka Ahaksi—the forgetting sickness or Alzheimer's disease as it would soon come to be known. The disease was apparently ravishing the poor old woman and she was cowered in the corner of her living room holding a butcher knife for protection when Dee walked in with the kids.

"Who are you and what's your business here?" the skinny, sickly looking old woman asked.

"Momma, it's me Dolores, your daughter, and I brought your grandchildren to visit."

"I have grandchildren?" she asked as if to herself. "I always wanted grandchildren."

"Well, you have quite a few, Momma, and I brought four of them with me," she said placing her arms around the children huddling around her, not quite sure what to think about their grandmother's current state of mind.

Dee put her kids to work cleaning up and reorganizing their grandmother's home. Dean went outside and started cutting the yard with the old, open-blade push-mower while Tonya started working on the kitchen. Micah got the easy work straightening the living room and folding the clothes while Frankie got stuck with the bathrooms—not a scene the little boy was well equipped for.

Meanwhile Dee phoned her brother Truman for the first time in several years. "Sorry to bother you Truman but Momma is not doing well. When's the last time you've been out here to see her?"

"It's been a few months, I talked to her on the phone a couple of weeks ago; she sounded fine," Truman insisted.

"She just greeted me and the kids with a butcher knife; she doesn't even know who we are. And her house looks like the city dump. I've never seen such filth and you know Momma doesn't live like that," she explained. "I'm taking her home with me, we need to figure out what to do about her house."

"I don't know if that's a good ideal with you and Beck fighting and fussing all the time," Truman responded coldly.

"First of all, what Beck and I do isn't what you would refer to as 'fighting.' It's more like training for boxing and I'm the bag but I'm sure you see it as my fault, big brother. That really doesn't matter though, Beck is gone and he's not coming back anytime soon."

"I wasn't implying it was your fault, Dee, but doesn't it take two?"

"No, Truman, not with Beck Hayden it doesn't and all I've done is spend the last seven years running from place to place trying to hide to keep him from killing my kids and me. Again, I know I shouldn't expect my big brother to understand or be there to help me or anything."

"What am I supposed to do, Dee?"

"Oh, I don't know, start by not thinking I'm some domestic squabbling tramp and find out what's really going on when your sister and nephews and nieces are being terrorized and beaten on a daily basis for nearly a decade. I mean, you are the high-falutin', well-connected banker—the only reason he's gotten away with it for so long is because he is friends with that Al Amiss, maybe some of your friends, you know like the mayor, could have helped, who knows?"

"Well, Dee, I didn't know what was going on and I guess I wanted to keep my nose out of it. Anyway, how do you know he's not going to be back?"

"Some lady cop from the EBRPD came by here and befriended Anna Rae. Officer Tauzin, I think," she explained "Anyway, Tauzin and her partner investigated all the hospital visits and disturbance complaints and somehow got somebody to put pressure on Amiss, now it seems like he's protecting us personally. Beck was banned from entering East Baton Rouge Parish for five years so he's off doing some work near New Orleans and I haven't seen him in six months."

"If you can get her to go home with you go ahead and take her. I'll talk to David and we can all figure out the best thing to do long term. Do I need to send someone out to clean the house up and get it in order?"

"No, I've got my crew on it, they'll have it in shipshape in no time, if Momma doesn't scalp 'em first." They laughed together for the first time in decades.

Thirty-Two

Mr. *Flint and his family*—a foreign wife, who barely spoke English and two daughters—lived three doors down from the Hayden's home on Eastgate. He was a middle-school teacher and troop leader of the Boy Scouts. Like many in the neighborhood, Flint would learn of the exile of Beck Hayden. But unlike most, he took the opportunity to offer assistance to the family and suggested to Dee, whom he met out at the mailbox one day, that she have the older boys join his troop—Cub Scouts for Frankie—where he could offer a guiding hand.

"Boys need a positive role model, structure, camaraderie, that's what the Scouts are all about."

"Why do you care, Mister?"

"I didn't have a father growing up," he lied. "I just know what it's like, and you know, we're neighbors," he reassured her.

"I'll talk to the boys and we'll think about it. Thanks for caring." She was genuinely appreciative.

"Let me know how we can help either way," he said walking back to his home.

Dean and Micah would join Mr. Flint's Boy Scout Troop and Frankie would join the Cub Scouts until he was old enough for the regular Scouts—one of the activities of the Scouts, Frankie's favorite—was ushering LSU home games at Tiger Stadium during the fall. If Frankie wasn't born to bleed Purple and Gold, it would only take one trip to Death Valley—the first of many—to create a lifelong fanatic. For over a year Dee would entrust the boys to Mr. Flint one night a week and every other weekend for scouting trips or whenever the Tigers were playing at home in the fall. He and his wife would also become regular babysitters for Dee; she thought they were a godsend, until they weren't.

What Dee was about to learn, what the EBRSO, the School Board, and the local press were about to learn is that Mr. Flint was a serial pedophile.

He had taught, coached, and mentored over a thousand children over the last decade. Eventually it would be known that he had molested, abused, and otherwise defiled at least fifty of them. He sought out the younger children, specifically fatherless boys, preferably ones who had suffered some abuse—they were easy prey and could be manipulated to keep his secret. He abused them at school, on scouting trips, and once the Haydens moved into the neighborhood—which would cause his downfall—in their own home.

One summer day in 1978, Dee had left Micah, Tonya, and Frankie with the Flints while she dropped Big Dean off at Sonny's on Florida Blvd.—now sixteen, though they thought he was eighteen, Dean had landed a job in the kitchen at the new Bar-B-Q restaurant—she then went into work for a big shindig that was happening at the hotel and Orleans would be kicking.

Flint also knew that Anna Rae was tending bar that night so she would not be stopping by unannounced, as she did so frequently.

Once Dee and Dean were down the road, he left Tonya and Micah with his wife and daughters and took an eager Frankie down to the Hayden house to work on some Cub Scout badges. Once there, he told Frankie, the youngest of the Hayden children, it was time for him to be a big boy like Micah and Dean. He ordered the seven-year-old boy to stand at attention. When he complied Flint said they were going to play the secret big boy game and he told him to take his clothes off—Frankie was instantly scared, he didn't know what was happening but he didn't understand why his clothes needed to be off for any game, so he didn't do anything. Flint assured him that Micah and Dean had played before and it was a necessary part of the game so reluctantly he started taking his clothes off—Flint then wanted he and the little boy to touch each other's private parts. When Frankie would not cooperate, he picked the little guy up and threw him on the bed.

As Frankie was kicking and screaming, he heard the door to the master bedroom—where they were—swing open.

"What in the hell is going on here?" Shouted James (JJ), Dee's eldest son, as he pushed the creep away from his little brother—James, who Flint didn't know, had stopped by to pick up some mail which Dee had left on the counter for him.

"Oh, Uh, I was just helping my nephew here get dressed after his shower, who are you?"

"I'm his big brother, you lying freak," James said as he tomahawk-chopped Flint in the neck, dropping him to his knees—growing up with Beck had toughened James, and motivated him to take up karate, which he now used to kick the living crap out of the disgusting pedophile he found in his momma's house doing God-knows-what, for God-knows-how-long to his little baby brother.

The aftermath was unreal. The EBRSO, led by the family's 'old friend' Al Amiss—eager to prove to Dee that he was sorry for letting Beck abuse them and genuinely incensed by the nature of Flint's creepiness—and a frenzied Baton Rouge press started turning over every rock they could on the teacher, scout leader and mentor. Before long there were dozens of former students and scouts coming forward to accuse the pervert.

It was a nightly news story for months and every segment on TV started with footage of Frankie—who really didn't like the attention—and the Haydens' little home on Eastgate. More than a few reporters walked up to Frankie playing in the yard or swinging on the tire hanging in a tree near the road to try to interview the poor victim for live TV; it was mortifying—Dee's "baby" was now the poster child for sex-abuse. For the first—and only—time (ever) she missed Beck, who was enraged and badgering Amiss on the phone every day.

"That's real good, Al, just fabulous, you get me kicked out of the parish and leave my kids prey to some disgusting pedophile, and I have to watch it helplessly on the damn news, reporters hounding my little Frankie like some weirdo paparazzi!" he would bark at his old friend.

"Look, Beck, no way we could see this thing coming but I promise you, your family is safe now, I've got 'em under surveillance for protection 24/7."

"Get one of your real estate boys to help Dee find a new place to live and keep it quiet. They need to get out of there and disappear for a while, it's just awful over there, they can't even go outside."

"I've asked T.D. Bickham to have one of his gals call Dee," Amiss informed Beck.

On another call Amiss told his friend, "Tell you what though, Beck, that skinny, little, long-haired stepson of yours, James, JJ, whatever his name is, he beat the hell out of that creep, I mean good, you'd have been proud."

"Yeah, he doesn't have much to pack a punch with but if you piss him off, he's crazier than me on a drunk." Beck said. "I tell you what else is true, good sheriff; you had better hope I never lay eyes on that Flint dude; I can tell you that much. You won't have a choice but to lock me up for keeps."

"You just keep working down there in LaPlace and keep your nose clean. The creep will be getting what he gave in Angola soon enough, he'll be a yard slave up there. And I promise, I'll look after your family until this blows over."

"Thanks, Al. Hey—do another favor for me, if you see Legend, tell him I'll send the rest of his money this Friday when I get my draw." Beck asked, mainly because he wanted Al to know he was taking care of his business and paying his debts.

"Will do, Beck, talk to you later."

Thirty-Three

L inda Hall, *a real estate agent and top associate* at the T.D. Bickham Company, would help Dee locate a brand-new, three-bedroom brick house with an enclosed garage and a big yard on the edge of the Parrish—on London Avenue in Village Coté, the newest development off of Stevendale Road—where Dee had experienced first-hand the flood of 1957.

"Isn't this a major floodplain?" Dee asked

"Not on this side of the tracks, the road in and the two middle neighborhoods are below the floodplain but the elevation of Village Coté is higher and these houses didn't flood last March when the Amite hit its highest point ever," Hall informed, reassuringly.

"Well, if the only road in floods, how do we get out?"

"Good question." Hall showed Dee the development master plan; "Hamilton Avenue—which runs parallel to London Avenue, currently dead ends but as you can see, they are getting ready to build a new by-pass—the Central Throughway—and Hamilton will be extended to access the bypass and Greenwell Springs Road." *Said extension wouldn't come to pass for nearly two decades.*

"That makes me feel a little better."

"Well, this should make you feel really good then," she promised, then explained. "Mr. Bickham has authorized me to sell you this house for your budget price of $50,000, even though it has already appraised for $69,000. That's barely over cost, best deal I've ever seen and instant equity."

Dee was already sold, but Linda continued. "And I'm not sure who you know, but someone is looking out for you. Our mortgage partner is willing to do an 80/20, 100 percent financing, that means you'll have two low-interest mortgages but you will not have to make the customary down payment, which would be about $10,000."

"That's great," Dee said signing the purchase agreement. "That means I can afford to buy us some decent furniture with the money I was saving for the down payment."

In early October two off-duty sheriff's deputies helped Big Dean load one of the deputies' pick-up truck and Dee's station wagon with about thirty packed boxes, her mother's armoire, a china hutch, a television console that would go in Dee's new master bedroom, and the matching set of bunk beds from the boys' rooms. Everything else, which wasn't a lot, would be loaded into a box truck—belonging to one of Amiss's construction buddies—and taken to the landfill on Flannery Road.

Deputy Barlow sat a block away in his personal car, on the lookout for any nosy reporters.

None showed up and the Hayden family was moved into their beautiful new home that Sunday afternoon—with their handful of belongings and the hope for a simple, quiet life.

On Monday morning a Sears, Roebuck delivery truck showed up with their new furniture. A ten-piece, double-stuffed sectional sofa set that could and would be organized into countless configurations.

A beautiful combination television/stereo/turntable console—with a high-quality, diamond-tipped needle—built into a beautiful mahogany cabinet with velvet and decorative, intricately crafted wrought-iron speaker covers integrated into the cabinet.

There were also four large, matching bookcases, in the same mahogany finish as the console, which would serve as the family's open library and knickknack/pictorial display. The dining room table was selected to match the antique china cabinet from Kelli-Kay's old homestead and the beautiful, smooth, poly-finished cedar armoire was placed in her bedroom.

There was a new king bedroom suite for Dee and queen sets for both Kelli-Kay and Tonya—Kelli-Kay was now living with Dee full time despite protests from Truman, who wanted to keep her in a nursing home. The garage was sealed off, carpeted, and converted into a huge bedroom and game area for the boys. With no Godzilla around to smash and break the place into smithereens the family's 1,800 sq ft modest home felt like a luxurious mansion.

Narrator's Note*: Kelli-Kay Crockett, nanny to the Crockett children, would spend most of her final years in Dee's house in Village Coté. She spent a few months in a nursing home, paid for by Truman, but Dee and the kids wanted her at home with them as much as possible until her peaceful passing in 1980. She was a faithful, proud, and beautiful woman. She would be sorely missed.

Dee loved her wonderful new home and she worked her butt off to keep the mortgage(s) paid, lights on, and cupboards full. The kids all had chores—which included helping to take care of their ailing grandmother who, in her final years, rarely remembered who they were but only occasionally threatened to scalp them—and for the most part—with the possible exception of the boys' room—they kept the place spotless.

Kelli-Kay also called Tonya by the name Dana quite frequently. Dee would never admit to understanding why she made such a name mix-up but she knew without question that while Kelli-Kay couldn't remember much of anything anymore, deep down she would never forget the beautiful baby girl they had kissed goodbye over a decade ago.

The kids found their new environment to be a big adventure. There were legions of kids in the Village and across the railroad tracks there were three other neighborhoods full of kids. The neighborhoods were surrounded by over a thousand acres of woodlands, trails, creeks, and the Comite and Amite River Basin.

Some of the kids had motorcycles—which would include Micah after that Christmas—mopeds, go-karts, and the recently invented Honda three-wheelers. Everybody had bicycles, and Frankie got a Sevylor five-man, whitewater-certified river raft when Micah got his motorcycle. The land, lakes, rivers, and streams surrounding the area were teeming with bike trails, kid-made racetracks, tree forts, fishing holes, a couple of semi-sandy river beaches, rope swings, bonfire pits, and party spots galore. Micah and Tonya had a ton of friends from the get-go, and Micah was one of the most popular kids in school. He was a neighborhood rock star.

Frankie, now Frank—because "little Frankie Hayden" was the lead-in to virtually every news story or TV segment dealing with the Flint case—on the other hand, was still ridiculed regularly and got into a number of fights with other kids that picked on and tried to bully him. When Micah—or Tonya for that matter—was around no one would dare bother him, but he was three years younger than Micah, two years younger than Tonya, and they were always with the older kids. Frank had to make his own way.

J.R. Browder and his brother, who they called Bouchy, started giving Frank "Little Frankie" a hard time on a regular basis. One night by the ponds, where some of the kids were hanging out by campfire, they started ribbing Frank about the Flint episode and J.R. smacked him in the back of the head, calling him a queer. Frank shoved J.R. to the ground and started walking home. Bouchy then tackled Frank and the two Browder boys beat him up pretty good while a few of their buddies egged it on.

When Micah found out about it, he and his friend Rusty went to confront the Browder boys. Bouchy was in his front yard, working on the family's project—a large, handcrafted, three-cabin, triple-deck houseboat which the neighborhood kids referred to as Browder's Ark—with two of his brothers, there were seven of them all together, and one girl—Micah's age—who, like most of the girls that age, was in love with Micah Hayden.

The Browder boys were all a little shady by reputation, but they stuck together like the Mexican Mafia and it didn't take long before the insignificant squabble turned into what would be nearly a decade-long family feud. It wasn't like the deadly Hatfield and McCoy dispute of the early twentieth century, but there were enough altercations, fisticuffs, and touch-football-turned-tackle-turned-all-out-brawls between the two families and their friends in the neighborhood to classify it as the Village Coté Civil War. The VCCW would culminate in the ignominious destruction of Browder's Ark; who caused its spectacular demise—the Haydens, the Thibodeaux brood—who had their own feud with the Browders—or if one of the Browders pulled an inside job remains a mystery to this day. Frank might know but he's not telling.

Ultimately Frank would recover from the Flint experience. James had shown up in time to save him physically but the aftermath—ridicule, accusations, and speculation—is what haunted him, and shaped him. For years kids would pick on him, call him a homo, and question his gender role. He learned to ignore it for the most part but there were many times—which tended to get him into trouble in school—that the picking was met with kicking and to the tall, lanky boy that would eventually stand 6 ft. 7 in., kicking came naturally. He would also become the antibully, protective of weaker and smaller friends.

There would also occasionally be a reporter who would show up out of the blue, looking for a follow-up story—they would be run off by Kelli-Kay if she was lucid, some member of the Hayden family, or Mrs. Dottie, a neighbor and close friend of Dee's—but that too died down and after a couple of years Frank was just another Village Cote kid. Until Beck showed up again, that is.

Thirty-Four

The BREC is the Recreation and Park Commission for EBR Parish, which develops, maintains, and operates 184 (modern figure) public parks, community facilities, and recreational leagues throughout the parish. From the age of six through High School—whether it was on a school-sponsored BREC team or for the Middle/High School official team—the boys played football, until one by one they each quit in protest—open rebellion—against their dad, the "Motivator," Beckett T. Hayden. He wanted desperately to live his gridiron dreams vicariously through the boys, particularly Micah and Frank.

James, as he was known back then, was as fast as a loose woman in a honky-tonk and would light up the Friday Night Panther Pride as a scatback and slot receiver for Woodlawn High. Big Dean was, as his nickname might suggest, BIG—by the age of 16 he stood 6 ft. 5 in., and weighed over 300—and he was agile with a high football IQ. He was the starting blindside tackle on every football team he ever played for but like James, and much to the dismay of his stepfather and his high school coach—Gene LeSage, at Belaire High—Big Dean refused to play football in his senior season.

Micah Hayden—his teammates called him Mike—became somewhat of a BREC-league superstar as the go-to wide receiver for the Junior and then Senior BREC Buccaneers, and then for the Broadmoor High School varsity team. If James had been thunder, Micah was lightning. In his sophomore year at Broadmoor he ran an official 4.36 seconds, forty-yard dash and when he caught the football in the flat there was simply no catching the kid. Broadmoor fans, as had the BREC fans at Memorial Stadium and other local venues, would call it playing "Mike Ball" when the Bucs' offense was on the field.

Micah would later be diagnosed with dyslexia and other learning disabilities—yet he was never identified as a special-needs child during his school years and he basically made it to his senior season functionally illiterate, though he was very street smart, with common sense. Nonetheless, it would appear that his athletic talents had bought him a few extra swings at the (learning) curve. He would, however, like James and Dean before him, choose to discontinue his football career. In a new twist, Micah dropped out of school all together and went to work framing houses, while making real money hosting X parties (Raves, as they would come to be known) in various local warehouses.

By 1980 Frank had played for the pee-wee Buccaneers for two years and was now a second-year member of the Southeastern Panthers. He had been moved all over the field from the defensive and offensive line to tight end and even safety. He wasn't gifted with the speed of James and Micah nor the solid frame of Big Dean, but he was tall, had big dependable hands, and once he caught the ball, the first or second tackler usually wasn't enough to bring him down. If Coach Dickie, now Southeastern's Head Coach, needed a few yards for a first down or a touchdown, the ball was going to the 'Frank Tank.'

Thirty-Four

It was at a playoff game in Memorial Stadium—the same stadium where Frank had taken the bone-shattering press-box plunge—that Frank heard a familiar voice from the sideline.

"You've got to get low with that shoulder, like I taught you, boy," instructed Beck, with dark shades and a high-sitting, coach's style cap on his head.

"Dad, you're here, I thought you couldn't come back?" an excited ten-year-old asked his Big Dad that he had been missing.

"Well, I'm not supposed to be, but I wanted to see your game and what they don't know won't hurt them." Beck—Big Dad, not Godzilla—was back and Frank was glad to see him.

He was in town to see his son's playoff game—versus the Ascension Parish Champion Gators, sponsored by St. Amant High School and quarterbacked by All-Parish QB, Paul Boudreaux—but he was also there because his old friend Billy Cannon wanted to discuss a business opportunity. They would meet at Robert Brunet's Restaurant on Flannery Road, the Galley, after Frank's big win, in which he scored the winning touchdown. Dee reluctantly allowed Frank and Tonya to go with Beck, since he promised he had not had a drink in over a year. Micah refused to go, opting instead to "go in to work" with his mother.

Robert "Bobby" Brunet—a retired NFL running back—knew Billy more from his legendary status around Baton Rouge than from when their paths had crossed briefly in 1970 when Brunet was a league rookie and Cannon was a retiring superstar. Nonetheless, he would treat Billy and whoever he was with like old friends and roll out the VIP treatment—Legend was accustomed to it, though he really didn't care for all the fuss.

Beck was also well known to Bobby, as he had been a regular at the Galley's Oyster Bar and Cocktail Lounge prior to his exile. The bar on the front half of the property was attached by a long hallway that contained all of the Brunet's, mostly Bobby's, trophies and memorabilia including a framed Washington Redskins jersey and one from Louisiana Tech, both bearing the #26 and the name R. Brunet.

"Beck, it's good to see you again and you and Billy are my special guests today, just promise me you will not drink too much?" Brunet pleaded. Bobby had witnessed firsthand the kind of destruction an inebriated Beck Hayden could disseminate.

"No problem, Bobby, I'm not drinking anymore, I just brought my kids in to see Billy and to celebrate Frankie's big win," he said placing his arm encouragingly on his son, who was still garbed in his grass-stained jersey and his padded football pants. "Meet my youngest son and future LSU Tiger; they call him the Frank Tank Hayden."

"Nice to meet you, son. You don't let your old man change your mind; I know he's an ole Rebel," said Bobby extending his hand.

"You got it, Mister Brunet; it's nice to meet you too."

After meeting little Tonya, still wearing her cheerleading uniform, the three were led to the large semi-private booth where Billy Cannon was waiting, signing an autograph as they approached.

"Frank Tank!" hollered the living legend as Frank ran toward his hero. "What do we tell your old man?"

"Geaux (go) to Hell Ole Miss, Geaux to Hell!" everyone laughed, except Beck, who just shook his head.

"Fine thing to teach my kid, Dr. Cannon."

"Hey, the kid's a Tiger, that's just how it is!"

"Yeah, yeah, how's Little Bill doing? Is he going to be a Tiger like his old man?" Billy Cannon Jr., Little Bill to his family, like his father was a powerful athlete and as a four-sport letterman at Broadmoor High School. Billy Jr. was one of the hottest recruits in the nation.

"I don't know; he might go play baseball for the Yankees if I can keep him away from some of those losing teams that are lining up to draft him."

"Just tell them all not to waste a draft pick because he's going to be a Tiger. Who wouldn't believe that, and then let Old Steinbrenner know that it might be worth taking a chance on him anyway, you never know, kids change their minds all the time, and what not . . ."

"Hmm, that actually might work, Beck, it might be a little ruthless but I don't want my kid stuck with some worthless team that uses him up and he's got nothing to show for it."

Several MLB teams would eventually file a grievance with Commissioner Bowie Kuhn after the Yankees drafted Cannon Jr. in the third round. The teams claimed that they were intentionally misled by telegrams sent from Cannon, the elder. Kuhn voided the contract that had been negotiated in secret and Billy Cannon Jr. decided to play football. He would commit to an LSU rival, Texas A&M, breaking the hearts of Tiger fans, including ten-year-old Frank Hayden.

They ordered a table full of Cajun-style seafood and feasted on Brunet's finest cuisine and the kids drank Coca-Cola until they were about to pop. Beck, also drinking Coca-Cola, then sent the two pre-teens to play darts on the other side of the bar, while he and Mr. Billy talked a little business.

"So, what's up, Billy? What's this opportunity you wanted to talk with me about?"

"Well, it's not what you'd call legal, Beck, but I've got a buddy that can print really good counterfeit money and I'm thinking about setting up a small operation. What do you think?" Billy asked his old friend, who had watched his back since high school.

"Damn, Billy, counterfeit money?" Beck questioned. "I don't get why you need to do something like that?"

"It's easy money, Beck, and frankly I need a lot of cash with some of these real estate deals and business partnerships I've gotten into. I've been sued so many times I can't see straight. My practice is doing fine but I'm going to wind up losing it and everything else if I don't do something, and fast."

"You know me, Billy, I'll do whatever you need me to, I just don't want to see nothing bad happen to you; those boys up at Angola don't play from what I hear at Parish Prison and frankly I wouldn't want you to go there either." Beck cautioned. "And what about Al, is he going to look the other way?"

"I don't know, Beck," Billy contemplated. "He's into his fair share of closed-door business but I don't know if he'd go for a counterfeiting deal. I thought about having you approach him but hell, he might put you back in jail just for asking."

"No doubt, no way I'm going to Amiss with that. It's probably better if I move the money over in St. John's Parish or down in New Orleans. I know some old boys down there, better to keep it out of Baton Rouge if possible," Beck suggested.

"I agree, I was thinking, you know that development deal we were looking at out by where you used to live, next to Jones Creek? I still own that land, we'll bury the money out there and whenever you're ready to move it you can dig up whatever you need. We can access it through all those little trails from Shenandoah and no one would ever notice the coming and going."

"Can you trust this printer? Do I know him?"

"No, he's a neighbor, John Siglets, but I trust him," Billy assured.

"I'm in but let's just keep it between us, Billy. I wouldn't trust too many people, especially if I were you."

"What's that supposed to mean?" Billy demanded.

Thirty-Four

"You know what I mean, Legend, you've got a million friends who all want to partner with Billy Cannon, put your name on barbells or your picture in an ad, but they're not getting sued when things go south, you are. It just seems it's hard to know who you can really trust."

"Yeah, you're right about that, we'll keep it between just us," Billy promised.

"All right, let's *print* some dough."

Thirty-Five

Dr. *William Abb Cannon would withdraw* $15,000 from his orthodontic practice's bank account and give it to John Siglets, a mediocre counterfeiter but first-rate con man. Nonetheless, the $100 bill plates were very high quality and had Siglets chosen to invest in a similar quality paper they might still be *making* money, but he was already in hock to some Texas bad guys so he used about a third of Billy's money to keep the alligators at bay.

In April of 1981, Siglets showed up to a crawfish boil at Cannon's home carrying a green metal Igloo cooler.

"Bring some cold beer, Johnny?" asked the jovial legend.

"More like cold hard cash," the charismatic convicted felon responded, lifting the lid to reveal its contents.

"Don't bring it to my house, man, are you crazy?"

"Sorry, just thought nobody would think twice about a couple of neighbors with a beer cooler at a cookout."

"Well, let's put this in the trunk of my car, we can check it out later."

Cannon would distribute a third of the $1.5 million in counterfeit $100 bills to Beck, who would sell the $500,000 for 25 cents on the dollar. The money was spread via Beck's New Orleans connection to Atlanta, Memphis, Charlotte, and a few other major southern cities. Beck would keep 20 percent and return $100,000 in real cash to Billy. Simultaneously, Cannon shipped the other two-thirds, $1 million, to Bill Glasscock, an associate, in Florida. Glasscock had promised 40 cents on the dollar and agreed to a 15 percent cut of the real money.

He was unable to deliver on the promise and after he had moved the bills and taken his cut, plus "expenses" Glasscock returned just over $120,000 to Billy. It was a lot less than expected, but added to Beck's return it was still a windfall return on the initial $15,000 investment, actually a little over $35,000 all together with subsequent cash payments made to Siglets "to keep things moving" but the return was just what Cannon needed.

It would motivate Billy to include more accomplices in the money changing operation—much to the chagrin of Beck—and a "broker" from Thibodeaux, Louisiana—Cannon had done legitimate business with him in the past, but knew he had connections—Tim Melancon and another man in Florida, Charles Whitfield—an investor with interests in everything from hog farming to shrimping to real estate.

Beck didn't know either of them and warned Billy that it was better to limit the distribution to one or two trusted sources that could get it moved out of state, like his New Orleans connection.

"But you're only getting 25 cents on the dollar, Beck. These guys can do 35 or 40 cents."

"Like your buddy Glasscock did?" Beck asked rhetorically. "Listen Billy, you open this thing up and it'll be a lot harder to control. We're not career criminals, we don't know how to run a criminal organization and we don't need to. My guy in New Orleans is well connected and he has no idea where the money is coming from so if he ever double-crosses us he can only point the finger at me. They'd put me in jail for a few years and that'd be that but if you ever got tied to this, well, you know."

"I know Beck, and I trust you, but I trust these guys too, they're good, I promise," assured the overconfident legend.

"It's your call because it's also your legacy on the line; just keep me out of everything with your new partners, I'm only working with you."

The accomplices and really the whole operation turned out to be anything but good. The phony bills started showing up all over Baton Rouge and in concentrated areas in South Florida. The US Secret service started tracing the bills during the summer of 1982; just a little more than a year from its inception, and the Feds were tracking the country's largest counterfeiting scheme, to that point, and watching every move made by its leader, the former Heisman Trophy winner, College and Pro Football Hall of Famer, Legend and Hero to the entire State of Louisiana and successful orthodontist, Dr. Billy Cannon.

EBRSO was initially involved in the investigation but once Cannon was identified as the main suspect the US Assistant DA in charge, Rand Miller, asked Sheriff Al Amiss to back away and keep his officers out of the loop, fearing they would tip-off the suspects. Amiss protested and was offended by the implication but ultimately felt that the best move for him, politically, was not to interfere with the Feds. He did warn Cannon that he was being "looked at" by the Feds, though he claimed ignorance as to why. Billy planned to follow up with the sheriff to see what he could find out but the good sheriff, J. Al Amiss died suddenly on February 6, 1983.

The Feds would keep their distance for a few more months, building their case and casting a wide net. The net, an effort to catch every fish swimming in Cannon's would-be school of want-to-be crime bosses, would recover $150,000 in phony bills, flip one accomplice, set up an undercover money buyer, and ultimately lead to the July 9, 1983, arrest of Louisiana's hero.

By the time Billy was arrested, he already knew that at least one of his cohorts had turned on him and he was ready for the whole thing to be over, come what may. The one thing the Feds didn't seem to know about, and Billy would not fill in the blanks, was the connection to the pipeline through New Orleans. They knew funny money was showing up throughout the South and even in the Northeast, but they assumed it was just trickling from Glasscock, Melancon, and Whitfield's pipelines.

In retrospect Billy really wished he had listened to his old friend and he knew that Beck would take the fall for him if he could. But since it was Billy, not Beck, in Federal custody it would be Billy that fell on his own sword. Dr. Cannon cooperated immediately implicating all his conspirators, save Beck Hayden.

He led investigators out to the site near Jones Creek where he and Beck had buried nearly $4 million in Igloo beer coolers. He verified the warehouse address of the print operation in Texas and fingered Siglets, who, in turn, gave up his suppliers. When the Feds were unable to find the cash, even with a map, Dr. Cannon waded through the snake-infested creek to show them where to dig and by the time it was over, the Feds knew everything, arrested everybody, and had recovered just over $6.5 million of the illegally printed funds.

They knew everything, that is, except the New Orleans connection, and they arrested everyone but Beck.

Beck would be at the Federal Courthouse when Billy was sentenced and as the two men made eye contact there was a feeling they both had, that no matter how loyal they were to each other, and no matter how much one would suffer to protect the other, they knew their "good ole days" were passed and they would never enjoy those times again.

The ride was over; it was time to get off. As Cannon left the courthouse on his own recognizance with time to arrange his affairs, minutes after being sentenced to five years in a federal prison, Ray

Thirty-Five

Termini, a mutual friend of Cannon and Beck Hayden, nearly hit a flaming flatbed pickup truck as he drove away.

"Was that Beck's truck, what's he doing here?" asked Termini.

"Like everyone else, I reckon, here to say goodbye to the old days."

"Well, I damn near hit him."

"Yeah, Ray, we noticed; as a getaway driver you get an F!" Billy and the rest of the somber passengers—which included his lawyers and his son, Little Bill—laughed for the first time in months, though only Billy really understood the irony.

Billy and Beck would never see each other again and while Beck would escape the counterfeiting scheme unscathed legally, it would however be a catalyst to reignite his old demons and he would fall further than ever.

Billy, on the other hand, would face the music and it would have far-reaching consequences for his whole family. But he would ultimately crawl then climb back to respectability and decades after he had been coined a "Counterfeit Hero" by *Sports Illustrated*, ESPN's *Outside the Lines* would run a widely well received story entitled "The Redemption of Billy Cannon."

A grown-up Frank, accompanied by his wife, would read and discuss the OTL article with Beck, as he laid—on what proved to be his death bed—in the VA Hospital in Jackson, Mississippi, in 2011. It was there that Beck would for the one and only time in his life admit to having been a horrible father, husband, and friend and he asked his youngest son for forgiveness. Frank had long moved past his childhood and offered his old man comfort and his forgiveness as best he could. But for a man that had hurt and damaged so much and so many, true forgiveness would have to be granted by his Maker.

Forgiveness was one thing, but now that this story is being told, I need to take you back again to that time in the life of Dee and her brood, times that are hard to forget . . .

Thirty-Six

❧

In the spring of 1982, a time when Beck was flush with cash, before the counterfeiting scheme had been uncovered and nearing the end of Beck's court-mandated exile from Baton Rouge, he showered his family with gifts and tried to heal their hurt with whatever his money could buy. His business was doing well so Dee never thought the extra cash might be a product of ill-gotten gain.

After a brief second courtship, Dee allowed Beck to move in with the family at their home on London Avenue. The younger kids were happy to have their Big Dad back, though Micah was very apprehensive at first. Big Dean let it be his excuse to move out and he and a friend, Ricky "Skills" Seals, moved into a small apartment in the Belaire neighborhood behind Sonny's Bar-B-Q, where Dean was now the kitchen manager.

Anna Rae and James protested vehemently and became frustrated when their arguments fell on Dee's deaf ears. Nonetheless, Anna Rae—who'd always been the second momma of the Dempsey/Hayden

Bunch—resolved to keep a close eye on her family and would keep her three youngest siblings with her family whenever possible.

Anna Rae's resolve might have saved Tonya's life. Two days before Thanksgiving Anna stopped by to pick up Tonya—the kids were out of school for the week—as the two were to do the grocery shopping for the holiday feast they were planning.

When Anna Rae arrived, she found Tonya in the driveway speaking to her friend Peggy and two older boys—young men, a more appropriate description—who were apparently inviting the naive young Tonya to join them for a joy ride.

"Dad said I could go, Anna, you don't really neeeeeeed me to go shopping, please don't make a big deal out of it, okay?" Tonya pleaded.

"I'm sorry, no," Anna insisted. "What is your name, buddy, and how old are you?" Anna asked the driver and oldest looking of the duo.

"You're not in charge, Anna! Don't worry about how old he is." A defiant Tonya barked "DADDY!" She stormed into the house to get Beck, who virtually always let Tonya have her way, while Anna interrogated the threesome blocked, by her car, in the driveway.

"Listen, lady, we don't want any trouble, we're just going to hang out with some friends at the arcade," the boy who identified himself as Rodney said innocently.

"Sorry, buddy, but you are too old to be 'hanging out' with these little girls. Tonya is only fourteen, and how old are you, Peggy?" Anna demanded.

"Sixteen, but I'm almost seventeen," Peggy answered as if she were a year away from social security.

"I told you, Anna!" Tonya said triumphantly, storming back to the scene with Beck in tow.

"Just let her go, Anna, they just want to go riding around, they're not hurting anybody," said Beck who really didn't seem to care.

"You can't be serious, Beck?" The older kids had long ceased calling him Dad. "These boys should be in college somewhere, not chasing around a high school freshman."

"Listen lady, I just turned seventeen and Kenny is only sixteen. We're not some old guys!" protested Rodney.

"Great, prove it," Anna demanded extending her open hand. "Show me your driver's license!"

"Uh, well, umm, I left my wallet at home," stuttered the stubble-bearded fellow.

"That's what I thought. Beck, if you let her leave, I'm calling the sheriff and we both know you don't want them poking around!"

Beck was not amused by the threat, but he reluctantly sent an infuriated Tonya inside and he told the boys to leave. Anna pleaded with Peggy not to go but she told Anna to mind her own business. Anna would regret not calling the police anyway, but she moved her car and let the trio ride off down London Avenue.

According to the *Morning Advocate*, they would stop at the 7–11 convenience store on Stevendale Road (less than a mile from the Hayden's home), where at least one of the young men proved, by way of picture ID, that he was old enough to buy alcohol. The three would then spend the afternoon and evening driving as far as St. Gabriel and the Court of Appeals of Louisiana, First Circuit, would later find the facts to include that the one-car accident occurred at 9:45 pm and Peggy Barrett died approximately five to ten minutes later as a result of her injuries.

Both Rodney Teston and Kenneth White suffered noncritical injuries. Teston was taken to Our Lady of the Lake Hospital in Baton Rouge, and White was taken to the East Ascension General Hospital in Gonzales, Louisiana. Blood-alcohol tests were administered by Louisiana State Police to Rodney Teston and Peggy Barrett, with readings of .14 and .11, respectively.

Sister of Sorrows

Earlier in the same year Frank had been at Anna Rae's apartment—where he had gone to spend a week during the summer—when his appendix ruptured. Being that the Hayden boys had been taught to be tough and not to complain over minor injuries, his appendix had been ruptured for over sixteen hours before he crumpled into a fetal position in Anna Rae's living room, causing her to rush him to the Our Lady of the Lake Regional Medical Center.

By the time he was admitted, a very slow process that day, and prepped for surgery his appendix had been ruptured for nearly twenty-four hours causing internal bleeding and an infection that would leave the child hospitalized for nearly two weeks.

Beck would pay all the hospital bills, as Dee would say, "without batting an eyelash," and he would visit his son at least twice a day. During one of his first visits Beck showed up with a brand-new color TV, an Atari 2600, and a handful of video-game cartridges to go with the console. The kid was still feeling nauseated from the explosion of his internal organs, but he lay happily for hours playing his "super cool" new home video system.

Beck also handed Frank an LSU football schedule and told him to pick a few games to go to with his Old Man, who now had season tickets. Frankie picked Rice, Tennessee, and of course, Ole Miss, and he would talk endlessly of the upcoming season with anyone who would listen. One of the nursing assistants at the hospital was a junior and cheerleader at LSU. She told Frankie to be sure to come see her down at the field when he got to Tiger Stadium. He couldn't wait!

On October 9, 1982, during halftime of the Tennessee game Frank was sitting on the steps at the front of the section where his dad's seats were located, telling big stories to several of his buddies from the neighborhood—part of the Boy Scout Troop that met at the Stevendale Optimist Club—who were ushering the game. (Frank would later join this troop to enjoy the privilege of "ushering" the LSU games again.)

"I'm telling you, that girl right there gave me a sponge bath," Frank swore to his friends.

"You wish, big liar, that's a Golden Girl, she didn't bath anybody!" accused one of the doubting scouts.

"Shelly! Shelly!" Frank shouted, leaning over the chain-link fence at field level. "Do you remember me?"

"Of course, my little boyfriend Frankie!" she said kissing the now elated twelve-year-old on the cheek. She then gave her former patient a big hug and waved to all of Frankk's bewildered buddies—beginning the legend of Frank "The Lady's Tank" Hayden—as she trotted back to the rest of the cheerleading squad to somersault and tumble the boys' little hearts away.

Later that month, on the day before Halloween, the Tiger faithful would celebrate the twenty-fourth anniversary of Billy Cannon's hallowed run—and like most of the other preteen boys in the stands, Frank was garbed in his Halloween costume, a replica LSU uniform, throwback helmet and jersey stitched with the #20, and the name Cannon between the shoulder blades.

After Cannon was honored on the field he walked up to Beck and Frank at the fence line and shook his hand back and forth through Frank's sandy blond hair. "What do we tell your old man, Frankie?"

"Geaux to hell Ole Miss, Geaux to hell!" they both chided the ole Rebel.

"Yeah, we'll see about that," Beck responded. "I like Johnny Reb's chances tonight!"

LSU routed the Rebels 45–8.

The next week LSU would go to Tuscaloosa, Alabama, and do something that had become a rare occurrence. They dominated the National Championship-contending Crimson Tide and beat them (20–10) for the first time in twelve years and only the third time since

1958, when Billy Cannon had led the Tigers to what would be its only recognized National Championship, until 2003.

For the Tigers in those days, beating Alabama and Ole Miss made it a good year, and for Dee, having her family back together with a sober and successful Beck made it a great year.

All told, 1982 was an excellent year for the Hayden/Dempsey Bunch. The next, 1983, would be different.

Thirty-Seven

Beck, *seeking advice on how to invest* the extra cash he was making, and seeing how enamored Frank and all the neighborhood kids were with his Atari game console, was easily convinced by a local investment banker—a VP at one of Truman Crockett's LNB branches—that the $3 billion gaming industry was a safe bet that would garner a huge return on his investment.

Shortly before Christmas, Beck placed $45,000 in an investment account—which he would call the kids' college fund—that would be invested in a technology mutual fund, which focused mainly on the video and computer gaming industry and the largest holding of the fund was Atari, Inc.—Atari was soaring.

The Haydens rang in the New Year with an Orange Bowl party at their house on London Avenue where they would hoop, holler, and ultimately agonize over LSU's loss to Nebraska.

About three weeks after the Orange Bowl, Beck got a phone call from Billy Cannon letting him know that Al Amiss had warned him to watch out for the Feds.

"I don't know, Beck, he claimed he didn't know why, just told me some Feds were poking around. He didn't say anything about you or the money."

"Well, what else would they be poking around about?" Beck growled.

"I don't know, Beck; I've had quite a few deals go south recently and some of the partners, well?"

"Damn it, Billy, why do you trust all these clowns?" Beck asked rhetorically. "I've got a deal set up for tomorrow with the boys down in New Orleans, I dug up the money last night, what should I do about that?"

"Well, nobody else knows about you, I haven't told a soul so if someone has talked to the Feds, they are just looking at me," Billy reasoned. "Did anybody see you going to the creek?"

"Not a chance. I hiked over two miles through my kids' old bike trails and went out a different way. It also didn't look like those trails had been used in years. If you haven't led anyone back there, then no one knows where to find it but me," of that, Beck was sure.

"Then be careful, make your deal and sit on the real cash until all this blows over. If the Feds come for me, they'll never know you were involved," Billy promised.

"I'm not worried about you, Billy; I'm worried about your trusting nature," Beck chided.

Beck would carefully conceal the funny money by wrapping six stacks—$20,000 per stack—of cash in Visqueen plastic, placing them in his precast foundation pier mold and then filling the mold with lightweight concrete. He would also position several short lengths of #4 rebar in the piers, so they would have the weight of a true concrete pier, should anyone examine them.

The next morning, dressed in concrete- and mud-stained coveralls and steel-toed work boots, Beck and a helper loaded his flatbed with a few pieces of equipment, a bundle of rebar, and the ten piers, along with ten full-strength piers. He could barely tell the difference in the two and he had fashioned both. Once the truck was loaded, strapped, and flagged for highway safety Beck set out to complete a small project near LaPlace. He studied his rear view, got on and off the interstate a dozen times, doubled back at least twice, and once he was certain he was not being followed he found a pay phone and called Mosca's Restaurant in Avondale, near New Orleans, where what was left of Carlos Marcello's Mafioso, including Beck's connection, regularly met to discuss their various criminal and business endeavors over the best Cajun-Italian food in the country.

"Have your boys stop by the job site, there will be ten concrete foundation blocks on my truck. Load them and put your toolbox inside my big job box, it'll be open. Close it and take the key with you. The blocks look and feel solid but one good smash with a sledgehammer and it will crack like an egg, a cash-laying egg, that is."

"We can only do fifteen cents on the dollar this time Beck, the paper on these bills isn't that good and we're having to spread the bills out more than we'd like" said the thickly accented voice on the other end of the phone.

"Come on, man, I can go twenty cents, you can move it for that."

"Seventeen cents is the best I can do, take it or leave it."

"Come get it."

On Wednesday of that week, January 26, 1983, Beck walked into LNB and deposited $30,000 into his business account and placed another $174,000 in the kids' college fund. His investment banker, who seemed quite pleased to report that the Gaming Fund had grown over 4.5 percent in the short time his money had been invested also asked, "Hey, did you hear that Bear Bryant died?"

Beck had grown tired of the 20-to-10 jokes (the final score of the last LSU vs. the Bear's Crimson Tide Football game) and was waiting for the punchline.

"No, seriously, he had a massive heart attack, he's gone."

Beck, like most non-Alabama supporting college football fans, respected the Bear, whom he'd met twice during the recruitment of Billy Cannon. The Bear had been a living legend, now he was just legendary.

Eleven days later—February 6th—Beck's good friend: political insider, protector, enabler turned recovery mentor and motivator, Sheriff J. Al Amiss, passed away.

At the funeral Sheriff Lloyd Johnson, from St. John's Parish dropped an atomic bomb on Beck.

"Sorry to break this to you here, Beck, but the council is going to reject your change order on the bridge—*the Luling-Destrehan cable stay bridge constructed on I-310 over the Mississippi River*—said they didn't approve additional funding for the stronger steel."

"Seriously, Lloyd, the parish's own engineers said the sections we tied had to have the stronger steel, the GC told me to do it, and I've already done the work, that work cost me over $80,000 extra. That's enough to put me out of business."

"I'm sorry, Beck, I made your case and I agree with you, but they said it's a federal contract and it's pretty clear, you have to get it in writing. I tried to argue but the Parish President said the DOT would cancel your upcoming contracts too, if you try to litigate."

"Can they do that?"

"I'm afraid so, Beck, you might need to swallow this one and try to make it up on some of the upcoming work."

"Hell, I don't know if I can afford to work for the Government, do I get to not pay taxes . . . ?" he asked with as much sarcasm as he could muster.

Thirty-Seven

Beck knew he would need to transfer most of his share of the money in the college fund into his business account in order to cover his vendor bills and make payroll. He was not a happy man and he didn't intend to fall off the wagon completely, but he needed a drink to calm his nerves.

Thirty-Eight

After the funeral, still dressed in the only suit Frank would ever see him in, Beck stopped by a watering hole on the edge of Baton Rouge. It was the last building in EBRP, before crossing the Amite River. The front half of the building was a convenience-and-package store; but the hallway past the bathrooms led to a dimly lit, seedy lounge that appeared to maintain a reddish, smoky haze the entire time Frank sat at the bar sipping a Coca-Cola next to his old man.

"Well, if it's not Beck Hayden, where have you been you big ole hunk of man?" asked a sultry woman with long legs, long hair, long eyelashes, and lots of cleavage.

"I've been working and trying to stay away from trouble like you," Beck said placing his arm around the woman's waist. "Meet my boy Frankie."

"It's Frank, Dad!"

"That's right, Beck, little Frankie here looks like big Frank to me," said the woman who had Frank's full attention. He would never remember her name nor if it was even spoken. All he would remember was that she leaned forward resting her lovely endowments directly in his lap, took his face into her silky soft hands, and slowly French kissed him right in the mouth. As she gradually lifted herself back up, she ran her hand between his legs and rested for a few seconds on his growing concern. "And he sure feels like a Big Frank!"

Frank was frozen; Beck erupted in laughter and the whole bar started making lighthearted jokes about Big Frank. When Beck ordered a round of whiskey shots he said, "Well, Big Frank, its time you had a drink with your old man."

On the way home, after three shots of straight whiskey, Frank wasn't sure if it was him or the car swerving until his dad ran the car into and out of the ditch on the side of Stevendale Road. Beck was able to get the car back under control but not before Frank slammed his head into the metal inlay on the dashboard of the restored 1968 Chevy Impala.

The three-inch gash above his right eyebrow started bleeding profusely and Frank took off his new white dress shirt—which Dee had purchased with the suit he was wearing for the funeral—by the time the Impala roared into the driveway on London Avenue the shirt was more blood-soaked than white and the suit had blood splotches all over it.

"What in the hell happened?" Dee demanded the second they walked in the door. "Is that alcohol I smell on you, Frankie?"

"It's Frank, Mom!" the inebriated twelve-and-a-half-year-old slurred.

"You got a twelve-year-old drunk Beck, have you lost your mind?" Dee fumed. "And what happened to his eye?"

"It's just a scratch, Mom."

"It's not a scratch; you're bleeding like a stuck pig, and I'm taking you to the hospital."

Beck grumbled something about a bitchy woman and the crooked government, but he worked really hard not to lose his temper, though

Thirty-Eight

he was on the edge of his personal control. He poured himself another whiskey while Dee walked out the door with the three youngest, en route to the medical center off O'Neal Lane. They hadn't been gone for more than five minutes before Beck passed out in his recliner with a half-smoked Viceroy cigarette burning in his hand.

Thirty-Nine

On Monday morning, April 7th, Beck headed out of town, in a driving rain, destined for LaPlace where he had a small commercial foundation to prepare and pour that week. He figured that day would be a washout, but the weatherman said the storm would be rolling out and there would only be a 30 percent chance of rain Tuesday and Wednesday so he felt pretty good about leaving. Plus he was tired of arguing over nearly burning the house down—he could get the nine foot burn in the carpet patched when he got home, he thought, and it was his La-Z-Boy that got destroyed. At least he woke up!

However, the storm would not roll out and when it was all water under the bridge; or over the bridges more accurately, the months of March and April, 1983, would be two of the wettest on record and the Amite River at Denham Springs would crest at its highest level ever, 41.5 feet on April 8th.

The flooding would stretch the Amite and Comite River boundaries all the way past Range Road in Denham Springs to Airline

Highway in Baton Rouge. Neighborhoods along Tiger Bend, Antioch, and Stevendale Road virtually disappeared under the murky waters. Dee had loaded a few things into her car and she and Tonya raced up Stevendale Road just as water started gushing over the short bridge at Steven's Creek.

Dee had reluctantly allowed Micah and Frank to stay behind sandbagging the back door and placing furniture and valuables on blocks in case the water got as far as their house. Dee realized she had made a huge mistake as she passed La Rouge Motel—no longer owned by the retired Hutchinses—and it was already being taken over by the National Guard. She looked off to her left toward the bridge into Denham Springs and she could literally see the river swelling over its banks and was now starting to submerge the bridge.

She parked her 1981 Oldsmobile Cutlass Supreme on the higher elevation of Florida Boulevard, which had become a parking lot, literally, as people were abandoning their vehicles in the middle of the main drag through Baton Rouge. Through the hammering downpour she crossed back over the service road and ran toward one of the marine amphibious vehicles. "My boys are trapped on London Avenue, please go get them!" she begged.

"Ma'am, we'll be headed into the neighborhoods as soon as the spotter helicopters can operate. You may want to stay up on higher ground or head a little further inland, though, the river is rising faster than I've ever seen!"

"How could I be so stupid?" she said to Brenda from the pay phone at La Rouge, where she had called her mother twenty-six years earlier, separated from her home and family by the same swelling river. "I should have known better."

"Don't beat yourself up, Dee, they'll be fine. Do you need me to pick you up?"

Thirty-Nine

"Come get Tonya, if you don't mind, I'm staying here until the boys are safe!"

The Haydens had watched the swollen rivers rise virtually every spring for five years. The closest it had ever gotten to the house was in '79 when the water had inched to about halfway up their sloped backyard to within roughly thirty feet of the back door. They had sandbagged each year as the water rose, but the sand was never touched by anything wet, save the raindrops.

When Dee kissed the boys goodbye she instructed them to head across the street to the Khan's two-story home if the water started getting close to the house. She now knew, however, that no house in the Stevendale area, on either side of the tracks, would be safe.

The boys, who were always up for a little adventure, had inflated Frank's river raft and tied it to the back door loaded with the two paddles, a green Igloo water cooler from one of Dad's job sites, and their scouting "survival" packs. They had also thrown in a hunting rifle and their dad's pistol. Everything was wrapped in a small, blue tarp to keep the packed items dry from the rain.

Micah had looked out the back door when his mother left, and the water was barely filling the small creek at the foot of the railroad levee that was the southern boundary of their yard and Village Coté. Now the water was just inches below the tip of the sandbags and the raft was fully floating in the deepening waters.

"FRANKIE! We have to go, buddy, come on get in the raft, now!"

The two boys got into the raft, draping the tarp over themselves as the rain kept beating down, and they watched in terrified amazement as water flooded over and submerged their sandbags and the little raft rose higher and higher. Pretty soon all they could see of their home was a few courses of the blondish brick at the top of the house and the reddish-brown shingle roof.

They paddled hard to keep from drifting away from the house and quickly realized they would have to do something to keep the driving rain from filling the boat.

"Paddle up to the roof!" Micah ordered.

They hurriedly set up the pup tent from Frank's survival pack and secured it into the bottom of the raft, creating a makeshift houseboat. They then tied the tarp to the tent as a lean-to running down both sides from the tent's peak. "Welcome to Micah's Ark," Micah said ushering his little brother back into the raft.

"Hey, it's my raft and my tent," protested Frank. "How come it's your ark?"

"Because I'm the big brother, that's why, now get in ya little monkey."

They took turns sitting below the lean-to tarp paddling the boat. It would take about two hours before the rising waters got to the tip of, and over the railroad levee so they tried to stick close to their house until they could row toward the front of Stevendale Road, near Florida Boulevard, where they knew—from past experience—that the rescue effort would be centered.

"Do you think Mom and Tonya made it past the creek?" Frankie asked.

"I'm sure they did, buddy, they'll be okay," Micah assured his little brother, hoping he was correct.

As they were circling their rooftop Frankie said, "Hey, let's paddle down toward the creek trestle, maybe we can cross over down there." The boys knew the tracks ran slightly downgrade past their home, as they had been riding the tracks on bicycles, motorcycles, and the trains themselves since they'd moved into the village five years prior.

"Good idea!" Micah agreed, and they paddled away from their family home, with the rain continuing to pour and the now—up to fourteen feet—deep water surrounding the railroad continuing to rise.

218

Thirty-Nine

As they made their way toward the wooden trestle—the rail bridge crossing a small creek on the western end of Village Coté—they could tell it was, indeed, submerged. More than that, they had paddled into what seemed to be a river current following the levee with eddy lines forming—hydraulics or holes in the current—the force of which was pulling them quickly toward the point of obstruction, where what appeared to be (class three) whitewater rapids cropping up in place of the eighteen foot trestle; Frank, the more experienced raft operator of the two, quickly assumed command of Micah's Ark.

"We have to paddle together, Micah; when I say, 'go' it means we both make one hard stroke forward, when I say, 'back,' we both stroke backward, one stroke. Left is only you, right is only me," recited the soon to be thirteen—he hoped—year-old, who had been on one whitewater adventure—on the Nantahala River, in Western North Carolina—he had also soloed up and down the Comite and Amite Rivers, as far as the Denham Springs Bridge, several times in his prized possession, the ten-foot raft which was now carrying them into some pretty rough-looking waters.

"Back, back, back, left," barked Micah's Ark's new captain.

The raft basically made a U-turn with the river current roughly four feet above the grade of the railroad trestle as they made the swing into what was now an even faster current that followed the power-line trail, which ran parallel to the tracks. On the starboard side of the power-line trail, wooded thickets now partially, if not totally, submerged, were creating obstructions and swirling hydraulics all along the whitewater gauntlet that stretched in front of them for nearly three miles, back past their home, on past the Stevendale Road crossing and over what used to be Blouin Road all the way to the main channel of the Comite River.

"Go, go, left, go, right, left, go, go," the captain guided.

The boys moved swiftly down the waterway toward the iron arches that marked the 150 foot crossing—the railroad trestle—which normally towered more than thirty feet over the river's surface. They could see various people trapped on their rooftops and as they crossed over what was Stevendale Road, Frank could see several motorboats moving to and fro further up what was now the Stevendale Canal.

"Back, back, back, right, right, right," they fought to turn the boat toward Florida Boulevard where the rescue effort was underway.

"Now go, go, go, dig, dig, go, go, go," Frank shouted, and the boys paddled as hard as they could but the current tugged and pulled. The tug-of-war went on for a good two minutes, but the boys were no match for the raging current and they were soon back in the center channel swirling toward the Comite.

"Micah, we've got to knock the tent down, we have to be in the center of the boat where we can control it better," Frank instructed.

"But this rain, it will fill the boat with water." Micah exclaimed.

"I know, but we have to control the boat, the river is going to be crazy. Drink some water now and fill the canteens from our packs; we'll have to use the Igloo to bail water out," Frank drilled, "and hurry!"

Micah hurriedly pulled the packs and guns out of the tent, checked the safety on the pistol and shoved the barrel into the front of his soaking wet jean shorts, wrapped everything else in the tarp and collapsed the two peaks of the tent back into each other, collapsing the tent into the floor of the boat. Micah lost his balance nearly tumbling into the raging water until Frank caught him with his oar and helped him regain his stability. "Hurry up with the water, we are about to hit those big waves," Frank prodded.

"I'm hurrying, little brother, just keep us in the channel."

As they rumbled over the whitecapped waves and started the dogleg into the Comite channel, Captain Frank was barking, "Right, right, right, left, go, go, dig, go!"

The boat jerked and wrenched and dipped over the whitecaps at a much faster pace now. Frank knew the turns and twist of the river quite well and even without the river banks and normal scenery he instinctively knew what was coming.

"Micah!" Frank shouted over the blare of the pounding rain and raging river. "Up around this next bend, that tree line to your left is going to disappear and the two rivers are going to come together, the water is going to get wild."

"This isn't wild?"

"No, not really," the little commander quipped. "It's about to get really nasty; and we cannot let the current drag us into the bridge. It'll flip us and drag us under. We are going to have to dig!"

"Right, right, go, go, go, dig, dig, dig, dig, dig, left, left, left, go, go!"

As they zoomed sideways over the bridge, Micah pushed them away from the top of the iron structure with the base of his paddle and Frank could see the sloped tar roof of the package store and lounge where the sultry woman had transformed little Frankie into Big Frank. He hoped she had made it to safety.

Forty

❧

Dee would never quite understand how they ended up in the main river channel, nor how they wound up so far from home. Yet, by the time word started reaching of the various sightings from the bridge near Denham Springs to the Amite River Diversion Canal, the boys had somehow wound and snaked over thirty-six miles down the Amite River basin through Woodlawn Park, Bayou Manchac, past Port Vincent and French Settlement, shot through the Diversion Canal and into Blind River, and by the time it was over they were navigating the mouth of the Blind River into Lake Maurepas.

Lake Maurepas, bordering Lake Pontchartrain and two links from the Gulf of Mexico, is a +/- 90-square-mile, brackish, normally shallow lake surrounded by over 110,000 acres of protected Wildlife Management Area. The protected area, owned by the Louisiana Department of Wildlife and Fisheries, was virtually unpopulated, save the protected wildlife, and a few hunting and fishing camps scattered about the streams, swamps, and tributaries feeding the lake.

The two boys had been paddling and baling the boat for more than seven hours; they were soaking wet to the point that their skin looked like the withered hide of a centenarian; and they were exhausted and they had no earthly idea where they were. The rain was still coming down, though it would slack to a mere drizzle periodically and the storm clouds seemed to be breaking. There wasn't much of a shine through the clouds but they estimated that they would have about two more hours of daylight before the setting sun would leave them alone in the dark, in what looked and smelled like the gulf of Mexico to them. They hadn't seen anything that looked like civilization for over two hours and they knew they couldn't make it back up the river.

"We've got to find somewhere to set up a camp, Frank, there is no way we can hike out of this swamp in the middle of the night and I don't think we want to cross this ocean."

"Do you think we're in the ocean, really?" Frank asked looking around as if he was sure a Great White was going to swallow them up, river raft and all.

"Not really, but it ain't the pond back in the Village, is it?" Micah retorted

"Guess not."

They skirted the lake along the southwestern banks; after about twenty minutes Micah noticed a small tributary that had a stilted, rusting, tin-roofed shack standing over fourteen feet above the lake's flooded surface. There was a small floating dock—that would rise and fall with the lake—with a ladder leading to a trapdoor in the floor of the structure that appeared to be a hunting camp.

The small camp seemed structurally sound with thick pine pier stilts, log joist and framing; with cypress- and cedar-trim siding and fascia, locked down hurricane shutters, covered with what appeared to be dusty screened windows all around the building and one door leading to a rocking-chair porch surrounding all four sides. But the only way into the camp or onto the deck appeared to be through the trapdoor which had a padlock on it.

As Frank was emptying the contents of the raft so he could flip it over and tie it down to the dock—BLAM—a shot rang out from the .22 caliber Plinkerton Micah had drawn from his waistband. The water moccasin—having taken the bullet right in the center of its blocky, diamond-shaped head—did a nervous death spiral and disappeared under the murky brown water about ten feet from Frank's bare feet.

"Put your hiking boots back on, Frankie."

"Okay, Jesse James, but my name is FRANK!"

The second shot—BLAM—went point blank into the belly of the Master Lock hanging from the latch on the camp's trapdoor and the padlock fell open permitting the two worn-out boys to climb into the dry, dusty camp.

Much to their surprise and delight the camp had working power and the refrigerator—next to the small kitchenette—had two jugs of Kentwood spring water, a large jar of dill pickles, and two six-packs of Budweiser beer.

"Jackpot," said a relieved Micah tipping back one of the Kentwood jugs, "Oh, that's good, and cold!" he said approvingly to his little brother who was looking through the armoire next to the door.

"Towels, blankets," Frank reported.

The big, open room was furnished with a card table, half-dozen chairs, a sofa, and two beds. On the wall opposite the kitchenette there was a gun case filled with fishing rods and equipment, but no guns. There was also a bathroom with a toilet and a standup shower. Among the decorations were several, mounted mallard ducks, a bigmouth bass—twenty pounds according to the plaque—and two embalmed alligator heads, one was as big as Micah, they surmised.

There was no hot water, but the clean shower and towel dry was a godsend to Frank who then wrapped himself in a clean blanket that he had taken from the armoire in the great room. His clothes—which had been showered with him—were now as clean as he could get them, wrung out and laid over several chairs for drying.

Micah was sitting at the card table with the pickle jar, some stale crackers he found in the cabinets, and two open beers.

"Here you go, Captain, have a beer," Micah said sliding a beer toward his little brother.

"Mom would kill me, she'd kill us both," he feigned a protest as he picked up his cold bottle of Bud. "That's nasty," he said. "Now I see why Dad likes whiskey."

"Drink a couple of them, it'll taste better."

Micah would clean his clothes and body the same way Frank did, and the two boys, wrapped in their clean blankets, would knock down a six-pack and pass out within about two hours of reaching the camp.

Forty-One

"**Why did you leave them at the house, Mother?**" Anna Rae demanded.

"I didn't know, oh my god, I didn't know it was going to be like this, we have to find them." Dee lamented.

"Michael will find them; we just need to pray they're okay," Anna tried to reassure her.

Michael Bullion and his brother Gene were searching the flooded zone for the two boys, and like the thirty or so rescue boats motoring about the area, they would find individuals and families stranded on many rooftops. They helped Dennis and Dewayne Sheppard—neighbors from two doors down—into Gene's sixteen foot Bass Tracker. Like the Haydens, they had been caught off-guard by the flash flooding and only Dottie and the two younger children would flee the Village in time.

"I saw them in Frank's raft," Dewayne—Frank's best buddy—told the men. "They were on the other side of the tracks in the current and they were really moving, I don't know if they made it all the way to the river but they were headed that way."

Once they delivered Dewayne and his father safely to the higher elevation where the National Guard was basing operations, Michael, a Marine reservist, spoke to the Guard commander and was able to ascertain that two boys in an inflatable raft had been spotted near the Denham Springs Bridge. The commander radioed to the other command posts along the flooded zone and one more sighting was reported, almost four hours earlier near Port Vincent.

"Holy smokes, Port Vincent, they are going to wind up in the Gulf of Mexico, if they don't drown," Gene surmised.

"We have to go find them, Gene!" Michael stated

"I'm with you, brother; we are going to run out of daylight soon, so we need to load up on supplies and fuel up."

Michael updated Anna Rae and Dee—Tonya was at Aunt Brenda's house by now—and they all hustled to get Gene's boat loaded with a few supplies, some food, water, sleeping bags, etc. . . . . Michael, the weekend Marine and former Eagle Scout, always had a survival pack in his truck along with his Browning double-action handgun. He strapped the holster around his shoulder and laced his Rambo style Buck knife to his thigh. Already wearing his camouflage slicker, Anna Rae's gung-ho husband was ready for the rescue expedition, or war if need be.

The two men set off down the still raging river in the 16 ft. aluminum boat with a 50 hp Mercury outboard motor capable of speeds of more than 30 mph; though they would have to navigate the river in a much more cautious fashion and their speed of descent down the river basin would have to be more methodical as they worked their way through alcoves and tributaries, searching high and low for the two teenage boys who were currently and sufficiently lost.

The men knew the boys had made it as far as Port Vincent so they snaked the river as fast as the rapids—which the rigid aluminum boat had to navigate more carefully—would allow. They would make it to Port Vincent in a little over two hours, but they felt like they had been riding a bucking Brahma bull virtually the whole way.

They then moved at a slower yet steady pace staying to the right side of the waterway—they felt they could come back up the other side if they were unsuccessful on the way down river. As the rain finally started abating, they had made it as far as French Settlement and were nearing the Diversion Canal. They debated whether they should stay in the river channel or follow the stronger current; settling on the main river channel, reasoning that the boys would have been closer to center channel as they approached and the canal looked much more daunting at the entry point.

What they didn't account for was the fact that the boys weren't intimidated by the river; they just didn't have enough strength to paddle the little inflatable out of the overpowering current.

Just past a huge bend in the river, after passing the canal they saw several boats and a Marine AV moving in and out of the river from a landing on the other side of the waterway. As it was starting to get dark they decided to go find the outpost—which had been set up on Highway 16 near Kitchen Road—to see if the boys had been found by any of the rescue teams.

They had not but a report came from a rescue team that had been operating near Pierre Bayou on the Diversion Canal and they reported seeing two young boys in an inflatable moving through the canal at approximately 3:35 pm.

"If they were in the canal they likely flowed into Blind River and assuming they stayed with the current, which is hard to get out of even with an outboard motor, they could be somewhere in Lake Maurepas by now," opined the Marine major in charge of the outpost.

"Is there anywhere for them to find a phone or civilization once they get to the lake, Major?" Michael asked the commanding officer— who he knew from weekend drills.

"Afraid not, Bullion, that lake is massive and it is surrounded by a million acres of swamp," he exaggerated, though it might as well be a million acres to two teenage boys lost in the middle of it. "If they made it to the lake let's hope we can find them as soon as possible. I've got a bird with a moonbeam en route."

"Permission to fly shotgun with your spotter, Major?" Michael, the reserve lieutenant asked.

"Are you still enlisted?"

"IRR, on the ready, Sir."

"Ten-four, Bullion, I'll arrange it with the Coast Guard, it's their bird."

"Thank you, sir!" Michael said saluting the major.

Michael found a pay phone and updated Anna Rae and then did a "live" interview for an Action News reporter who was on the scene at the rescue outpost.

"We're live in Port Allen tonight, near the edge of the swollen Amite River Diversion Canal as this Marine Reservist prepares to join a rescue team in search of two teenage boys from Baton Rouge who were last seen in an inflatable raft a few miles from here fighting the river's powerful current . . ." The reporter began. "Tell our audience why this search is important to you, Lieutenant Bullion."

"These two boys are my brothers-in-law, they're good kids, and I don't think I can go home to my wife without them. If you've seen them or have the capacity to look for them please help us find Micah and Frank Hayden!" Michael pled his case over the howling wind and the chopping sound of the Euro HH-65 Dolphin helicopter landing in the background.

"There you have it, Louisiana, from this flood-ravaged region, one Reserve Marine wants to go home to his wife but needs to find her brothers first, believed to be lost in the raging floodwaters somewhere between here and Lake Pontchartrain, and bring them home safely to do so."

Forty-One

Michael thanked the reporter and waved for the camera as he began strapping on a Marine-issue flight jacket and climbed on board the orange-and-white US Coast Guard (USCG) rescue bird. He tightened the chinstrap on the flight helmet and a booming voice could be heard over the communication system's background static and the partially muffled sound of the whirling 18 ft. rotary blades.

"Welcome aboard, Lieutenant Hollywood, you ready to roll now?" the captain asked through the comm.

"Ten-four, Captain," Michael said as he secured the locking mechanism on his harness. "Sorry about the show, sir, fly your bird when ready."

The HH-65 was equipped with an 18 MCP (Million Candlepower) "Moonbeam" spotlight and an early version of NVTI (Night Vision Thermal Imaging) and when the beam of light hit the water below a 40 ft. diameter of the surface was daylight visible from the chopper hovering about 60 feet above the surface.

They chopped their way through the thick, rainy night scanning the river's surface and surrounding banks with the illumination of the powerful spotlight. The NVTI was only effective from about twenty to twenty-five feet, due to heavy rains and the lower temperature of the chilly spring night. Several times they saw movement along the banks and moved in closer with the aircraft to get a heat signature. In one case it was a nutria rat—a beaver-sized rodent indigenous to the region—frantically swimming against the current, slowly regressing downstream with the current it was fighting; every other heat signature turned out to be alligators moving around near the river's edge, trying to find suitable refuge from the rising waters.

"There are a lot of gators down there, I hope they're not hungry," Michael said into the comm.

"You mean you hope they are 'still' hungry," the moonbeam operator deadpanned.

"Not funny, Corporal," barked the captain. "Shut your pie hole and find those boys before I feed you to the gators."

"Yes, sir, sorry, Lieutenant Bullion!"

"No sweat, Corporal, just keep looking."

They worked their way through the diversion canal, down the Blind River basin, and within an hour they were scanning the mouth of the Blind and the western shoreline of Lake Maurepas. As Michael got his first whiff of the foul-smelling, salty, brackish water and looked out into the endless darkness of the ocean-like water's surface he began to feel a sense of hopelessness.

"How far could they have gotten?"

"My guess is not very far, once they made it to the lake, if they got this far," the captain started, in a matter-of-fact tone. "The river current would have pulled them downstream quick, fast, and in a hurry but once they made it through the mouth of the river down there they'd be relying on paddle power for the most part."

"Our best bet is to scan the shorelines in both directions for a few miles and then work our way through the edge of the swamp a few hundred yards in, I can't imagine they'd venture too far into the swamp at night," the spotter suggested.

"Sound like a plan, Bullion?" the captain asked Michael, keeping the concerned family member involved in the hunt.

"Roger that, Cap, but please cover as much ground as possible."

As they scanned the tributary where a wet, rusting tin roof covering a stilted hunting camp appeared, they picked up a few heat signatures. As they moved closer, they picked up three large alligators moving to and fro in the water around the camp. They really couldn't get a reading from inside the camp as the tin roof acted as a sufficient shield blocking the first generation NVTI but from the looks of the camp it was deserted with no sign of life.

Forty-One

They quickly moved on along the shoreline and no one noticed when a naked boy ran out onto the camp's deck waving and screaming frantically in a failed attempt to catch the attention of the rescue crew.

"There are a few camps along the shore and into the swamp like that one back there," the captain informed. "If I was them I'd be trying to find a place like that to lay my head until dawn."

"I was thinking the same, that camp looked promising at first," Michael lamented.

"We'll find them, Lieutenant, just keep an eye on that TI screen."

"10–4."

Forty-Two

*F*rank awoke hearing the chopper hovering over their stilted haven and as he opened his eyes the beam from the massive spotlight on the search craft lit up the swamp camp like high beams on a dark road. But before Frank could get to the door and onto the deck the chopper had moved on surveying the lakeshore with its massive shaft of light.

"Put some clothes on, would you?" Micah—still wrapped in his blanket asked his little brother as he stepped on the deck, who hadn't bothered to put clothes on before passing out or running, screaming onto the deck trying get the attention of the rescue chopper. "They can't hear you, but they'll be back."

"You think so?" Frank asked, not so sure himself.

"I hope so; get dressed and turn all the lights on so they can see us if they do come back."

The boys would spend the rest of the night on the covered porch, high above the lake, in their sleeping bags, with a flashlight from their pack in hand, hoping the whirling rescue bird would make a second pass. It would not and by dawn the boys were beginning to think they were stranded for good.

"What are we going to do, Micah?"

"I don't know, buddy. We could stay here and hope they come back, or try to hike out of here, or we could paddle back up the river but I don't think we can do that."

"No, we're not going back the way we came, that's for sure. Where do we hike to?"

"We'll we've got nothing but water that way, the river's back there so I guess we hike into the woods over here?" The older boy said, uneasily.

"Hey, this is a hunting camp, maybe there is a map somewhere."

"Let's see."

They did not find a map, but they did find a pair of binoculars in a drawer at the bottom of the gun cabinet. Using their survival knives as climbing spikes Micah climbed one of the support pillars to the base of the roof deck and squirreled his way around the fascia and onto the tin roof. From the peak of the roof Micah surveyed their surroundings and the fifteen-year-old son of Godzilla had never felt so small.

Even with the powerful vision of the 10x50 binoculars he could not see across the lake; maybe it is the ocean, he thought. Back from whence they came, he could barely discern the lake from the mouth of the raging river, but it was clear that it was anything but passable. Moving due south away from the camp, he could barely make out a straight line on the horizon. He assumed it was a highway of some sort, which he determined would be their destination. About a mile to their east there appeared to be a small drainage canal of some sort and with the binoculars he could follow the treeline on either side of the canal. It seemed to go straight toward the highway so that would be their route.

Forty-Two

He continued to survey the area for a few minutes and the more he looked, the more frightened he became. In their immediate surroundings he located two LARGE alligators ominously gazing in the direction of their little nesting spot. "Stay in the camp!" he hollered down to his little brother.

"I'm on the dock, fishing." came the response.

"Well, be careful and stay on the dock, or you might be the catch."

Micah kept an eye on the gators and kept surveying the isolated swampland they found themselves lost in. For fifteen minutes he found literally no sign of human life. Other than the gators, a rat—nutria—about the size of a farm hog, and a huge watersnake, he didn't see much life at all; though he felt like the place was teeming with lurking creatures just waiting to devour the two boys. He also thought the clover-covered ground—that existed all around the northern side of the camp and to the east where he intended to hike toward the drainage canal appeared to be moving. It was eerie and what he didn't realize at first was that the clover-covered ground was actually colonized giant salvinia and hyacinth growing and floating on the surface of the swamp.

"I caught breakfast," Frank announced from below.

"Coming down," Micah responded.

As Frank filleted then fired the two smallmouth bass he had proudly angled, his big brother let him in on his discoveries. "We're not on the shore of a lake, we're on the edge of a swamp," he said. "And I think we are surrounded by water for-ever!"

"What do you mean, there's grass all over that way and trees, there's forest for days." the confused little fisherman asked.

"Let me show you something," Micah said motioning Frank to follow him onto the porch surrounding their elevated perch. He found a terracotta flowerpot that weighed about twelve pounds with the dirt in it, picked it up, and held it over the east side porch railing. "Watch this."

He dropped the flowerpot to the ground below and it hit the plant covering and quickly disappeared under the surface creating a little splash and a ripple that moved through the coverage for about ten feet and then the water disappeared again beneath the salvinia carpet.

"Holy cow, I almost went for a walk on that stuff!" Frank exclaimed.

"We won't be walking anywhere and I'm not sure how safe we are in the raft," Micah said handing Frank the binoculars and pointing him to the direction of the bank where he had seen the two big alligators sunning, now there were three. "One of those monsters is bigger than our boat."

"Uh, I think they all are!" a stunned Frank offered. "Do you think the helicopter will come back?"

"I don't know, buddy, but I don't think they'll expect to find us way out here."

Forty-Three

They debated over their breakfast bass and finished off one of the jugs of water. "We really don't have enough food and water to stay; no way I'm drinking what's coming out of the tap, it smells worse than the ocean lake," Micah surmised and they decided to paddle their way up the canal and toward the highway he had spotted some eight to ten miles south.

Before they left, they took a white bedsheet and a black magic marker they found in the camp and wrote: "HELP—Gone up canal" with an arrow pointing toward the canal entrance and hung the sheet over the deck hoping it would be seen by the rescue copter, should it return.

They repacked their survival bags, strapped the packs onto their backs, climbed back into Micah's Ark, and embarked into the murky lake, following the edge of the swamp—marked by the congregating salvinia and hyacinth—and made their way toward the canal. As they approached the entry, they could see it was blocked by a layer of the seemingly ubiquitous plant life.

"You think we can we go through it?" Frank asked

"I think so, it's pretty creepy and I don't like it, but it moves, and we don't really have a choice," Micah responded.

They cautiously approached the dense, donkey-ear-shaped plant gathering and as they pushed their little ark into the thick, the botanical rug parted before their vessel. The paddling, however, was laborious and it took them nearly an hour to get through about 150 yards of the invasive plant.

As they were about halfway through the salvinia, a broad-banded watersnake launched itself from its disturbed hyacinth perch into the front of the raft, just about causing Micah to launch himself into the hyacinth.

"NO!" Frank shouted at Micah who was now aiming the Plinkerton at the snake. "You'll sink the boat."

Frank pinned the snake's head into the crease of the raft with the blade of his paddle; with his free hand he grabbed the hissing and angry serpent—that was giving off a distinct musky smell—by the tail and in one motion he flipped the unwanted passenger from the ark about forty feet back into its botanical palace.

"What was that funky smell?" Micah asked as they settled back into their rowing positions.

"The smell of us drowning if you pulled that trigger," Captain Frank scolded.

They were happy to see the open water as the botanical blanket of death was now behind them. What was in front of them was miles of black murky water, lined by walls of tall cypress, tupelo, and Chinese tallow, all seemingly growing straight out of the swamp water. Even with the heat of the sun bearing down on them and burning their exposed skin, the canal was dark and ominous. Every few minutes a swell in the water would pass under the raft, pushing the boys toward the starboard swamp wall. They would hurriedly paddle back to the center and onward—not wanting to be too close to the forest to see behind the trees, and they both knew stories of snakes dropping from tree branches into unsuspecting boats below.

The beleaguered boys rowed the raft toward what they hoped was an accessible highway or some other sign of civilization while a swarm of mosquitoes feasted on their withered skin. They had been moving down the eerie flowing strait for about three hours and with the binoculars they could now confirm that it was a highway they were approaching, but the massive concrete columns holding the highway high above the murky water were taller than the towering tree walls currently staring down at them.

"It's got to be the spillway," Micah said referring to the Bonnet Carré Spillway—a flood-control structure that diverts floodwaters from the Mighty Mississippi into Lake Pontchartrain, Lake Maurepas, the low-lying swamplands—where the boys currently found themselves—and ultimately into the Gulf of Mexico. In reality, the highway they were striving to reach was Interstate 10, which literally rises over forty feet out of the swamp and stretches for over sixty miles unreachably high above the land or water below. The boys had traversed the bridge a few times with their mom going to and from Biloxi, Mississippi, and Frank—who had a bridge phobia anyway—had vividly and fearfully imagined being tossed over that bridge into the watery oblivion below; he really hated that bridge.

"So, we were in Lake Pontchartrain?" a suddenly terrified Frank inquired.

"I guess so, buddy. I always thought Pontchartrain was on the other side of the freeway but that wasn't a river we were in, and neither is this, it's a flood channel!" he said as another ripple bumped them toward the side of the swamp and he suddenly realized that the water was rising and the trees were getting a little shorter with each bump. "And I'm pretty sure they have opened the spillway."

Forty-Four

"**W**e've got to refuel, *Bullion,* plus it's almost dawn, we'll be able to see a lot more in the light," the captain reassured Michael as they temporarily abandoned the lake search and headed toward Air Station New Orleans in Belle Chase, Louisiana, on the West Bank of the Mississippi River, near New Orleans, where the USCG's SAR (Search and Rescue) Southern Command is located.

"Let's hit the head and grab some chow over at the mess hall, Lieutenant," the captain suggested. "The ground crew will have her ready to fly by 0600."

"Ten-four, Captain, but I really want to get back out there; with the spillway opened they'll be in the Gulf of Mexico before noon."

"Roger that, Bullion, as soon as we have a bird ready, I'll get you back out there."

"We've been doing all we can, Anna, but it's hard at night. We'll being taking off again in few minutes, I promise; I will not stop looking until we find them and I know Gene will keep scouring the river channels . . ." Michael updated his sleep-depraved wife, who'd been up all night watching the local news and CNN which was covering the floods nationally.

"You're not the only ones looking, after you did that interview hundreds of people started showing up at the Port Vincent Outpost offering to help. There are probably fifty boats ready to start searching at dawn."

"Wow, that's awesome, well hopefully we can find them fast, the lake is really going to deluge today as they've had to start opening the floodgates on the spillway."

"I know, it has been all over CNN, the whole country is praying for you and the boys and the governor promised to send in the Nation Guard to find them if necessary!"

Michael and the captain with a fresh copilot and a diver instead of the spotter lifted off in the refueled HH-65 dubbed "the Guardian" at precisely zero-six hundred (6:00 am) and made a beeline for Port Vincent.

"We'll start back at Vincent and head back down channel, retracing our path from last night. We have to assume they are in or near the lake, but I don't want to miss anything."

"Roger that, my wife tells me we're going to have a fleet of civilian search parties this morning, that might help."

"Ten-four, the Post Commander confirmed forty-two search vessels preparing to launch at 0700; he wants to let us get ahead of the confusion."

"Sounds like a good plan"

They circled over the Outpost and headed back toward the Diversion Canal. Michael tried to make out Gene's boat in the Chaos below but it was impossible to discern which of the many Bass Trackers lumped in with every other type of riverboat below—he would later learn that Gene had spent the entire night "jack-lighting" (searching with a spotlight) along the river's banks and was well ahead of the media-drawn search parties.

They made it back to Lake Maurepas and it was now almost impossible to determine where the river ended or the lake began as millions of gallons of murky flood water were pouring into the lake from the Blind, Tickfaw, and Amite Rivers on the lake's western banks while the Bonnet Carré Spillway poured hundreds of millions from the Mighty Mississippi into Lake Pontchartrain to the east.

They followed the western shoreline—which was about a half-mile further inland than it normally was—and methodically searched every channel and tributary making their way all the way around the lake to the point where the canal banks connecting Maurepas and Pontchartrain had completely disappeared under the murky flood waters creating a singular, unforgiving, choppy, and whitecapped body of water.

"I really hope they didn't get this far, Captain," Michael opined solemnly.

"Yeah, I hate to say it but there's no way an inflatable could hold up in those waves."

They scanned the muddy waves for a few minutes, almost relieved not to find any sign of the boys or their raft near the merging of the two massive lakes and continued around to the southern point of Maurepas.

The helicopter crew came across the entrance of the Reserve Flood Channel at approximately the same time as one of the search boats—an aluminum Jon boat, a wide, flat-bottom boat, with an aircraft engine and propeller mounted in a metal cage behind the operator's perch—found the camp with the SOS sheet pointing toward the canal.

As another ripple swayed the boys' raft, Frank was beginning to think the murky, blackish-brown water was going to swallow them whole; and then he heard the faint chopping sound of the whirling HH-65 rescue helicopter working its way up the channel.

"They're coming, Frank; they're coming for us!"

"Thank God!"

As the helicopter approached the boys were being pushed faster in the channel and into the trees. They paddled frantically to keep from being pushed through the swamp's cypress prison gates when the helicopter pilot, realizing their peril, climbed higher in the sky above them. The copter circled high above the boys, keeping a watchful eye on the little inflatable and its two occupants. There was another helicopter that made a few passes, but it never got close enough to push the raft.

After about ten minutes of watching the crafts hover above they heard another chopping sound behind them. The airboat approached from the same direction from which the boys had traveled.

"I 'spect you'd be the Hayden boys?" asked the bearded boat operator who had killed the deafening engine and glided quietly up to the boys from about two hundred yards out.

"Yes, sir; and boy are we glad to see you!"

The boy's climbed onboard Mr. Mitcham's airboat—Mitcham, from Ponchatoula, Louisiana, worked on an alligator farm, literally wrestling with the gators, when not hunting them in the swamps. He knew these waters well.

"You boys know where you are?" Mitcham asked.

"Lake Pontchartrain?"

"The Spillway?"

"Well you're both close, you are in a flood-relief channel in Maurepas Swamp, which is part of Maurepas Lake. It connects to Pontchartrain, the Gulf of Mexico, and to the Bonnet Carré Spillway— they've got the spillbays open, all 350 of them. In a few more hours you won't see anything but the tips of these trees, and a million snakes and gators will not have anywhere to rest on dry land—your little boat there would look like an island oasis," the swamp wrangler chuckled.

"Glad you got here when you did!" an appreciative Frank explained.

"Amen!" chimed Micah who had just finished tying down the now mostly deflated raft to the front of the Jon boat.

Mitcham flipped a switch bringing the engine and propeller to a rotating roar. He pulled back gently on the handle of the tall throttle stick in his hand and pushed it forward and the boys were suddenly flying across the water, skimming inches above the waves. It was an uneasy feeling, like riding on the back of their dad's flatbed, just faster and with a million homeless snakes and Jurassic-era, man-eating reptiles afloat, Frank was holding on for dear life.

As they rapidly approached the elevated freeway Micah realized that his hope of reaching the highway and receiving assistance would have been utterly futile as there would have been no way for the boys to scale the towering support columns and it would have been nearly as impossible to garner the attention of the passersby zooming across the freeway at 70 mph.

The swamp captain zigzagged around the columns of the two elevated roadways—one for east and one for westbound traffic—and on the other side they skimmed right into another relief channel and followed it several miles to its end at Airline Highway, near Reserve, Louisiana.

The helicopter landed in a field about two hundred yards from the channel's end and Michael Bullion, their brother-in-law, jumped from the helicopter and ran toward his found and rescued family members.

"I'm glad to see you two little urchins!"

"Man, are we glad to see you too Michael. Are Mom and Tonya okay?" Micah asked as soon as they hugged.

"They're fine, everybody is fine, just worried about you guys. Heck, half the state is worried about you; you've been all over the news," he said pointing up to the other helicopter that had been following the action.

A satellite vehicle had just pulled up to the roadside and a reporter was asking if he could interview the boys and their brother-in-law. Frank wanted no part of it and Micah just wanted to go home but they agreed to take some footage of the boys on the airboat with Mr. Mitcham and together with Michael if the reporter promised to use the name Frank, no Frankie.

"You may remember little Frankie Hayden from the Flint abuse story we began reporting back in 1977," the story began. "Well, today, an alligator farmer and airboat captain, with the help of the Coast Guard and a Marine Reservist, located and extracted little Frankie, who goes by the name Frank now, and his older brother Micah from the Maurepas Swamp. The boys were forced into a small, inflatable raft when their home near Stevendale Road flooded and that raft carried the two boys, 13 and 16, into the Amite River, more than 40 miles downstream and ultimately into the 92-square-mile lake and then into the 110,000-acre swamp which like the Amite River Basin, is experiencing its worst flooding in recorded history."

Lizzy (Elizabeth Boudreaux) watched the news report in her family's den in their home near Gonzales, Louisiana, just fifteen minutes from where the boys landed in the airboat. She couldn't explain the overwhelming joy she felt watching this family reunited on the television news show.

"They found those boys everybody was looking for! They are in Reserve (La.) on Airline Highway," she reported to the rest of the Boudreaux family, who had all been at the Port Vincent relief post the day before when the inflatable raft swiftly passed by and when the young Marine queried everyone possible, including them, trying to figure out where they might be.

"Oh, thank God, I had been praying for those boys!" Julie said sincerely.

248

"Me too, can you believe they floated down river all the way from Baton Rouge and spent the night in Swamp Maurepas?"

"They must be brave little boys, sad about that disgusting teacher!" Julie opined.

The family watched the story and resolved to continue their volunteer efforts, as their community too had been hard hit by the flooding that ravaged the Hayden family.

"Mom, can I go work with the Catholic kids in Baton Rouge?" Lizzy, a sixteen-year-old with a driver's license and a car, asked. "There is a youth group that is meeting Saturday at St. Louis King of France and going to help some of the families near Denham Springs where those two boys are from."

"I guess so, dear, if you promise to be careful and stay out of trouble!"

"Of course!" said Lizzy smiling.

Forty-Five

There was another flood—that would add to the Hayden's devastation—that April. Atari, Inc. would flood the market with twelve million Pac-Man video game cartridges even though less than ten million game compatible consoles had ever been sold, reasoning that Pac-Man's popularity would drive additional game console sales. The poor quality of the home version of the game—Frank played his twice before declaring it total garbage—led to pitiful sales and many of the units sold were returned by irate customers seeking a refund. This led to the first major drop in the kids' college fund.

"You told me this thing was bulletproof, now you're telling me I've lost over $70,000?"

"It's just temporary, Mr. Hayden, one bad game is not going to wreck a company like Atari and the other stocks are still doing fine," the investment banker assured. "Besides, you don't lose money in investing until you sell; stocks go down, stocks go back up, it's the nature of the beast. Ride it out and you'll make the $70,000 back and then some."

The banker showed Beck a memo from Atari, Inc. announcing their partnership with Steven Spielberg who had granted Atari the rights to create the video game version of *E.T.*, the blockbuster movie of 1982. The company expected E.T. to be ready prior to that year's Christmas season and promised its stockholders that returns would be enormous.

Beck decided to ride it out; the account was below the amount owed to Cannon at that point anyway so he was hoping the stock would rebound.

Not a happy man, he left LNB to drive out to the family's home on London Avenue. Dee had called him Wednesday night at the roadside motel where he was staying temporarily—she and the kids were staying at Brenda's house—and told him that Stevendale Road was reopened for the first time in over a week. He knew that water had gotten into the house, and he knew it was somehow enough to wash his boys damn near down to the Gulf of Mexico—although he still found a way to chastise and excoriate them for their little misadventure—but he really wasn't prepared for what he found.

The house and all its contents were utterly destroyed. The National Guard had gone through opening most of the windows, the ones that weren't broken, in an effort to let the place dry out. The water had abated days before but the furniture, what hadn't floated away, was still soaking wet and virtually everything in the house, including the walls and ceilings was covered in silt and a fuzzy, black and orange-brown spotty substance, and Beck could barely breathe as he walked through the ruins. Even the ceiling fans had a layer of silt on them and the blades had the wilted curvature of palm leaves hanging from an island tree. The popcorn-finished drywall ceiling was bowing downward and clumps of it had falling onto the muddy swamp below that used to be the carpet.

"I sure as hell hope you got good insurance when you bought this place," he said later that day when he met Dee at the house to survey the damage.

Forty-Five

She was already in tears, "I did, I even made sure we had flood insurance, but the agent is now telling me that our claim will be rejected because we are in a known floodplain!" she sobbed.

"Damn it to Henry Frick, woman, can't you do anything right?" Beck snapped.

"Maybe if my husband hadn't been drunk or kicked out of town, he could have helped me figure it out!"

They had their first fight since Beck's exile—it would not be the last—but Beck was still on the wagon, so he apologized for flying off the handle and they both calmed down.

"I've got some of my guys on the way to clean the place out and we'll figure out how to get it restored. I can call on some of my contractor buddies and I'll see what kind of deals we can get."

"How long do you think it will take?" Dee asked, still in tears.

"Well, I've got a big draw due tomorrow, once I make payroll and pay a few vendors I should have a good chunk left over. If we pay cash we can get it all done in a couple of months, I think."

"Okay, please get it done as fast as you can, I don't want to stay at Brenda's too long and it'd be nice to have us all back together."

Beck's crew showed up right before lunch and they started gutting the place. All the furniture, most of it not more than a year old, was ruined. The doors on Kelli-Kay's armoire had swollen to the point that the doors had to be smashed to get it opened. The wooden book cases and sectional sofa bottoms were placed in the front yard to dry out, in hopes they could be refinished, but the cushions were all trashed; mattresses, box springs, linens, clothes, carpet, drapes, art work, Frank's fish tank, books, knickknacks. It was all gone. Locke's burial flag, still folded, was found in the master bathtub, covered in mud and mold.

The sheetrock on the walls and ceilings had to be stripped to the darkening yellow-pine studs; all of the carpet, padding, and vinyl flooring was torn out and tossed onto the mountain of debris at the end of the driveway by the street—it would take the parish three months to remove all of the foul-smelling, snake, rat and bug attracting debris mountains from the Village—and most of the doors and cabinetry were warped.

About the only thing left was the brick exterior, the frame, and the roof. Everything else would be starting from scratch.

Beck's six-man crew showed up the next morning, Friday, April 18th, at 7:00 am to complete the demolition. Michael Bullion—a skilled carpenter—had arranged for a few days off and was there with a friend who had agreed to help. Beck arrived promptly and he laid down his plan for the day. Michael, his helper, and one of his apprentices would turn the garage into a woodworking shop, once everything was cleaned out of it, and they would begin to repair, sand, and refinish the doors, cabinets, and the bits and pieces of wood furnishings that were salvageable. The rest of his crew would finish demolishing the mold-infested materials and get the place clean and ready for remodel.

He had to drive over to LaPlace to pick up the draw and then he would return to LNB to cash the check so he could make payroll. Then they would take the flatbed and the box truck up to the Lowes Building Material and Lumber yard on Florida Blvd. to pick up the materials—insulation, drywall, finishing materials, some cabinetry, ceramic tile for the kitchen, laundry, and bathrooms, ceiling fans, wooden draw-down blinds, and a few other items they would need, all totaling a little more than $18,000—the draw would be more than $40,000 and after payroll, vendor payables, and equipment payments he would have enough to cover it with a few dollars left over. Everyone got to work, and Beck hit the road.

At 9:45 am he made it to the office of the developer, Joe Milligan, who owed him more than $80,000 in total; $40,000 was supposed to be waiting for him at the receptionist desk but the receptionist informed him that Mr. Milligan was gone for the day; and he had not left anything for Beck or for Hayden Steel and Foundations.

"There is supposed to be a check here for me and I don't have time for any of Joe's games. You get him on the phone and tell him I need my damn money!"

"I'm sorry, Mr. Hayden, I don't know where to reach him," the intimidated receptionist said.

"Look, Missy, no offense, but I need to talk to somebody who can either get me my check or get Joe's lying ass on the phone."

"There's no need to cuss at her, Mr. Hayden," said the older gentle-men—in a double-breasted gray suit with a skinny red tie—who stepped from the conference room, "she's just a receptionist."

"And who are you?"

"I'm Joe's partner, Fred Carter, why don't we go to my office where we can talk."

Mr. Carter informed Beck that the highway bonds they were counting on had been canceled and they were putting the development on hold.

"That's all well and good, Mr. Carter, but I've already tied all of the steel and more than half the concrete is formed and poured, you gentlemen owe me $80,000 and I need at least $40,000 of it today as agreed!"

"We just don't have it, Mr. Hayden, we put all of our funds into the site and utility work, which the DOT funds were supposed to reimburse us for, so we could pay you for the foundation and build the shell." He showed Beck, who was fuming already, the rejection letter from the DOT to prove what he was saying.

"First," Beck said looking at the letter, "how do you green-light a project you can't afford if you don't know that the funding is secured?"

"We had assurances."

"From who?" he demanded. "And second, this letter is dated ten days ago, why am I just hearing it?"

"Well, we were trying to work it out and Joe is still out trying to raise the funds."

"Bullshit, you crook, you all waited because you knew I would pull off the job and you were hoping I'd finish the concrete before my draw was due and I would have if my kids hadn't been lost in the damn swamp!" Beck stated, his temper now in full bloom.

"Now listen, buddy, I'm not a crook; we were just trying to raise the funds to make it right," Carter protested.

"So, you knew you didn't have the money, you knew the DOT turned you down but you went ahead and let me place $80,000 worth of concrete and steel on your site, knowing I can't take it back and you don't think you're a damn crook?" Beck snapped and the conference table proved to be an inadequate barrier between the two men. By the time the St. John's sheriff's deputies arrived Mr. Carter's red tie matched the better part of his previously white shirt, with most of the blood emanating from his nose, which was now broken. He also had a black eye and Beck was working on business development for Mr. Carter's oral surgeon.

Forty-Six

Beck was booked for aggravated assault, property damage, and disturbing the peace. He would spend the next four days in the Gretna, Louisiana, jail and on Wednesday morning the judge set a $10,000 bond, cash only, since Beck wasn't a parish resident. Carter and Milligan's attorney would later agree to drop charges in exchange for Beck forfeiting his profit and overhead for the project. The developer would pay the vendors direct for the material, and was supposed to pay for the cost of the labor, which Beck provided payroll reports to back up his figures but like his profit and overhead, he would ultimately never see a dime for his crew's labor.

That Monday, while Beck was sitting in jail awaiting arraignment, Commodore International announced price reductions of its personal computers, the Commodore 64 and the entry-level system, the VIC-20 to $199. The VIC-20, having sold 800,000 units in 1982 was the hottest-selling personal computer on the market and it was specifically designed to be compatible with the Atari 2600 joystick.

With added memory, better graphics and more game options sales were expected to soar.

By the close of business Tuesday Atari's stock and the kids' college fund had fallen another 60 percent. It was in a virtual freefall and the oversaturation of gaming consoles was starting to show up in the quarterly reports of Mattel, Apple, Magnavox, Gemini, and others. By the end of the year a $3 billion industry in 1982 would be reduced to just over $100 million in total revenues. It would be known as the North American Atari Crash of 1983 and would cause a near depression in Japan's economy, forever remembered as the Atari Shock.

By Wednesday, there was slightly more than $12,500 left in the fund, and his business account was drained. He owed more than $50,000 to vendors and even when fully collected he only had about $25,000 in unpaid contracts, not counting what he would never be paid from Carter and Milligan. To top it off he owed Billy Cannon $160,000 and Beck expected him to call for the funds at any moment.

Hayden Steel and Foundation Contractors was a bust, he couldn't make payroll, and though they got the demolition nearly done, his crew walked off the job at the Hayden home on London Ave and now he couldn't even afford to buy the materials to do the remodel himself. He hadn't been drinking but he was ready to kill somebody, smash Tokyo, breathe fire, and take on King Kong.

Dee cashed out the investment account—which had been worth well over $250,000 just a couple of months prior—and paid the $10,000 bond, securing Beck's release from jail. She then gave him the $2,500 that remained, $120 of which he used to retrieve his Impala from impound, and once he acquired his keys, he rode off in the foulest mood Dee had ever seen. He didn't bother to say goodbye and she didn't bother to ask where he was going.

By Friday night, Beck had been drinking—barely slept it off and drinking again—for over forty-eight hours. He was pretty much out of money, though he thought about wading through the still partially flooded Jones Creek to dig some up, and he felt it was time that he explained to Dee, just why it was all her fault that he was a failure. He proceeded to drive his vehicle, completely inebriated, to the Baton Rouge Hilton.

Dee was working a cash bar, her twelfth shift that week, and at the security desk he demanded that they go find his wife so he could discuss a pressing family matter with her.

Reluctantly Thomas Tally, a former USL—University of Southwestern Louisiana—defensive end, who was playing semi-pro football and working part-time security at the Hilton, went to the Grand Ballroom to summon Dee to the security desk, which was located at the back entrance right next to the employee cafeteria.

"I think he may have been drinking, Ms. Dee," Tally—a tall, muscular young man with a sandy blond mullet—explained.

"Great, if he gets out of hand, please call the police immediately," she pleaded.

"I will, I promise."

By the time she made it to security Beck was already arguing with Tally's watch partner Billy Prescott. "Beck, can we talk outside; these boys don't need to hear all of our problems?" she asked, as if promising to work out whatever Beck's problem was.

Once outside Beck raged at her for a good five minutes about every flaw, or perceived flaw she had, he basically blamed her for all of their problems, he blamed her for everything that happened to Frankie, for his fall at the stadium, the Flint thing, for the flood—as if she made it rain—and for Micah and Frankie getting lost in the swamp. He blamed her for his own business failures and then he demanded to know where he was supposed to come up with $160,000 to pay Billy with.

"What in the Henry Frick do you owe Billy Cannon $160,000 for?" Dee managed to ask in shock.

"We were making money together and I put some of his money in the kids' college fund, which is now gone."

"And that's my fault, how?" still not realizing that he meant literally "making" money.

"Well, it's your brother's bank that lost it, that little crooked investment guy probably fixed it with your crooked brother!"

"I asked you not to go to my brother's bank in the first place, and even so he didn't make the stock market plunge but we can talk about all this later, I have to get back to work," she said starting to walk away.

Beck grabbed her arm, "You're not going anywhere damn it; you're going to listen to me for once in your damn life!"

As she pulled away, Beck reared back and punched her square in the cheekbone, knocking her to the ground—one of her back teeth dislodged and she started bleeding tremendously—and Beck was snarling and cussing at her as he reached down and grabbed her hair in his hand snatching her head back to expose her face as he reared back and punched her again.

Tally and Billy Prescott came flying through the windowed, brown double-doors and Tally tackled Beck as if he was a flat-footed quarterback; the two tussled for a few minutes—leaving both nicked and bruised—until another security guard and the first of six EBRPD officers showed up to help subdue Beck—which was no easy task.

Prescott helped Dee to her feet and walked her back into the hotel where she would be treated from the first-aid kit at security. She refused to go to the hospital saying that she had to finish her shift. Claiborne Smith, the MOD—Manager on Duty—was adamant that she seek treatment, again she refused.

"Sorry, Smitty, I'm going back to work," Dee said, still holding gauze in her bleeding mouth. "I have mouths to feed and a house to rebuild and I can pretty much guarantee that this worthless SOB is not going to help me, so . . ." The determined woman went to the ladies' room to spit-up blood for a few minutes, fix her hair, and cry.

The tooth was dislodged but not completely out so she tried to push it back into its socket, which was painful but she was tough. She washed her mouth out one more time, bit down on a wad of gauze, put on her Foster Grant shades to cover her darkening eye, and went back to her station. She kept her mouth closed for the rest of the night—except when she could run back into the service corridor and wash her mouth out at the coffee station sink—and served drinks with a smile.

She wrote "sorry, can't talk, dental work" on a hotel notepad and showed it to people if they asked her questions that she couldn't just nod or smile to answer.

EBRPD hauled a belligerent and defiant Beck off to the Parish Prison drunk tank. Claiborne Smith—an African American gentleman who respected Dee as a capable manager—and Thomas Tally showed up at Beck's arraignment to seek a restraining order on behalf of the Baton Rouge Hilton and to see to it that the charges against him were pursued.

The restraint order was granted, and Beck was sentenced to thirty days in EBRPP where he would stew over all the injustices done to him, and the audacity of that "uppity Negro" showing up at court for his arraignment. Dee must be sleeping with him, he decided. And though nothing of the sort ever happened, nor was there any evidence to suggest it had, Beck—a lifelong Democrat who had stood up at a 1981 School Board meeting to vocalize a hateful and racist protest of the busing plan the EBR School Board was implementing to begin desegregation—would shamelessly accuse her of sleeping with Smitty and call her a "nigger lover" from that point on.

"No doubt, he'd be a better man to have than you'll ever be!" Dee would retort when he would say it to her, virtually guaranteeing Beck's rage and abuse.

Forty-Seven

The Hayden family was now—and would remain so for the duration of Frank's childhood—ostensibly poor, dirt poor. The floods had washed away virtually everything and anything they had. The restoration of the home on London Avenue would take over two-and-a-half years, as Dee, Michael Bullion, and the children would complete small projects whenever Dee could buy a small amount of the needed materials. Michael would obtain extra materials from completed job sites and would provide most of the insulation and over half of the drywall one or two pieces at the time. Michael and Anna Rae would do all they could before moving to Atlanta, Georgia, with their two babies—Michael Jr. and Miechelle Elisabeth—in the fall of 1984.

They wouldn't complete the final finish sanding of the drywall or prime and paint the walls until spring of 1985. New carpet and padding—to cover the chalky concrete foundation they had been walking on—would be the family's Christmas present that year from

Dee; Beck never participated in the remodel, once he and his crew walked away from the demolition.

For the previous Christmas, 1984, one of James's friends—from his church—had volunteered to popcorn the ceilings. He got the gypsum pops all over the new ceiling fans, the lights, the woodworking, and whatever furniture they had. Frank and Tonya would spend three weeks cleaning up behind the guy and to this day, there is likely hardened popcorn mud in the nooks and crannies of that house.

The engine and piping of Micah's Yamaha YZ125 motorcycle—which was chained to the air conditioning unit in the back yard when the rivers annexed Village Coté—was irreparably damaged and the motorbike would never be ridden again. It rusted into oblivion for another year or two before being carted off to the dump.

The kids had very few clothes, as most of it, too, was destroyed or gone. Frank, already wearing a size thirteen shoe at the age of twelve, would soon grow into a size fourteen, which was virtually impossible to find other than via catalog order, in those days. As a result, the kids—the three youngest—each had one pair of shoes and Frank's would be at least a size too small. In fact, from the time he was 13 until he moved to Atlanta in 1989, when his shoe size was a 15DDD, Frank never owned anything above a size 13D shoe. By that point his toes were permanently scrunched and virtually every toenail was "in-grown".

Dee would bring home leftover banquet food and/or baked goods whenever she could, and she bought Kraft macaroni-and-cheese by the case. Dee worked all the time; she worked doubles nearly every day and weekends and holidays were the busiest. She really didn't have a choice; Beck was worthless for all intents and purposes, though he would show up every so often—unless he was working out of town or in jail—and scream at the kids for perceived inadequacies, administer drunken discipline, which usually meant just taking swings at Micah or Frank—Tonya was spared most of the physical but not mental abuse—until Dee came home, then he'd go after her with a violent zeal.

Beck's addiction, his rage, and the so-called discipline along with the sheer desperation of their mother turned Dee's three youngest children into a pack of fearless, the devil-be-warned warriors. They would fight with each other like cats and dogs, but they would also protect each other and their mother like grizzly bears protecting their cubs. Beck's brutality was met with whatever adolescent equivalent his sons or daughter could muster. They lived in a war zone.

One of the battles occurred shortly after the flood of 1983. The kids were out of school for Memorial Day when Dee and Tonya had gone to pick up Frank from Big Dean's apartment where he was dangerously doing backflips off of the soaking wet, metal ladder handles that rose above the deep end of the Newport Villa's community swimming pool. On the way home Dee spotted Beck's clunker of a pickup truck—the flaming flatbed had been sold along with his Impala and most of his equipment—outside of a honky-tonk on Florida Boulevard.

Beck had promised Dee money for the kids and to help with the remodel of the house on Friday, but she hadn't heard from him since. Thinking it was too early for him to be inebriated, as it was just a few minutes after noon, she pulled in next to his truck—which was alone in the front parking area—and after ordering Frank and Tonya to stay in the car she began walking toward the entrance. She heard muffled screaming penetrating the thick cinderblock walls and her initial instinct was to turn around and leave.

Hesitantly she pulled on the front door handle as the belligerent, defiant, and angry sound of Beck's voice began to reverberate in her eardrums—even the one predominantly deafened by a past beating administered during a similar sounding tirade—with psychotic ranting and raving. The terrified bartender, who recognized Dee from previous husband search-and-retrieval missions, immediately pleaded with Dee to take her husband home.

"Sorry, buddy, you got him this way, you deal with it," Dee said, as Beck continued to rage barely glancing in her direction and she closed the door heading back to the car. As she opened the car door, she heard the ranting of the lunatic rage through the front door and Beck started screaming at her to come listen to whatever it was that he was trying to say. Without answering she quickly slid behind the wheel of her car, turned the ignition, and put the car in reverse.

As she sped out of the parking lot Beck was running beside the car banging on the glass screaming at her to stop. She didn't and she prayed he wouldn't follow her, but she could see from the rearview mirror, just a few seconds later that he was swerving his way out of the parking lot following right behind her.

She sped home and pulled into the family's driveway just seconds ahead of the nearly out-of-control pickup truck and she ran into the house ushering her two teenage passengers, both of whom wanted her to drive to the police station rather than home, as they got inside the house Dee locked the front door behind them and she ran to the back door to make sure it too was locked.

As Beck started banging on the front door Dee ordered the kids—including Micah, who had emerged from the boys' room to investigate the commotion—to go into her bedroom where they could lock themselves into the room and the closet. Dee followed her children into the closet and began closing the door behind them to the sound of breaking glass as Beck continued his assault on the front door. Micah pushed his way past Dee and exited the closet holding Uncle Locke's rusting shotgun—one of the few flood surviving heirlooms.

She tried to grab him but Micah pushed her back into the closet and closed the door behind him. "Stay with Tonya and Frankie!" the sixteen-year old ordered his mother as Tonya started tugging her back into the closet.

By now Beck had started making his way to the back door and with a cast-iron mold that he had pulled from the back of his truck he smashed every window on the garage door and along the side of the home. Micah reached the living room, raising the gun to his shoulder as he traversed the living room.

Smash! Smash! Smash!

After breaking the dining room windows Beck started pounding with his iron mold against the back door, which barely held its ground under the behemoth's hammering. As the glass panes fell to the uncarpeted concrete on the inside of the house the barrel of the shotgun hit him right on his raging mouth.

"If you don't leave now, I swear I'll blow your freaking head off Beck Hayden!" Micah bellowed as he stared at his drunken father through the broken door light and through his own tearing and now bloodshot eyes.

Dee's blood ran cold as she heard the exchange and she pulled free from the grip of her two youngest. As she exited the bedroom, BLAMM!

She would never be sure if the shotgun blast was a warning shot or a legitimate attempt to end the Hayden family wars once and for all time but that particular battle was ended by it and Beck hightailed back to his vehicle and drove off inebriated, enraged, and shaken.

Dee wrapped her arms around Micah, who was still holding the smoking gun through the broken glass, and she tried to console her shaking son.

"He's gone, honey, let's put the gun down," she pleaded with him.

Micah lowered the gun and asked his mother why she put up with him for all this time. The question went unanswered as Micah turned and went back to his room and locked himself inside, with the shotgun, and started cleaning up broken glass.

Dee felt and heard her beautiful son Micah change that day. He had always had a protective and surviving spirit. He'd been through the father-mother battles and the father-anything-that-moved conflicts but that day he fought back in a most ominous way, that day his young rage reached a crescendo, that day he pulled the trigger and both he and his parents knew that he would not miss again, intentionally.

Dee had endured enough, and she knew that she could no longer subject herself or her children to the monster. She decided to buy a handgun and learned how to use it, and she was determined to fight back the next time Godzilla appeared.

She also attempted to file for legal divorce that summer and learned that she had never been legally married to the monster in the first place.

She was, nonetheless, granted a common-law dissolution and awarded full custody of the three minor children. Beck was also ordered to pay child support of $600 per month. Beck—who had been drinking since lunch—was served the papers on a Friday afternoon at the aging La Rouge Motel—where he would live periodically through the mid-eighties—and the court order threw him into yet another psychotic rage.

He stormed down the stairs, climbed into his pickup truck, and raced the 1.2 miles from the motel to the now partially restored home on London Avenue. "Where in the hell is your damn momma?" he screamed at Micah who was in the garage staining one of the recently repaired doors for the house. Michael Bullion and Anna Rae were in the master bedroom finishing sheetrock with Tonya, and Frank was sanding another door to prepare for staining.

"She's not here, Beck," Micah replied coldly, wondering where his mother had hidden the shotgun.

"Beck?" he snapped at the sixteen-year old. "Who the hell are you calling Beck, boy?"

"Well, you're not much of a father, so pardon me if I don't call you Dad!" Micah said defiantly.

All hell broke loose as Beck charged into the garage after Micah, who quickly armed himself with a 2x4.

"I'll take your head off you miserable SOB!"

"Give me that board, son!" Beck demanded, trying to corner him.

Frank, running up behind Beck, shouted, "Why can't you just leave us alone!"

Beck took a swing at his thirteen-year old son, Frank, grazing him on the top of the head as Frank leaned back away from the blow. Before Frank could rebound Micah walloped Beck in the back of his neck and head, slamming him into the wall. Beck regained his balance and charged at Micah like a raging rhinoceros and the 2x4 landed another thundering blow to the side of his head and arm that Beck had raised to try and fend off the contact.

Michael Bullion made it into the garage as the three Haydens were swinging at each other wildly. The combat-trained Marine took about three steps and launched himself behind Beck and wrapped his slightly muscular but very powerful arms around his head and neck and brought Godzilla down with a full headlock in effect.

"My God, Beck, is everything a barroom brawl with you?" Anna Rae screamed in dismay as she followed her husband to the scene.

"Back up guys, it's over!" Michael said to his brothers-in-law as he was pressuring Beck into submission. "I'm going to let go, Beck," Michael promised, "if this is over?"

"Okay, okay, damn it; let me go," Beck responded. "But you can tell your damn momma this ain't over!" He snapped to Frank on the way out, though he would go back to La Rouge, pack his bag, and flee Baton Rouge and the state of Louisiana to avoid making the child support payments he was now ordered to make and to avoid answering for the violence that had just unfolded with his teenage boys.

As he left the scene, Mr. Jones from next door stood in his driveway, gun in hand. "Are you boys okay? I called the police."

"Yes, sir, we're fine," Micah said cynically. "Just a typical Friday afternoon at the Hayden's place."

It had become typical, too typical for entirely too long, the younger Hayden children barely knew life without violence and struggle. Not that the older children had it much better, but they remembered a lot of good times before they witnessed Beck's fall and they each made their way out as soon as they were able. Even they couldn't know what it was like to live an entire childhood at the violent and turbulent bottom.

Any and every waking moment had the potential to erupt into all out warfare, abuse was an accepted way of life, but competent adult supervision was virtually nonexistent. For Micah the only answer was to fight, Tonya chose flight, and Frank just wanted to make it all right. Frank had loved his Big Dad; Beck had been Frankie's first hero, his model to follow in becoming a man himself. But now having survived towering falls, every sort of abuse, raging storms, flooding rivers, snake- and gator-infested swamps, and more bloody family battles than he could remember, the boy, perhaps a young man at the ripe old age of thirteen, had an epiphany.

It was at that point, not that he knew exactly what it meant or the changes he would one day make in his own life to make it so, but that was the day that Frank James Hayden, the youngest son of the Sister of Sorrows, decided that he would be nothing like his father, Beckett T. Hayden, though he would grow up to look just like him. From that day forward the most positive thing Frank could ever say about his father was that he provided the model for what not to be.

Frank's journey from that turbulent bottom in the wilds of Southern Louisiana and a dysfunctional upbringing to places he never dreamed would be tumultuous, treacherous, and maybe even triumphant but that's a whole other story, stay tuned . . .

End Part II

270

Epilogue I

"This is Dolores; I hope you weren't on hold too long, how can I help you?" Dee said answering the blinking line in her office at the back of the service corridor of the Atlanta Sheraton, Northwest. She was hoping whatever it was could be quickly handled as she had several events underway and needed to get back to her guests as quickly as possible.

"My name is Lizzy; I mean Elisabeth Boudreaux," the caller identified herself and added, "I believe you are my biological mother."

Dee let the words fill her head and as she fell into and then sank into the big, black leather office chair behind her desk she mumbled "this wasn't supposed to happen; how . . . how did you find me?"

"Well, it was a challenge at first but I've known who you are for a long time," Lizzy explained. "I just never knew how to reach out, if I should or if I wanted to; the reason I'm calling now is that my husband and I are expecting our first child in a few months and I wanted to have all of our family medical history."

"Um, okay, I can tell you whatever you need to know about my medical history," Dee offered awkwardly then hesitantly asked, "So how are you, do you have a good family; have you had a good life?"

"So far I have, my parents took good care of all of their children, including me, and though I've had my ups and downs, I think I turned out okay," Lizzy opined. "I also have a wonderful husband and we are looking forward to raising our child together."

That's so good to hear," Dee said sheepishly and then apologetically asked, "So what do you need to know about me? I'm fairly healthy and haven't ever had any diseases or disabilities, save making some bad decisions along the way."

"It's good to know that you have been in good health. I need to know about both sides of the family if possible. Has any of your or my biological father's family had heart disease, cancer, you know things like that, and are all of my biological siblings healthy . . . ?"

"I'm sorry, Elisabeth, I can tell you about my history and I'll tell you about my children, if you promise not to contact them directly but I can't help you with information about your father."

And so, began a distant and limited relationship with Dee and the child she had placed for adoption all those many moons ago. Still scandalized by her hidden secrets and stubborn from years of abuse and her own obstinacy, Dee had a hard time opening up to Lizzy. She promised that she would tell her children, Lizzy's biological siblings, of her existence when she could get them together and she answered some of Lizzy's questions about the decision to place her for adoption. But she made Lizzy promise not to contact her siblings or other family members and she refused to answer questions about her father.

As Dee hung up the phone from her first call with Lizzy, with tears streaming down her face, her handsome 6 ft. 7 in., 25-year-old "baby boy" Frank appeared at the office door sporting a fresh, clean-cut hair style, dressed in a pair of gray slacks, and a new, pressed *Auto Glass Professionals* logoed golf shirt.

"Hey lady," he said noticing the tears as he moved toward his mother for a greeting hug. "Are you okay?"

"Yeah, I'm fine, honey," she fibbed. "I, uh, I was just having a crazy conversation with your brother, Micah. You know how it is with him."

"Yeah, sorry, is he off of his meds again?"

"I guess so, but he's still at the hospital in Rome (Georgia) so at least he's being cared for."

"Well, I hope you weren't arguing with him, Mom. You know it can be hard to tell who's crazier, the crazy person or the person arguing with the crazy person," Frank said, citing a loving lecture he had repeated more than a few times to his dear ole mom.

"I don't argue with him, Frank. I just can't agree with all that crazy stuff he says about us," she retorted.

"It's called arguing, Mom. You'd both be better off if you would just ignore the stuff that doesn't make sense, let him know you love him, and move on with the conversation."

"I know, I know, let's talk about something else, you look nice, how is everything with your business?"

"Really good actually. I just landed a huge account with one of the car auctions. I'm going to need to hire one or two more technicians I think, I'm hoping I can talk Dean into working with me."

"Well, maybe you can talk to him this weekend, are you coming?"

"To Anna Rae's house for the shindig? Yeah, I think so, is James still flying in? I may have someone I want to introduce to everyone."

"Oh really, so you're dating again?" Dee asked hopefully.

"Well, you know my faith, Mom. I only believe in dating if there is a purpose for it so let's just say I have met someone that I might be interested in. If we do start dating I'll let you know."

"Okay, well we're all having dinner Saturday evening but James is coming in Friday night, the last I heard, Dean and his family will be there and supposedly Tonya is getting a weekend pass from the halfway house so we'll all be together."

"Okay, Moms, I've got to go but I'll see you Saturday, love ya!"

"Love you too, honey, just make sure you come Saturday, I need to talk to all of you guys about something important."